PRAISE FOR

"A winner from first page to last. Lee Goldberg has singlehandedly invented a new genre of thriller. At once nail-bitingly suspenseful and gut-bustingly hilarious . . . but never less than a pedal-to-the-metal, full-on page-turner. *Fake Truth* is clever, edge-of-your-seat entertainment that I read in one glorious sitting. And that's no lie!"
—Christopher Reich, *New York Times* bestselling author

"Timely, satirical, and funny. Lee Goldberg's *Fake Truth* is deftly ironic and painfully observant."
—Robert Dugoni, *New York Times* bestselling author

PRAISE FOR *KILLER THRILLER*

"*Killer Thriller* grabs you from page one with brilliant wit, sharply honed suspense, and a huge helping of pure originality."
—Jeffery Deaver, *New York Times* bestselling author

"A delight from start to finish, a round-the-world, thrill-a-minute, laser-guided missile of a book."
—Joseph Finder, *New York Times* bestselling author of *Judgment*

"*Killer Thriller* is an action-packed treasure filled with intrigue, engaging characters, and exciting, well-rendered locales. With Goldberg's hyper-clever plotting, dialogue, and wit on every page, readers are in for a blast with this one!"
—Mark Greaney, *New York Times* bestselling author of the Gray Man series

PRAISE FOR *TRUE FICTION*

"Thriller fiction at its absolute finest—and it could happen for real.
But not to me, I hope."
—Lee Child, #1 *New York Times* bestselling author of the Jack
Reacher series

"This may be the most fun you'll ever have reading a thriller. It's a
breathtaking rush of suspense, intrigue, and laughter that only Lee
Goldberg could pull off. I loved it."
—Janet Evanovich, #1 *New York Times* bestselling author

"This is my life . . . in a thriller! *True Fiction* is great fun."
—Brad Meltzer, #1 *New York Times* bestselling author of *The House of
Secrets*

"Fans of parodic thrillers will enjoy the exhilarating ride . . . [in] this
Elmore Leonard mashed with *Get Smart* romp."
—*Publishers Weekly*

"A conspiracy thriller of the first order, a magical blend of fact and it-
could-happen scary fiction. Nail-biting, page-turning, and laced with
Goldberg's wry humor, *True Fiction* is a true delight, reminiscent of
Three Days of the Condor and the best of Hitchcock's innocent-man-
in-peril films."
—Paul Levine, bestselling author of *Bum Rap*

"Great fun that moves as fast as a jet. Goldberg walks a tightrope
between suspense and humor and never slips."
—Linwood Barclay, *New York Times* bestselling author of
The Twenty-Three

FAKE
TRUTH

OTHER TITLES BY LEE GOLDBERG

The Diagnosis Murder Series

The Silent Partner
The Death Merchant
The Shooting Script
The Waking Nightmare
The Past Tense
The Dead Letter
The Double Life
The Last Word

The Monk Series

Mr. Monk Goes to the Firehouse
Mr. Monk Goes to Hawaii
Mr. Monk and the Blue Flu
Mr. Monk and the Two Assistants
Mr. Monk in Outer Space
Mr. Monk Goes to Germany
Mr. Monk Is Miserable
Mr. Monk and the Dirty Cop
Mr. Monk in Trouble
Mr. Monk Is Cleaned Out
Mr. Monk on the Road
Mr. Monk on the Couch
Mr. Monk on Patrol
Mr. Monk Is a Mess
Mr. Monk Gets Even

The Charlie Willis Series

My Gun Has Bullets
Dead Space

The Dead Man Series
(coauthored with William Rabkin)

Face of Evil
Ring of Knives (with James Daniels)
Hell in Heaven
The Dead Woman (with David McAfee)
The Blood Mesa (with James Reasoner)
Kill Them All (with Harry Shannon)
The Beast Within (with James Daniels)
Fire & Ice (with Jude Hardin)
Carnival of Death (with Bill Crider)
Freaks Must Die (with Joel Goldman)
Slaves to Evil (with Lisa Klink)
The Midnight Special (with Phoef Sutton)
The Death March (with Christa Faust)
The Black Death (with Aric Davis)
The Killing Floor (with David Tully)
Colder Than Hell (with Anthony Neil Smith)
Evil to Burn (with Lisa Klink)
Streets of Blood (with Barry Napier)
Crucible of Fire (with Mel Odom)
The Dark Need (with Stant Litore)
The Rising Dead (with Stella Green)
Reborn (with Kate Danley, Phoef Sutton, and Lisa Klink)

The Jury Series

Judgment
Adjourned
Payback
Guilty

Nonfiction

The Best TV Shows You Never Saw
Unsold Television Pilots 1955–1989
Television Fast Forward
Science Fiction Filmmaking in the 1980s
(cowritten with William Rabkin, Randy Lofficier, and Jean-
Marc Lofficier)
*The Dreamweavers: Interviews with Fantasy Filmmakers of
the 1980s* (cowritten with William Rabkin, Randy Lofficier, and
Jean-Marc Lofficier)
Successful Television Writing (cowritten with William Rabkin)

FAKE
TRUTH

LEE GOLDBERG

THOMAS & MERCER

Text copyright © 2020 by Adventures in Television, Inc.
All rights reserved.

Published by Thomas & Mercer, Seattle

www.apub.com

Amazon, the Amazon logo, and Thomas & Mercer are trademarks of Amazon.com, Inc., or its affiliates.

ISBN-13: 9781542014694 (hardcover)
ISBN-10: 1542014697 (hardcover)
ISBN-13: 9781542093118 (paperback)
ISBN-10: 1542093112 (paperback)

Cover design by Mike Heath | Shannon Associates

Printed in the United States of America

First edition

To Valerie and Maddie:
what I feel for you is true.

CHAPTER ONE

Syria, Virginia. July 11. 2:30 p.m. Eastern Daylight Time.

It had been four days since author Ian Ludlow and his research assistant, Margo French, saved the lives of the presidents of the United States and France and four hours since they'd left the Oval Office, where the leader of the free world privately expressed his gratitude for their heroic actions.

Nobody would ever know what Ian and Margo had done, and Ian was fine with that. In fact, he was still having a hard time believing any of it had actually happened. It was the kind of outrageous adventure that Clint Straker, the freelance superspy in his bestselling series of novels, had every day.

But not Ian. He didn't have the body or the training for it. He was a flabby Californian in his thirties who had learned everything he knew about covert spying from James Bond, Jason Bourne, and Austin Powers.

And yet here they were, riding with CIA director Michael Healy and his two bodyguards in a bulletproof black Suburban on a country road through a forest in the hills outside Syria, Virginia. The road ended at a remote log cabin, where another black Suburban was parked out front.

"What is this place?" Ian asked.

"A CIA safe house," Healy said. He was a clean-cut man in his fifties who appeared so wholesome that Ian was sure he could pass as a high school teacher, a Mormon missionary, or the reliable love interest in one of those Hallmark Channel movies.

"In Syria," Ian said, sounding skeptical.

"Virginia," Healy said.

"Still, you have to appreciate the irony."

"I don't see it," Healy said.

Ian did and he wished he could use it in a novel. But when he agreed four hours earlier in the Oval Office to share his future plot ideas with the CIA, just in case some of them might come true again (as they already had twice, in a *big* way), the arrangement came with the promise not to reveal any government secrets he might learn.

"What if the safe house was in Moscow, Maryland, or Lebanon, Pennsylvania?" Ian asked. "Would you see it then?"

Healy straightened up. "How did you know we have safe houses there?"

"I didn't."

Margo laughed. "It's nice to know that there's someone in the CIA besides me who has a sense of humor."

She was in her twenties, naturally slim, with short crow-black hair that looked like she'd angrily trimmed it herself with a serrated bread knife, which Ian thought was a real possibility. He'd also frequently thought about sleeping with her, but that was definitely an impossibility, since she was gay.

When Ian met Margo a little over two years ago, he was on a promotional tour for his latest Straker novel and she was the professional dog walker and aspiring folk singer his publisher had hired to drive him to book signings around Seattle. He'd just learned in the past few days that, in the year since then, she'd been secretly recruited by the CIA and was using her job as his researcher as a cover. It was a ridiculous plot twist that could have come right out of one of his thrillers.

"It's no joke," Healy said. "If some idiot intentionally located safe houses in places that share the names of enemy states and cities, then it's a pattern that can be discovered by our adversaries and puts the assets we are protecting in mortal danger. Every one of those safe houses has to be shut down. Ian, you've proved your value to us once again. We need the perspective of someone outside looking in."

Ian wasn't sure he wanted to be that guy. It was too dangerous.

The driver parked behind the other Suburban. The two bodyguards got out first to sniff the air for terrorists, snipers, and other potential dangers, and then, once they were satisfied it was safe, they opened the back doors for Healy, Ian, and Margo.

The three of them were met on the front porch by two CIA agents wearing stiff new John Deere baseball caps, aviator shades, and untucked, loose-fitting Carhartt plaid work shirts over faded blue jeans, outfits that Ian figured were supposed to make them blend in with the locals. If that was the goal, then the agents probably should have parked a mud-spattered Ford F-150 pickup in front of the cabin instead of a spotless black Suburban with windows tinted darker than tar paper.

"She's inside and the cabin has been swept for listening devices," one of the agents said. "It's all clear."

Healy led Ian and Margo into the cabin, where Wang Mei sat, in a peasant blouse and blue jeans, on a log couch with leather-upholstered cushions. It wasn't exactly the appropriate wardrobe or setting for the beautiful young daughter of an imprisoned billionaire and one of the most famous actresses in China.

She held a mason jar of ice tea in her hand. Of course the glasses were mason jars, Ian thought. The cabin was like a production design-er's idea of a mountain retreat. All that was missing was an elk's head mounted on the stone fireplace.

"This is a surprise," Mei said when she saw Ian and Margo. "I didn't think I'd ever see you two again."

She didn't strike Ian as too excited about it, either.

"Not even at the *Straker* premiere?" he asked. She was one of the stars of the big-budget movie adaptation of his books, which had just started production in Hong Kong. That was where he'd met Wang Mei and helped the actress defect to the United States, which had probably killed the movie, though he hadn't been keeping up on Hollywood news lately. Mei had brought with her a microSD card hidden in the flesh of her thigh. That was something Ian was definitely going to use in one of his books.

The microSD card contained decades-old hidden-camera footage of Vice President Willard Penny, then a young politician, cavorting in bed with two naked Chinese women. The Chinese had been using the film for decades to blackmail Penny into doing their bidding. Now Healy was using Penny to feed the Chinese false intelligence.

"If they finish the movie, which I doubt they will, I won't be in it," Mei said. "I'm expecting to get a new identity and then be sent off to Wyoming to live in a double-wide and work at Walmart for the rest of my life."

"Is that what you want?" Healy asked.

"What I want doesn't mean anything to you," she said, a sharp edge to her voice. "I defected to deliver a punishing blow to China and perhaps stop President Xiao from achieving his dream of ruling there for life. But you betrayed me."

"Oooh," Margo whispered to Ian, "this is going to be good." And then she went to the refrigerator, pulled out the pitcher of ice tea, and helped herself to two mason jars from a kitchen cabinet.

"On the contrary," Healy said. "We acted immediately on the information you gave us on the microSD card, saved the lives of two presidents, and undermined a scheme that Xiao spent decades, and billions of dollars, to achieve. Isn't *that* what you wanted?"

Margo poured a jar of ice tea for Ian, and then one for herself, while they watched the show.

"No, it wasn't," Mei said. "I wanted to destroy Xiao to avenge my parents, who he has imprisoned for life. But you blamed ISIS for the assassination attempts, not Xiao, and you didn't expose his plot to the world. He walks away unscathed, and in November that party congress will let him become dictator."

Healy waved off her argument. "That's only the way it seems. The fact is, you've dealt Xiao a fatal blow that will eventually destroy him and his government. He just doesn't know it yet."

"*Eventually.* That's nice," Mei said. "I hope I'll still be alive to see it. When do I go into hiding?"

"You don't," Healy said.

"Then I definitely won't be alive to see it."

Ian thought she was probably right about that.

"Your life isn't in any danger," Healy said. "Penny told the Chinese that you brought us no actionable intelligence and that you're just a spoiled, neurotic heiress who played us for fools."

"And you think they believe him?" Mei asked.

Margo spoke up. "Why not? Half the story is true."

Ian quickly asked a question to distract Healy and Mei from Margo's caustic remark. "What's China saying about her defection?"

"Not a word," Healy said. "Not even through back channels. They don't seem to care that Mei is gone."

"They care," Mei said. "Xiao will send assassins to kill me. I have to disappear."

"You have to do the opposite," Healy said. "You're going to put a spotlight on yourself. You and Ian will go public, telling the world about your daring escape from Chinese oppression, maybe even imply a romance to tug at America's salacious heartstrings. It's a win-win for everybody."

"How do you figure that?" Ian asked.

"The Chinese will be shamed, you will sell a bazillion books, and the studio will put *Straker* back into production to capitalize on the publicity, turning Mei into an international star."

"Posthumously," Mei said. "The Chinese will kill me before the movie comes out."

"They wouldn't dare," Healy said.

"They just tried to kill two presidents," Margo said to Healy. "But you think they draw the line at killing an actress?"

Healy got up, got himself a mason jar, and casually filled it with ice tea. If he was angered by Margo challenging him, he wasn't showing it. "It would be a public relations nightmare, right before the party congress. Xiao won't want that."

Mei said, "So he'll kill me after he becomes ruler for life."

"Why would he bother if he already has what he wants?" Healy brought the pitcher over to the couch and refilled Mei's glass, playing the polite host. "Besides, the fact that we didn't put you into hiding, and that you're going public, reinforces Penny's story that you gave us nothing, so we tossed you on your ass."

"Isn't that what you're doing?" she asked.

"You'll be with Ian and Margo, at least until the movie resumes production. After it wraps, your new life begins. You may not even need our help to get on your feet." Healy took a sip of his ice tea. "Or we can just forget all that and you can go off to your double-wide in Wyoming."

Mei looked past Healy to Ian. "What do you think?"

Ian thought about Healy's scenario as if it were a story being pitched to him for one of the TV series that he'd produced before he became a novelist. He considered whether the action naturally developed from the characters, and their established motivations, or if they were being shoehorned into a contrived narrative for the convenience of a lazy writer.

"I don't see any holes in the plot," Ian said. "I could write it."

"Okay," Mei announced. "Then I'll do it."

Ian was flattered that she was willing to bet her life on his story sense yet again. But then it occurred to him that the truth was probably that she'd rather die than work at a Walmart in Wyoming.

"Excellent," Healy said and turned to Ian. "I'm going to take you at your word."

"What word is that?" Ian asked.

"That you'll write it."

"I didn't mean it literally."

"This is your scenario now. You run with it." Healy set down his mason jar and headed for the door. "I'm leaving now and taking Mei's security detail with me. The CIA can't be directly involved in what comes next. Good luck."

And on that note, Healy walked out.

CHAPTER TWO

Top Chef Catering. Khimki, Moscow Oblast. July 11. 9:30 p.m. Moscow Standard Time.

The headquarters of Top Chef Catering was a ten-story, deep-blue monolith in Khimki, a bedroom community eighteen miles northwest of the Kremlin, and was known in Russian intelligence circles as the Kitchen.

It wasn't called that because the first two floors of the tower were devoted to preparing meals for the Russian military, hundreds of grade schools, numerous prisons, and the International Space Station. It got its nickname because floors three through ten were devoted to cooking up covert operations that were too hot for even the feared GRU to touch, even with oven mitts. The Kitchen's present mission was running an internet troll farm that employed four hundred Russians to spread propaganda on the web.

The Kitchen belonged to Leonid Morzeny, who began his career running a prostitution ring, expanded into blackmail and loan-sharking, and then took an unexpected turn into catering when he seized Top Chef from a now-deceased borrower who couldn't settle his debts. Morzeny broadened the catering business into institutional food service, bribing and blackmailing politicians to win lucrative contracts, then shrewdly approached the GRU with the idea of laundering cash through his company to fund their covert operations abroad. The GRU jumped at it. That successful relationship evolved into Top Chef becoming the cover for various off-the-books intelligence operations, secretly funded by outrageously inflated government and institutional food service contracts so there wouldn't be any direct ties to the Kremlin if things went wrong.

Morzeny was forty-five, regularly shaved his head to keep it Jeff Bezos bald, and always wore the Steve Jobs black-sweater-and-blue-jeans ensemble. He believed that emulating the style cues of successful men subliminally prompted others to see their qualities in him.

Today he was consciously trying not to trip on his Air Jordans, which he wore with the laces untied, Jay-Z style, as he strode into his tenth-floor conference room. Falling on his face would seriously undermine the oligarch's authority with his "generals." That was what he called the six computer geeks—unshaven, pale-skinned, and largely unbathed twentysomethings—who sat around the conference table. They were awaiting their orders from him on how to deploy their soldiers, the hundreds of internet trolls toiling in the floors below, in their war on Russia's enemies. His generals looked up at him with their bloodshot eyes, strained from countless hours staring at bright computer screens, as he stood at the head of the table.

"Good evening, gentlemen. We've enjoyed great success weaponizing free speech on social media platforms to disrupt the democratic political systems and institutions abroad. That fake news operation will continue. But now we've been ordered to take that operation to the next level."

His six generals traded looks. They had no idea what "the next level" was. Frankly, Morzeny hadn't known what it was, either, until he was told by the president himself over breakfast at the Kremlin. But he rolled his eyes, as if the answer was obvious and his generals were morons for not knowing it.

"We're going to manipulate the American people and their leaders with real fake news to achieve a specific outcome."

Petrov, a programmer adept at hijacking websites, raised one of his freakish arms, which was almost as long as his legs, and then spoke up without waiting to be called on. "Real fake news? What is that?"

"Reality that isn't real," Morzeny said. "I suppose you could call it fake truth."

"Like a movie," said Viktor, a shifty little man who excelled at creating doctored photos and videos for social media and, on his own time, liked to direct amateur skin flicks for Pornhub.

"Yes, but one that's played out in the real world," Morzeny said. "The way the Ukrainians faked the death of an anti-Russia reporter as a means of exposing the assassins who'd been hired to kill him."

"By the GRU," said Evgeny, who created fake social media accounts for nonexistent people and oversaw the posting of thousands of fake tweets each day. He had the nervous habit of chewing his fingers until they bled. His keyboard looked like a crime scene. "It was a major fuckup."

"The GRU prefers to look at it as a teachable moment," Morzeny said.

"So we're going to stage events," Petrov said, not raising one of his tentacles this time, "and then amplify them through social media manipulation."

"They won't be staged," Morzeny said. "They will be real."

Evgeny chewed on a scab on his left thumb. "I don't understand."

"We are going to take several real events and wildly amplify them until they come together to form one compelling narrative that leads inevitably to our desired result. It's not a new idea. In the 1890s, a revolution was raging in Cuba. American newspaper publisher William Randolph Hearst had his reporters exaggerate what was going on in their stories to whip the public into a frenzy and spark the Spanish-American War. Why did he want a war? To sell more newspapers. And it worked."

Viktor asked: "What is the specific outcome we want to achieve?"

"The first steps in the rebirth and reunification of the Soviet Union."

"Is that all?" Petrov said, his sarcastic comment generating some anxious laughter among the generals. "Where do we start?"

"As with any story, it begins with the plot." Morzeny went to the door and opened it, ushering in a guest with a wave of his arm. "For that, we're fortunate to have an expert to lead us."

And, to the astonishment of the generals, in strode Kirk Cannon, the American action movie star, writer, and director who'd fled from the United States to Russia a decade ago rather than face eighty years in prison for drugging and raping women. He'd become the president's personal martial arts instructor and continued to pursue his passion for filmmaking and sex with unconscious women.

Cannon, whose given name was Floyd Gruber, wore an elaborately embroidered Japanese silk kimono over his three-hundred-pound girth, and his crude oil black hair was tied into a tight man bun. The sixty-year-old actor had injected so much Botox into his face that Morzeny thought he looked like a wax museum version of himself.

Cannon dropped a four-hundred-page screenplay on the table with a heavy thud that got everyone's attention.

"This is our script," he said in English, having never bothered to learn Russian, and in a near whisper, because it forced people to concentrate when he spoke. Everyone in the room was fluent in English, of course, which was how they were able to write and produce social media posts that seemed authentically American. "We will need a Mexican sociopath, a patriotic Texas rancher, a barbaric drug lord, and a blowhard TV pundit with a huge, devoted audience of ideological sycophants."

"We already have one of them," Morzeny said in English. "The others might take a little time to find."

"The president has given us six months," Cannon said. "We have an unlimited budget and a crack team of GRU special forces agents under our direct command. If Paramount Pictures had given me that kind of support, I'd have ten Oscars by now."

"The hell with Oscar," Viktor said. "I think you're the greatest film-maker who has ever lived."

"Thank you. But what I did before were just movies. This is going to be my enduring masterpiece," Cannon said. "And my revenge."

CHAPTER THREE

Syria, Virginia. July 11. 3:40 p.m. Eastern Daylight Time.

After Healy left, Ian spent thirty minutes pacing outside the cabin, thinking about his next move, and then used Margo's burner phone to call Larry Novak, his literary agent in New York.

"Where are you?" Novak yelled into his ear. "I've been trying to reach you for days."

"Sorry, my life has been wild and this is the first chance I've had to catch my breath."

"I've left you six thousand messages. Do you have any idea what you've done?"

"No, I don't. I've been off the grid." That was true. Ian had been held *incommunicado* in a safe house since his return to the United States and had been so caught up with saving the country from being overthrown by the Chinese that he hadn't thought about the blowback on his writing career. "Fill me in."

"Is Wang Mei with you?"

"Yes."

"Shit! Then it's true."

"What's true?"

"That you ran off with the female star of your damn movie. Pinnacle Pictures has shut down production on *Straker*, not that they had any choice. The Chinese government kicked the cast and crew out of Hong Kong and banned the release of Pinnacle's movies in their country. Thinking with your dick could cost Pinnacle hundreds of millions of dollars."

Ian could visualize Novak, a native New Yorker, wearing his ever-present Bluetooth earbuds, angrily pacing his Sixth Avenue corner office and underscoring his words with broad hand gestures in his own personal sign language. "Is that all?"

"This isn't funny. There are probably a dozen process servers sleeping on your front porch right now. The studio wants your balls and your money. Your publisher is shredding your book contract, and oh, by the way, we don't represent you anymore."

"It wasn't an affair, Larry. It was a defection."

"Bullshit," Novak said.

"I'm calling you from a CIA safe house in Virginia." Ian told him about Mei's political troubles in China and a heavily redacted version of their escape from Hong Kong. He left out the part about saving the president of the United States from assassination.

"That's incredible," Novak said. "When will the CIA go public with this?"

"Never," Ian said. "They're a spy agency."

"Is Mei willing to go to the media with her story?"

"I don't know." Ian pretended to hesitate for a second. "I might be able to talk her into it."

"Do it, because otherwise nobody will believe you and going public with this is the only thing that can save your ass," Novak said. "Will the CIA contradict you when this comes out?"

"They'll say that they can neither confirm nor deny the story."

"Perfect, because that's just another way of saying yes, it's all true," Novak said. "How soon can you two get to New York?"

"We can be there tonight . . . if she agrees to come with me."

"Guilt her into it," Novak said. "Tell her if she doesn't do this, you'll end up destitute, living under an overpass, and begging for change outside of Trader Joe's. I'll start lining up national television interviews for you to do tomorrow."

"You can make it happen that fast?"

"This is breaking news and it's got it all: international intrigue, celebrity, and sex. I could get you on the air tonight if you're up for it."

"Tomorrow is soon enough," Ian said. "Does this mean you're still my agent?"

"Of course I am. What a stupid thing to ask. But I do have a very important question for you."

"What's that?"

"Does Mei have a literary agent?"

LaGuardia Airport. New York City. July 11. 8:07 p.m. Eastern Daylight Time.

Ian, Margo, and Mei had taken an Uber to the Charlottesville Airport, where they caught a flight to LaGuardia that arrived shortly after 8:00 p.m. The only baggage they brought with them was psychological. A car was waiting for them outside the terminal, courtesy of Larry Novak, and took them straight to Macy's in Herald Square so they could buy some clothes. They got to Macy's less than an hour before closing time. Ian and Margo found what they needed in five minutes but Mei shopped until the manager pushed them out.

Their driver took them up to the Grand Hyatt on East Forty-Second Street, where Novak had reserved three rooms and left an envelope for Ian with the desk clerk that contained their itinerary for the next day. Their first interview was set for *CBS This Morning* at 7:30 a.m., and half a dozen more TV interviews were scheduled throughout the day, spread across Manhattan and among networks that covered the full political spectrum, from MSNBC to Fox.

Ian and Mei spent the next two hours in his room, rehearsing their stories with Margo, who played their interviewer, until they were sure they were telling just enough truth to make their lies and omissions credible. They didn't get into their beds until after two, giving Ian and Margo about three hours of sleep and Mei, who needed to get up early to do her own hair and makeup, only enough time for an hour-long catnap.

At 6:45 a.m., another driver was waiting outside the hotel to take them around Manhattan for their whirlwind day of interviews.

CHAPTER FOUR

Most news show sets looked like the bridge of a starship. But the set of *Cuomo Primetime* resembled a converted loft with brick walls, exposed iron girders, and window-framed flat-screen monitors that displayed a generic urban skyline. Ian assumed the point of pretending to broadcast from a renovated factory was to make the news, and the people delivering it, more relatable to the common working man, few of whom had ever been on a starship, and in those cases only for colonoscopies conducted by extraterrestrial proctologists.

Ian and Mei sat across a plexiglass table from Chris Cuomo, the host of the show, who faced the camera and said: "Ian Ludlow is the author of the *New York Times* bestselling adventures of freelance spy Clint Straker. But a few weeks ago in Hong Kong, Ian became the unlikely hero of a real-life espionage thriller, helping Chinese movie star Wang Mei defect to the United States."

While Cuomo spoke, the screens behind him swapped the urban skyline for covers of Ian's books and glamour shots of Mei from her various Chinese movies. Ian stole a glance at Margo, who stood off camera beside the show's female producer and a monitor that played a live feed of the broadcast. Margo seemed amused by it all.

"It's an event that went largely unnoticed by the media because it happened quietly, only a day or two before the attempted assassination of the president in Paris. But now their incredible story has emerged and the two key players are here to tell us about it. Let's get after it." Cuomo shifted his gaze from the camera to Ian. "Set the scene for us, Ian."

"It's simple, really, Chris. I went to Hong Kong to see the movie version of my book being filmed and to be in some publicity photos with the stars, Damon Matthews and Wang Mei. That's all that I was expecting."

Various movie clips of Matthews, the biggest box-office star on earth and also one of the shortest, dangling from helicopters, shooting guns, and wrestling with dinosaurs appeared on-screen behind them.

Mei said, "And I was preparing for the role of a lifetime, costarring in a Damon Matthews movie."

Cuomo glanced at Mei now. "But that's not the whole story, is it, Mei? The real drama for you was happening off camera. Your father, Wang Kang, is the Chinese billionaire who owns the studio that's making the movie and who vanished months ago."

"He didn't vanish," she said. "He was abducted by the Chinese government."

Cuomo feigned ignorance. "Why would they do that?"

"Because he's against President Xiao anointing himself leader for life at the party congress in November. My father believes it's a step backward for the Chinese people. So Xiao has silenced him and hundreds of others who might oppose his ascension. That is something I couldn't say until I was here, safe from Xiao's retribution. I have Ian to thank for that."

She smiled at Ian and squeezed his hand on the table. It was a smart move. Ian saw, out of the corner of his eye, a close-up of their hands on the monitor.

Cuomo narrowed his eyes at Mei and leaned forward, signaling his intent to drill down to the heart of the story. "You're a major celebrity in China, but after your father's disappearance, you were constantly accompanied by bodyguards, presumably for your safety. But the truth is they were actually Chinese agents making sure you never stepped out of line."

"I was essentially a prisoner," she said. "The only freedom I had was when I was in front of the camera, performing my part."

Cuomo turned to Ian. "And that's where you came in. What happened next?"

"One night on the set, she slipped me a note saying that she wanted to defect, that it was the only way she could make sure the truth got out about her father."

The essence of the story was true, though it was Mei's mother who'd approached him and Margo. Ian wasn't actually sure that Mei knew that she was defecting until it happened. They'd never discussed their plans with her.

Cuomo looked back at Mei. "You were taking a big chance coming forward to Ian. Why him? What did you think he could possibly do for you? He's a writer, not a spy."

"I knew from his books that he had the imagination to pull off my escape and I knew, from the instant I met him, that he was also someone I could trust." She stared soulfully into Ian's eyes and he wondered if it was true.

"What about you, Ian?" Cuomo asked. "Why did you stick your neck out to help her?"

"Because she wasn't just playing the character that Straker rescues anymore. She'd become her," Ian said. "I'm not Straker but he lives within me. His values are my values. He wouldn't walk away from Mei and neither could I, not if I wanted to live with myself."

It sounded so good that Ian almost believed it himself. He didn't dare glance at Margo because he knew he'd see her choking back laughter.

"C'mon, Ian," Cuomo said, pointing his pen at him. "You had to know that was insane. There's a big difference between writing about an action hero and being one."

Not as much as you'd think, Ian thought.

"I'm not an action hero and never will be. I tell stories. So that's what I did. I tweaked the plot," Ian said. "I took a car chase scene that she was in and rewrote it as her means of escape. When her bodyguards watched her speed away for the cameras, they didn't realize that she wouldn't be coming back."

"Or that you were in the car, too," Cuomo said. "How did you get her out of Hong Kong?"

"I've met a few real-life spies in my research and I reached out to them for assistance." Meaning he'd asked Margo to get word to her CIA contact in Hong Kong to make the arrangements. "But how we actually fled the country is top secret, for obvious reasons."

Cuomo didn't press the issue. "You two had quite an extraordinary adventure, like something from one of your books. Maybe that's where we'll learn the rest of the story someday."

Ian smiled. "You never know."

But Ian did. Cuomo was right.

CHAPTER FIVE

Their last interview of the day was on *The Real Story with Dwight Edney*, the highest-rated show on Fox News. Ian, Mei, and Edney sat on chrome stools at a white counter that resembled a kitchen island— Edney at one end with Mei and Ian to his right. Behind them was a video wall that displayed an ever-changing array of animated red, white, and blue graphics that repeatedly spelled out Edney's name in massive letters against the backdrop of an American flag.

Ian figured the story of their escape from Hong Kong would be red meat for Edney, a chance for the conservative pundit to show off his patriotism and rail against China, a frequent target of the barbed monologues that opened his show.

Edney wore his usual double-breasted pin-striped suit, an array of papers spread out in front of him that he marked with a gold-plated Montblanc pen, a signature part of his act. He had plump, rosy cheeks and a thin beard that looked like it had been drawn on his round, chubby face with a Sharpie to indicate that he actually had a chin.

A Maryland native in his early forties, Edney flaunted hair a shade of brown not found in nature and he spoke with a nonspecific southern accent of his own creation, one easily and often lampooned by comedians. In fact, Ian was having a hard time not adopting the accent himself as he responded to Edney's questions, which were virtually the same ones they'd already answered on six other programs.

"Straker wouldn't walk away from her and neither could I," Ian said, finishing his rote response to Edney's last query. "Not if I wanted to live with myself."

"Because you are an American," Edney said, "and you carry with you the enduring values of freedom and democracy that is our country's lifeblood."

"That must be it," Ian said and saw Margo, standing behind the robotic cameras, pretending to stick a finger down her throat. The only other person behind the cameras was the stage manager, a chubby guy in his fifties wearing a headset microphone.

Edney turned to Mei, who sat between him and Ian. "Basically, what you're telling us is that after your father's arrest on unspecified charges, you became a prisoner of the communist state. The bureaucrats allowed you to act in a big Hollywood movie as a form of global propaganda to perpetuate the lie that the Chinese people have creative freedom."

"I only had the illusion of freedom," Mei said. "I couldn't live like that. Nobody can. So I had a choice. Either escape that oppression or be slowly crushed by it."

"Everyone in Red China is a prisoner of oppression," Edney said. "That is the nature of communism."

"I realize that now," she said.

"That's an incredible story." Edney gathered his scattered papers, stacked them, and shifted his gaze back to Ian. "It's like a plot from one of your books."

"It's even better than one of mine. I might have to steal it." Ian smiled and waited for Edney to thank them for being his guests and then go to commercial.

"If you do," Edney said, "you're going to have to make some changes."

Ian had put such a nice button on the interview that he was surprised that Edney was belaboring the point. Perhaps Edney still had a couple of seconds to kill before the commercial break. Well, Ian could roll with it.

"It's going to need more action and a lot more sex," Ian said, mainly because there wasn't any sex in his story. There hadn't been for way too long.

"I don't think that's the problem," Edney said. "What it really needs is a more sympathetic heroine. Because, let's be honest, who is going to care about her?"

Mei was startled by the remark, her eyes widening in disbelief. Ian felt an immediate need to protect her even as he realized, with an aching dread, that the entire pleasant interview had been a setup to soften them for the attack that was about to come.

"I care," Ian said. "Enough that I risked my life for her."

Edney dismissed Ian's remark with a wave. "That's because you're sleeping with her. You were blinded by lust. To the rest of us, she's the spoiled daughter of a corrupt businessman who made billions exploiting cheap Chinese labor, propping up a communist regime, and taking jobs from American workers. And now we're supposed to feel sorry for her?" Edney shook his head at the camera and then smirked at Mei. "How stupid do you think Americans are?"

Mei glared furiously at him. "I lost everything."

Edney sneered. "You deserved it, honey."

Mei slapped Edney across the face so hard that it knocked him off his stool. She ripped the tiny microphone from her blouse and stormed off the set, marching past Margo and the dumbfounded stage manager to the studio door, slamming it closed behind her. Ian removed his microphone and hurried after her.

"Wait." Margo grabbed his arm as he passed. "I want to see this."

They both turned to face the set. The stunned stage manager hadn't moved and was engaged in some urgent, whispered conversation with someone on his microphone.

Edney got to his feet, holding a hand to his bleeding nose, and yelled at Mei as if she were still around to hear him. "Go back to China and work for a few years in one of your father's sweatshops, you spoiled bitch, then you can come crying to me about oppression. We'll be back after this . . ."

The show went to a commercial for a drug that controlled irritable bowel syndrome, a product that Ian believed was a perfect match for the show. The stage manager rushed up to deal with Edney while Ian and Margo made their discreet, but hurried, exit from the studio.

"He makes a good point," Margo said as they walked down a bare, dimly lit corridor that led to the emergency exit from the building.

"You're forgetting that we have Mei to thank for saving the president's life and preventing the White House from becoming the Chinese embassy," Ian whispered, just in case there were microphones attached to the security cameras in the corridor. "She sacrificed everything for our country."

"Edney doesn't know that," Margo said. "But I do, and you know something? I still agree with him."

Ian gave her an incredulous look. "You agree with Dwight Edney?"

"Don't spread it around," Margo said. "I could lose my lesbian membership card."

"I'm sure there are conservative lesbians out there."

"Of course there are," Margo said. "They're as common as leprechauns."

They reached the fire exit, which opened onto an alley behind the building, and then they walked briskly out to the Avenue of the

Americas, where their limo was waiting, the engine running. Mei was already in the back seat, her face red with rage. They slid in beside her, and Ian told the driver to take them back to the Grand Hyatt.

"That was my last interview," Mei said. "Ever."

"Good idea," Margo said, scrolling through something on her phone screen. "That one will be hard to top."

"It was a disaster," Mei said. "He humiliated me in front of the world."

"Don't be so sure about that," Ian said. "There are a lot of people who've dreamed of slapping Dwight Edney and you actually did it."

"Ian's right," Margo said. "It's only been five minutes and you're already trending on Twitter."

"I'm *what*?" Mei asked.

Margo showed Mei the screen of her phone. "You're mentioned in 7,787 tweets. Just wait until somebody uploads a video clip of that segment. You'll be a viral sensation."

And less than an hour later, Wang Mei was.

It was the slap seen around the world. The YouTube video notched fifteen million views over the next forty-eight hours.

And by the end of the week, Pinnacle Pictures resumed production of *Straker* in Los Angeles, brought Wang Mei in to continue her role, and issued a press release that supported her "courageous escape to freedom from an oppressive regime." However, Ian was informed through his agent that he wasn't welcome on the set or on the Pinnacle lot, not even as a guest on the studio tour, because his "dick-driven, batshit-insane behavior" got the *Straker* crew thrown out of China, cost the production millions of dollars, and nearly killed the movie.

At least there weren't any process servers waiting for him when he got home.

CHAPTER SIX

It had been a long, horrible week for Dwight Edney. Not only did the Wang Mei clip go viral, but so did a *Saturday Night Live* skit about the notorious incident, with Melissa McCarthy playing him with an absurd southern accent and a beard that was drawn on her face with a Sharpie. In the skit, Edney was slapped so hard that he was sent backward in time to the Stone Age, where his political views were enthusiastically embraced by the Neanderthals, all of whom had his same hair color and accent.

But what really infuriated Edney was that the two videos drew a much larger audience than his show. Now he was going to get his revenge. He faced the camera, tapping his pen on the stack of papers in front of him.

"By now, you've all seen me getting slapped by Wang Mei, the spoiled Chinese movie star and billionairess who says that she fled her country to escape oppression. At least that's the story she'd like you to believe. Tonight I can reveal the *real story*. Mei is one of dozens of Chinese actors, singers, and sports figures who are under investigation by the communists for using yin-yang contracts. What are those? They're like a mobster's two sets of books and just as criminal. Mei made everybody she worked for draw up two contracts for her, one real and one fake, to hide what she was really paid. I have her yin-yang contracts for *Straker* right here."

Edney held up a sheaf of papers in each hand and went on to explain that the fake *Straker* contract paid her 10 million yuan, or $1.5 million, for three weeks' work while the real, secret contract paid her four times as much.

The Chinese government only saw the fake contract, allowing Mei to avoid paying nearly 8 million yuan in taxes on her salary for the film. She reportedly owed the government close to 100 million yuan in back taxes.

"Wang Mei was facing imminent arrest for tax evasion and probably years in prison. That's why she manipulated Ian Ludlow into helping her escape from Hong Kong." Edney smiled into the camera. "I don't blame Ludlow, a starstruck author, for falling into her honey trap and being bamboozled by a common criminal. But I saw right through her and I'm betting that you did, too. That, my friends, is the *real story*. I don't expect the left-wing radicals at Pinnacle Studios to fire Wang Mei from *Straker*, so tonight I am calling on the Justice Department to investigate the studio for blatant violations of the Foreign Corrupt Practices Act in the financing of the movie."

Edney smiled, pleased with himself, and then spent the rest of the show attacking the president for allowing NATO to use American taxpayers as their ATM. It was time, he said, for Europe to pay for their own protection and for the president to invest those billions of dollars instead in rebuilding our crumbling infrastructure. During the final commercial break, Edney got a text on his iPhone. His mother was waiting for him at home.

That was never good news. Cloris Edney came into Manhattan from the Hamptons only if she had orders to give him.

As soon as the show was over, he got into his limo and headed straight to his Upper East Side apartment building that overlooked Central Park.

Edney stepped into the elevator and immediately smelled his seventy-two-year-old mother's clinging, faintly nauseating scent, a mix of flowery perfume and the smoke from her hand-rolled cigarettes. It was how he imagined a rose garden would smell if somebody covered it with fertilizer, doused it with gasoline, set it on fire, and then put out the flames with buckets of horse piss.

Her scent was even stronger when he stepped into his apartment, which, after his third divorce, he'd decorated like the home of a British lord in dark wood, leather furniture, and oil paintings of landscapes and fox hunts. This was a man's world.

He found Cloris Edney sitting at the bar in his game room, smoking one of her cigarettes and nursing a brandy. The room was dominated by a pool table that he never used and a big-screen TV for watching football games and porn.

"What have I told you about smoking in my house?" Edney took the cigarette from her hand, tossed it in the sink behind the bar, then went looking for the can of Glade Cashmere Woods air freshener that he kept specifically for her visits. "Isn't it bad enough you killed Dad with it?"

"Your father didn't die from secondhand smoke. He died from all the solvents he inhaled in the cleaning business," she said. "Smoking saved me. The chemicals couldn't get past the charcoal in my lungs."

He found the Glade under the sink, but before he could spray it, she said: "But I will kill you with my bare hands if you spray that in this room while I'm sitting here."

"You're a feeble old lady," Edney said. "Your days of killing are over."

But he put the can away out of respect, since she had once been pretty good at killing, and he reached instead for a glass to pour himself a few fingers of Scotch.

"Is that how you thank me for giving you Wang Mei's yin-yang contracts?" she asked.

"Were they real?"

"Does it matter? Consider it a gift from the Kitchen." She reached into the large Chanel purse that was resting on a barstool, pulled out a fat manila envelope, and set it on the bar top. "Now they want you to shift your rhetoric in a new direction."

Unlike other Russian sleeper agents, Dwight Edney didn't have to worry about setting up clandestine meetings with his handler—because his handler was his mother. He could meet her anywhere, anytime, without arousing any suspicion. She'd once passed him a package of secret, coded documents on the street outside FBI headquarters just for the "fuck you" fun of it. The big drawback to the arrangement, though, was that Edney was a forty-year-old man who still took orders from his mother.

His parents were trained from childhood in Russia to become "espionage colonists" in America—sleeper agent couples that the GRU hoped would breed generations of deeply embedded spies in all levels of American culture.

Harold and Cloris Edney had arrived in Maryland in the mid-1970s and started a housecleaning and custodial business in Washington, DC, that allowed the two spies free, unfettered access to the empty homes and offices of politicians, lobbyists, reporters, and even several law-enforcement agents.

It was an intelligence bonanza.

Dwight was their only child and, from a very early age, he was groomed to become a journalist and someday help the Russians manipulate the media and, by extension, American public opinion. His big break came early, when he was just fourteen years old and working on his high school newspaper. He wrote Boris Yeltsin a letter, asking for an interview. Yeltsin not only responded but invited the youngster to interview him during his Vancouver summit with President Clinton. That opportunity, shrewdly engineered by the GRU, made Edney a national media darling, popularity that he was able to leverage into a successful journalism career.

Edney knew that in the eyes of his nameless, faceless superiors in Russia, his success on Fox News and his cultural influence completely overshadowed his failure to have offspring and produce another generation of homegrown spies. But not to his mother. Cloris took each of his childless divorces as a personal betrayal. She believed he was intentionally refusing to procreate to sabotage the long-term mission she and her husband had dedicated their lives to achieving.

She was right. It was his one act of rebellion. And besides, he hated kids.

Edney gestured with his glass of Scotch to the envelope his mother had set on the bar. "What's in there?"

"Secret Justice Department memos that reveal that hordes of drug-crazed, sexually depraved illegal aliens are streaming over the border, raping, killing, and taking American jobs."

"In that order? Or are they doing it all at once?"

"Don't be a smart-ass," she said. "Just do what you're told."

"I would be more effective at it if the Kitchen would share the big picture with me," he said, "whatever it is that they are trying to pull off."

"The less you know, the less likely you are to screw it up by revealing too much on TV. You love to hear yourself talk."

"The Kitchen is working in the dark, coming up with these grandiose plots in some back room in Moscow," Edney said. "They're *caterers*, for God's sake. They should talk to me. They don't understand the culture here as well as I do."

"That's why they have experienced spies like me to advise them," she said. "I've been here fifty years. I understand Americans."

"But you're still an outsider looking in," Edney said. "I *am* an American."

Cloris slapped him hard across the face, drawing tears in his eyes, but at least he remained standing this time and didn't have a nosebleed. This was the second time in a week that he'd been slapped by a woman and he didn't like it.

"Don't you ever say that to me," she said. "You are a Russian."

"Who doesn't speak a word of the language and has never set foot on Russian soil. My soul may be Russian, but in every other way, I am an American," Edney said. She started to take another swing at him but he grabbed her by her thin, age-spotted wrist. "I was born, raised, and educated here. That is a fact. It's also an asset that isn't being exploited to its full extent. I could be doing so much more for them than whipping up public anger. I shouldn't be a puppet. I should be one of the people pulling the strings."

He let go of her wrist, took a fresh glass, and poured himself a new drink.

She shook her head in disappointment. "You're arrogant and egotistical. You think you are smarter than everybody else. It serves you well on TV, but it will get you killed in the spy game. That's why you will always be kept in the dark about the part you are playing and why you'll talk to no one but me. It's your enforced ignorance that's keeping you free and alive."

"The FBI has no idea I'm a spy and even if they did, the worst they'd ever do is put me in prison. They wouldn't kill me."

"They wouldn't," his mother said. "But I would."

"Only because I haven't given you any grandchildren."

"Then you better knock up a woman soon." Cloris finished her brandy, grabbed her purse, and stood to go. "As a life insurance policy."

CHAPTER SEVEN

La Villa Contenta Resort. Puerto Vallarta, Mexico. November 1. 3:11 p.m. Central Standard Time.

Gustavo Reynoso raked the private beach. It was a dumb thing to be doing, but apparently the rich, self-indulgent American tourists who stayed in the resort villas expected the sand to be as smooth as carpet.

He wore a jaunty little panama straw hat with a flowered band, a short-sleeved guayabera shirt covered with brightly colored flowers, white shorts, white socks, and white sneakers. It was a resort uniform that made the dark-skinned, loose-limbed thirty-year-old look like a gay circus clown as he walked back and forth, pin-striping the sand with the tines of his rake and smiling as if this were the greatest joy of his life. This was the second-worst job at the resort, one step above cleaning the toilets, which is what he had to do after he raked the beach.

But he was lucky to have the work, considering that only two weeks earlier he had been released from the Topo Chico penitentiary in Monterrey after a seven-year stretch for rape. The resort didn't know that, of course. They didn't waste time doing background checks on losers willing to dress like a clown, rake sand in the blazing sun, and stick their faces in shit for forty pesos a day.

He'd been watching a blonde American woman in a string bikini who was sunbathing on a cushioned chaise lounge under a palapa. She was in her early thirties and had spent most of the day drinking cocktails and smoking cigarettes that she'd stubbed out in the sand, using the beach like her personal ashtray. But now she got up, her towel falling off the chaise, and dove into the surf to cool off. After a few minutes, she strode back onto the beach, water beading on her bouncing boobs and streaming in rivulets down her long, lean legs.

She approached her chaise lounge and looked with disgust at her towel on the sand as if it had landed on a pile of steaming manure. She caught Gustavo's eye, snapped her fingers at him, and pointed at the towel like it was his fault.

"Get me a fresh towel," she said.

Gustavo nodded, understanding the message if not the actual words, dropped his rake, and headed for the beach cabana where the fresh towels were kept.

"*Ándale!*" she said, snapping her fingers. "*Ándale!*"

Gustavo felt his skin burn with anger. Nobody had ever talked to him like that before. He grabbed a clean, folded towel and walked back toward her.

She snapped her fingers again, insistent, a scowl on her face. "*Arriba! Arriba!* I'm freezing here, Pedro."

He ran the last few steps, as if it were an emergency, and presented the folded towel to her. She had goose bumps on her skin and her nipples were hard.

The woman snatched the towel from him, sat down on the edge of her chaise, and dried herself off, running the towel over her breasts and down her stomach. She then spread her legs to dry her thighs.

His breath caught in his throat and he was suddenly aware of himself still standing there staring at her. He turned his back to the woman and went to retrieve his rake, hoping she couldn't see the tent in his shorts.

She snapped her fingers at him again. "Wait, Pedro. I didn't say you could go yet."

Gustavo looked over his shoulder. She held a plastic bottle of suntan lotion out to him, shook it, and gestured to her back.

"Do my back." She slid to the end of the chaise lounge, turned her back to him, and set the bottle beside her.

Gustavo was glad her back was to him and she couldn't see his obvious arousal as he returned to the chaise lounge. He picked up the bottle, squirted the lotion between her shoulder blades, and began to spread the warm lotion over her skin. It was the first time he'd touched a woman in years. As he worked on her firm shoulders, he imagined himself slipping his hands around her slender neck, forcing her facedown into the sand while she struggled helplessly underneath him.

He climaxed just from the thought of it, shocking and embarrassing himself. She turned, glanced at his shorts, and burst into laughter.

"Poor little man," she said.

She was still laughing at Gustavo as he covered his groin with his straw hat and rushed to the toilets, where he could work until his shorts dried and escape her humiliating, shrill laughter.

But he wasn't going to let it end there. He couldn't and still call himself a man. Gustavo watched from afar as she left the beach and returned to her villa.

Gustavo had a switchblade in the old, rusted-out Ford Escort that he lived in and that he'd parked in an empty lot thirty yards from the resort. After work, he went to his car, sat in the back seat drinking tequila until it was dark, then took his knife and crept back to the rude woman's secluded villa. He was still in his ridiculous uniform, so he wouldn't look suspicious if any guests saw him on the property.

The sliding glass door that faced the beach was open, letting in the ocean breeze through the screen. Tourists were so trusting. He peeked into the living room. It was empty and the only movement came from the ceiling fan moving the breeze over the rattan furniture. He could hear the shower running.

Gustavo eased open the screen and slipped inside. At almost the same instant, he heard the shower shut off. He moved to the bedroom door, stepped to one side of it, pressed his back against the wall, and waited for the woman to step out.

A moment later, she walked past him with a bath towel wrapped loosely around her naked, damp body. It was almost as if she was begging for it. He sprang on her, intending to hold the knife to her throat and force her to the floor for a lesson in respect. But things didn't go quite the way he planned.

She sidestepped him and yanked off her towel. The sight of her nude distracted him for an instant, an opportunity that she used to brandish the towel like a whip, expertly taking the knife from his hand and knocking him to the floor in three lightning-fast moves he never actually saw.

To his astonishment and dismay, he found himself flat on his back, the naked woman straddling him and holding the sharp edge of his knife under his shriveling scrotum. He knew his shorts wouldn't offer him much protection from the blade.

She leaned over, her bare breasts swaying in his face, and whispered into his ear in perfect Spanish what in English would translate to: "You like blonde women with big boobs, don't you, Gustavo?"

When he spoke, his voice was hoarse, a physiological reaction that probably had something to do with the knife under his wrinkled ball sack. "How do you know my name?"

"I know all about you and all of the women that you've raped."

"I've never raped anyone."

"So what is this? Room service?" She ran the edge of the knife along the contours of his left testicle and he thought he might cry. "You obviously can't control your impulses. Perverts like you are not welcome in Puerto Vallarta. There are two ways we can solve this problem. I can cut off your balls for a coin purse or you can go to the United States tonight and never come back. What's it going to be?"

He'd tried to get into the United States before and had been caught, and deported, five times. He didn't have the money to pay the coyotes to get him across the border again.

"I don't have the money," he said.

"I don't care," she said.

"Why are you doing this to me?"

"Because you're bad for tourism." She abruptly sliced through his shorts and jammed the edge of the knife up where his scrotum met his perineum, the tender skin between his genitals and his anus. One swipe and he'd be a eunuch. "Make a choice."

"I'll go," he squeaked. He'd find the money somehow.

"Wise decision." She stood up with the knife in hand, strode to the front door, and opened it. Two hard-looking men walked in past her, neither one of them paying any attention to her nudity. "Prepare Mr. Reynoso for the trip while I pack."

Gustavo sat up on his elbows and she whirled around, throwing the knife in the same motion. The knife tip stabbed the floor between his legs, a mere hair away from his crotch. His dick retreated so far into his body he wondered if he'd ever find it again.

One of the men lifted Gustavo to his feet and the other jammed a syringe into his shoulder. He was unconscious in an instant.

CHAPTER EIGHT

Ian's Spanish-style hacienda was nestled in a canyon on a secluded stretch of Mulholland Highway in the Santa Monica Mountains. He'd rebuilt the house exactly the way it had been before a gas leak caused an explosion that burned the place down. The explosion wasn't an accident, but that was another story. He'd added a six-foot-high stucco wall around the property, a wrought iron front gate, and security cameras, but otherwise the house appeared to be virtually the same on the outside as it was before.

Restoring the interior of his house wasn't so easy. Everything Ian owned had gone up in flames, including his vintage paperback collection, his framed Straker book covers, his James Bond movie posters, and a real human skeleton that he'd kept in his office.

He'd found a used bookstore that was going out of business, bought out their entire stock of mysteries and thrillers, and filled the shelves of his office with the old, yellowed paperbacks. It gave his workspace, and his true refuge, the right smell, but the books weren't the same ones he'd collected over a lifetime and that had shaped his career as a writer.

He'd framed his Straker book covers and a few James Bond posters and hung them on the walls. But the dust jackets weren't the originals that he'd framed with such pride and excitement as each new book was published. And the Bond posters weren't the creased ones with yellowed Scotch tape residue and multiple thumbtack holes in the corners that he'd got as a kid and brought with him to college, to every apartment he'd ever lived in, and finally to his own home. He'd found another human skeleton from India for $5,600 online, but it wasn't the same. It wasn't the mysterious set of sun-bleached bones, with a $250 price tag tied to the cracked jaw, that he'd stumbled upon in a Barstow antique store and that, in the years since he'd bought it, had often sparked his imagination.

The end result was that Ian didn't feel at home in his own house. It was like he was living in captivity in a zoo that had re-created his dwelling, less for his comfort than for the education of the visitors peering into his cage. Maybe that was why his writing was going so badly.

He'd been sitting in his office for weeks now, trying to come up with the plot for his next Straker novel, but he had nothing. For the last few days, Ian had tried the Lee Child approach, just writing and hoping a story would come to him along the way, but all he ended up with was fifty pages of Straker walking around, beating up muggers and purse snatchers and sleeping with the appreciative women that he rescued. Ian deleted it all.

Now he stared at his blank computer screen and listened to a Fox News report on the TV, which he'd kept on in the living room for company. He learned that China's president, Xiao, had been appointed ruler for life, the US stock market had lost all its gains for the year, the leader of the Vibora drug cartel had escaped from a Mexican prison using a tunnel under his toilet, and a senator in Oregon had decided to become a woman. Just another typical news day in which life was a lot more exciting than anything he was writing.

The theme music for Dwight Edney's *The Real Story* began to play just as his computer pinged and a window opened up on his screen, showing him the video feed from the motion-activated camera at his gate. A black Mercedes had pulled up in front of the house.

Wang Mei got out of the car, marched up to the gate, and leaned on the buzzer. Ian hadn't seen her, or heard from her, since she'd left New York to go back to work on *Straker*. He'd heard about the yin-yang contract scandal, of course, but it had flamed out after only a few days, overshadowed by more prurient and salacious news, and he had no idea how it had ended up.

Ian hurried to his front door and hit the button on the wall that unlocked the gates. It wasn't until he opened the door to greet her that he remembered that he was unshaven, barefoot, and wearing an open terry-cloth bathrobe over a T-shirt and sweatpants.

"If I'd known you were coming," Ian said, trying and failing to sound nonchalant, "I would have put on socks."

"Sorry I didn't call first, but I didn't know what to say."

"How about, 'I'm in the neighborhood, can I stop by and say hello?'"

"That's why you're a writer," she said. "Words come so easily to you."

"God, I wish that was true," he stepped aside and gestured for her to come in.

She waved to the limo driver, who drove off, and she stepped inside the house. "The truth is, the movie wrapped today and when I left the set, I realized I had nowhere to go. So I told the driver to come here."

"I'm glad you did," he said, closing the door behind her. "It's nice to see you."

Mei went down the hall and peeked into his office. "So this is where the magic happens."

He was about to say something self-deprecating, and sadly true, but that was when Dwight Edney spoke on the TV from the living room and she followed the sound of his unmistakable voice.

"The president is letting hordes of illegal aliens swarm over our borders to rape our women, rob our homes and businesses, and sell drugs for the Mexican cartels. Why hasn't he stopped it?"

Mei stood in front of the big flat screen, put her hands on her hips, and stared disapprovingly at Edney, who was tapping his Montblanc pen on the sheaf of papers in front of him.

"I'll tell you why," Edney said, looking into the camera and creating the illusion that he was talking directly to Mei. "Because it's the drug cartels, led by Arturo Giron, who are secretly financing his reelection campaign. It's a battle that Southwest Texas rancher Eli Tanner knows all too well because it's playing out on his land. Tonight you'll get the *real story.*"

Mei turned to Ian and pointed at the screen. "How is he allowed to say that about the president?"

"The first amendment," Ian said. "It guarantees the right of free speech."

"But it isn't true."

"Probably not." Ian picked up the TV remote from the coffee table and muted Edney. "Not that it matters anymore. You say things enough on TV and it becomes its own truth."

"You watch his show?"

Ian shrugged. "I find him inspiring."

Mei stared at him in furious astonishment. "You *admire* this man? How can you say that after the way he treated me? This was a bad idea."

She turned and headed for the front door.

Ian chased after her. "I didn't say that I admire Edney. I think he's an ass. But I get ideas for my Straker books by listening to insane conspiracy theories from guys like him and I could use a few ideas right now. Any idea would do, actually."

She stopped at the front door and faced him, some concern on her face. "The writing isn't going well?"

He closed his bathrobe, cinched the sash tight, and tied it into a knot. "I've never had such a hard time writing a book."

"What about telling our story and revealing China's plot to assassinate the president?"

"I tried using it but every time I added Straker into the mix, it became ridiculous."

"Straker has always been ridiculous," she said.

"Yes," Ian said. "But now I know it."

"That's a shame."

"What is? That I can't finish this book or that I've become so self-aware that I might never be able to write a Straker novel again?"

She shook her head. "That those are the reasons you can't write the book. I thought you were going to say that the reason you couldn't use our story was because you were afraid it would put me in jeopardy."

Ian wished he were that noble or, at the very least, had thought to say that, even if it wasn't true. He was always better at making up dialogue for his characters than he was for himself.

"You'd be in no danger," he said. "I could tell the truth, word for word, and no one would believe that's what really happened."

"But we know it did," she said. "That's actually why I'm here."

"I don't understand."

Mei lowered her eyes. "I have nowhere else to go."

"You're a billionairess," he said. "You could afford to stay anywhere you want."

"Most of my money is stashed in offshore accounts and it's not going to be easy to access it. All I have right now is my paltry salary from the movie."

"Which is either a million dollars or four million dollars, depending on which contract we're talking about."

"It's not about money," she said, ignoring his reference to the yin-yang scandal. "I could continue to stay at the Peninsula Hotel in Beverly Hills for years if I wanted."

"Then what is the problem?"

She met his gaze. "You're the only one who knows the truth, who I can be myself with."

"Healy and Margo know the truth."

"But you're the only one I trust," Mei said.

"You can trust Margo."

"She hates me," Mei said.

"She'd still die for you."

Mei smiled. "That sounds like something Straker would say."

"Because I'm the guy who used to put words in his mouth."

"It's more than that. You saved two presidents from assassination. You actually do what he does."

"That's probably why I'm having such a hard time writing the books," Ian said. "Now I know you don't have to be Clint Straker, and have his experience and special skills, to save America. You can just bumble your way through it like I did."

"I'm one of the few people who knows that about you." Mei took a step toward him and held his hands in hers. "Who else could you tell that to? Doesn't it feel good?"

He pulled his hands away from her loose grip. "What do you want from me?"

"To stay here until I feel safe and I know what to do with my life."

"You're going to be a movie star," he said.

"That hasn't happened yet. It may after the movie comes out or it may not. Until then, what do I do with myself and where do I go? I need time, in a safe place, to figure out my life."

Ian had sympathy for her situation but he also felt a nagging sense of déjà vu. The last time he'd let a woman stay with him, because he was supposedly "the only one who understood the truth" about her life, it was Margo. She'd claimed she was homeless, broke, and suffered from PTSD. It had been a lie. She'd turned out to be a CIA agent who was using him as her cover for her first mission.

"Are you a spy?" he asked Mei.

"Of course not!" She laughed. "How would that work anyway? Spies are supposed to move around in secret. I'm famous."

Ian was famous and technically a spy, but he figured he probably shouldn't tell her that. "Good point. I have a guesthouse out back. It's not much, just a bedroom, a kitchenette, and a bathroom."

"Thank you," she said and kissed him on the cheek. "I'll have the Peninsula Hotel send over my suitcases."

"I hope you like it," he said as he led her across the living room to the french doors that opened to the backyard. "But if you don't, feel free to redecorate, take out a wall, or add a second floor."

"I will," she said.

He was joking but he wasn't certain that she was.

CHAPTER NINE

San Diego, California. November 2. 10:00 p.m. Pacific Daylight Time.

Gustavo Reynoso awoke in the back seat of a panel van. He was dizzy and dry-mouthed, and all his joints ached. It felt like he'd been folded in half. Someone had changed him out of his La Villa Contenta shirt and shorts into a denim work shirt and jeans.

The woman who'd held a knife to his cojones turned around in the front passenger seat and tossed him a bottle of water. He unscrewed the top off the bottle and took a long drink, noticing now that one of the two men he'd seen in her villa was sitting beside him. The other was driving the van. There were palm trees outside and the signs on the passing storefronts outside were written in English.

"Where are we?" Gustavo asked, though he knew they were in the US. He would have known it even without seeing the street outside. The air was different in the States.

"San Diego," she said.

"How did I get here?"

"I packed you in my suitcase and took a private jet."

Her eyes were hard, not a trace of humor in them. Based on that, and the way every bendable part of his body felt, he believed her. He was thankful he'd been unconscious for the journey. The van pulled to a stop in the parking lot of a shopping center.

"This is your stop." She opened her door and got out.

He glanced at the man beside him, who nodded his permission, and Gustavo opened the sliding door and got out, too, a bit unsteady on his feet. The man in the van tossed Gustavo a gym bag. Catching the bag nearly knocked Gustavo down. She grabbed his forearm to keep him from falling.

"Take a deep breath and relax, Gustavo. We put a hundred dollars in your wallet and you'll find some clothes, toiletries, and another pair of shoes in the bag." She pointed down the street. "There's a homeless shelter around the corner with plenty of beds. Good luck."

None of this made any sense to Gustavo. "Why are you doing this?"

"Because you aren't welcome in Mexico anymore." Her hand was still on his forearm and she forcefully turned him toward the storefronts down the other side of the street, where he could see a Pilates studio with dozens of blonde women on mats doing pelvic curls in front of the picture window. "This is your home now."

The women in the studio were beautiful, fit, and limber. "I can live with that."

She smiled. "I'm glad to hear it, Gustavo, because if you ever return to Mexico, I'll kill you."

He could see in her eyes that she meant it. She let go of him and climbed into the van. The man in the back seat slid the side door closed and the van drove away.

Gustavo watched them go, then shifted his gaze back to the women in the Pilates studio doing one-armed side bends and he felt blessed. He decided that the woman who'd held a knife to his scrotum was an angel. For the first time in his life, the world seemed full of possibilities.

Top Chef Catering. Khimki, Moscow Oblast. November 3. 9:30 a.m. Moscow Standard Time.

Kirk Cannon was in the tenth-floor office the Kitchen had provided for him, looking down at the Moscow Canal, a toxic torrent of Russian chemicals and raw sewage, and then beyond it to the Moscow skyline on the opposite bank. It got him thinking about the wild Mississippi, about his hometown of Memphis, about the soul music coming out of the bars on Beale Street, and about how he'd probably never see the Mississippi, or Memphis, or Beale Street, or even the abomination that was the Bass Pro Pyramid on the riverbank ever again, when Leonid Morzeny sauntered in like he owned the place, which he did.

Morzeny was in his usual Steve Jobs outfit but he'd swapped his untied Air Jordans for a pair of white, red, and blue Pharrell Williams' Adidas Human Race N.E.R.D. sneakers with neon-yellow soles and laces and a drawing of a human brain on the heel. The man hated America, worked all day to undermine its institutions and society, and yet gleefully rolled his body in its culture like a pig in shit. It made no sense to Cannon.

"Gustavo Reynoso is in San Diego," Morzeny said. "Now all we have to do is wait."

The words broke Cannon out of his funk and reminded him why he was here. His country had betrayed him, driving him away for daring to follow his creative vision and refusing to compromise it by adhering to insipid rules of personal conduct meant for people without his gifts.

"If nature doesn't take its course in a week or two, you'll have to frame him." Cannon picked up a few script pages off his desk and handed them to Morzeny. "I've written up a scenario for you just in case."

Morzeny skimmed the pages and grimaced. "Let's hope it doesn't come to this. It would be better if things played out organically without our heavy hand."

"Which is why you dropped him off outside a studio filled with women in skintight leotards."

"We don't have much time and he is who he is," Morzeny said. "There's no downside in offering him the opportunity to be himself."

They might as well have dropped him off in a nudist colony, Cannon thought. These government bureaucrats were no different than the movie studio executives who'd given him "creative notes" on his scripts. The executives always insisted on hammering every emotional beat, underscoring every plot point, and foreshadowing each coming event with the subtlety of a runaway freight train loaded with dynamite heading toward an oil refinery. But this was real life he was writing and directing, not a movie, and the present situation did raise an interesting question.

"It makes you wonder about the concept of free will, though, doesn't it?" Cannon said. "Do we ever have a choice? Or are all of us simply playing a part someone else has written?"

"It's called fate."

Cannon smiled. "Is that who I am?"

Morzeny held up Cannon's script pages. "You are for Gustavo Reynoso."

And perhaps, Cannon thought, for everyone in the United States, too.

CHAPTER TEN

In Moscow, it was already tomorrow, but it was still yesterday in Malibu, where Ian was sitting on his living room couch and watching the nightly repeat of Dwight Edney's show.

For this episode, Edney was on location in Dunn, Texas, and instead of his trademark suit, he wore a Stetson cowboy hat, a red bandana around his neck, and a western shirt with rhinestone snaps. He was doing a walk-and-talk with Eli Tanner, a bow-legged Texan with skin like an old boot who'd obviously spent most of his fifty-some years outside on a horse. They spoke as they walked across the sunbaked dirt of Tanner's ranch toward a faded red barn.

"We're thirty miles north of the Mexico border but I've still got illegals running across my land every night," Tanner said. "They used to break into my house, looking for water and cash. I had to put bars on my windows to keep 'em out and install motion-activated lights to scare 'em away at night. Come daylight, I've found all kinds of trash out there—water bottles, tin cans, syringes, and even some corpses, illegals who died on their journey from sunstroke. Or they had their throats slit by one of their own."

"Have you called the Border Patrol?" Edney asked.

"I've called everybody with a badge and they don't do anything about it except haul away the dead ones."

"It's a national disgrace," Edney said.

"To be fair, the sheriff and the Border Patrol are decent folk who just don't have the manpower or the resources to handle the surge. Each deputy is responsible for covering a hundred square miles. It ain't humanly possible to do that. So I've had to protect myself."

"What does that mean?" Edney asked, but Ian was sure the pundit already knew the answer. That was why he'd dressed up like Roy Rogers and flew out to Texas with a film crew.

"Me and some of my ranch hands have started nightly patrols. We catch 'em and hold 'em here." Tanner led Edney and the camera crew into the barn, where he'd built a huge cage out of chain-link fencing on a concrete pad. The cage held a dozen weary Mexican men, who milled around or sat on metal benches that were bolted to the floor. The camera panned across their sunburned faces.

"We give 'em water and some food, because that's the humane thing to do," Tanner said, "then we turn 'em over to the Border Patrol, who send 'em back to where they came from. The thing is, I see some of the same faces again and again."

Edney put on his best solemn expression. "How does that make you feel?"

"Like I'm the one poor son of a bitch trying to plug all the holes in a leaking dam but more holes keep popping open. Pretty soon the dam is gonna give and everybody is gonna drown in the floodwaters."

"I hear you," Edney said. "What you're saying is that in this sun-baked corner of Southwest Texas, you're all that's protecting America from the immigrant hordes that want to rape our women, hook our kids on drugs, and take our jobs."

To Ian's surprise, Tanner didn't take the bait. "Naw, I'm just an ordinary man trying to protect his family and his land."

That was all Ian could take of Edney's show. Ian changed the channel to Buzzr and caught the middle of a vintage *Match Game '73* episode, hosted by Gene Rayburn. The game show was comfort food for Ian. He liked seeing the cheesy 1970s fashions and the celebrities of the era. The panelists this time were actors Bert Convy, Loretta Swit, Charles Nelson Reilly, Mary Ann Mobley, Richard Dawson, and Kaye Ballard. There were two contestants, a housewife and a dentist.

"Lester believes in *blank* even though he has never seen one," Gene asked the housewife.

"Fairies," she said.

The crowd roared with laughter. Gene fanned the question card in front of his face as if somebody had just cranked up the heat in the studio and said: "Well, Lester has never been on Third Avenue, I'll tell you that."

That was a joke that would never get on the air today, Ian thought.

Gene approached the panel for their answers. Bert Convy said "ghosts." Loretta Swit said "Martians," and then Gene got to Charles Nelson Reilly, a toupee-wearing character actor everybody knew was gay but who wouldn't publicly acknowledge his sexual orientation for a few more decades.

"Lester did see two at the church picnic but he didn't know that they were . . ." Charles whipped out his card: "Fairies."

Charles smiled wickedly into the camera. Take that, America.

That was when Mei came in wearing a silk bathrobe. She was beautiful. Ian tried to focus his attention on the TV.

"What are you watching?" she asked.

"An old game show called *Match Game.*"

"How is the game played?"

"The host reads a sentence that is missing a word. Two contestants try to guess what word the six celebrities will pick. The contestant who guesses correctly the most times wins some prize money."

On TV, Gene had moved on to the next question. "George Washington didn't brush his wooden teeth, he *blanked* them."

Mei sat down next to Ian on the couch and watched the show for a few minutes while four of the six celebrities wrote down their answers. "Americans find this challenging and entertaining?"

"It was a huge hit in its day."

"Who are the celebrities?"

"Mostly washed-up TV stars," Ian said as Gene turned to the contestant for his answer to the question. The contestant answered "soaked." The celebrities answered "sharpened," "waxed," "polished," and "filed."

Mei was confused. "What is the correct answer?"

"There isn't one," Ian said.

"This is a stupid game."

"That's what makes it fun."

Wang Mei climbed onto Ian's lap and straddled him, blocking most of his view of the TV. Her bathrobe fell open and he saw that she was naked underneath.

"If I become a celebrity in America," she said, "will I have to play this game?"

"No," he said, his voice catching in his throat.

"That's a relief." She kissed him. He was hard instantly. It had been a long time since he'd been with a woman.

Gene Rayburn asked the celebrities another question. "Because Lola was a spy, she kept a microphone hidden in her *blank*."

"You can answer this one," Mei said and shrugged off her bathrobe.

He'd seen her nearly naked before, in a shipping container on the way to Singapore, but it was much more erotic this time. He tried to stay cool.

"You're welcome to stay here," Ian said. "You don't have to do this."

She ignored his comment and began pulling down his sweatpants. He didn't resist.

The dentist answered Gene's question. "Bosom!"

The crowd shrieked and laughed at the naughty answer.

Mei reached between his legs and he almost climaxed at her touch. The only reason he didn't was because Bert Convy was watching him.

"Is she correct?" Mei asked.

Ian stared at her breasts. "No microphone there. So I guess you really aren't a spy."

"Keep checking."

Mei slipped him inside her, and again he nearly came but a quick glance at Charles Nelson Reilly kept him from letting go. She pulled his head to her breasts and moved rhythmically against him. He felt himself losing control and peeked under her armpit at the TV again. One look at Gene Rayburn was enough to kill his desire for a few more seconds. He nearly made it to the Super Match, but he came before the show's climax and her own, which didn't arrive.

"I'm sorry," Ian said, breathing hard. "It's been a long time."

"It's okay," she said. "It felt good."

"Why did you do this?"

"Wang Mei had sex with Ian because she felt *blank*."

Ian leaned back and studied her face. "Obligated? Lonely? Bored? Afraid?"

"There is no correct answer. Isn't that what you told me?" She climbed off him, stood up, and held out her hand. "Take me to bed and you can try again to fill in the blank."

He did as he was told.

They made love twice more that night. She faked an orgasm the first time, for his sake, but she wasn't that good an actress. It also reminded him that he wasn't much of a lover. He wasn't lousy in bed, but he wasn't Clint Straker, either. Perhaps nobody was, though there was certainly room for improvement. Ian always felt like he was blindfolded the first time he went to bed with a new lover. He fumbled around in the dark, hoping not to stub a toe or fall down a flight of stairs, rather than relying on instinct, his senses, and his expertise to find his way. Part of the problem, he knew, was his own eagerness and lust. Once past that, he could approach a woman like a story, finding the plot points that will inevitably lead to a strong, emotionally earned climax that was true to her character.

So the third time he made love with Mei, Ian relaxed and focused his attention on her, gently caressing and exploring her body. He worked his way down to the scar on her thigh where she'd hidden the microSD card. He licked the scar, eliciting an encouraging moan from her, and let his tongue trace a trail up between her legs, where he continued his explorations, slowly and tenderly, until she arched her back and her body quivered for a long, sweet moment. She barely made a sound, unlike the theatrical writhing and moans of her fake climax. And when it was over, Mei almost immediately drifted off to sleep.

And that worried Ian, who was relieved that he'd finally satisfied her but was concerned that she might only remember his two failed attempts. What if she woke up in the morning and thought her orgasm was a dream, the wishful thinking of a dissatisfied lover?

He fell asleep trying to think of a way he could tell her that it really happened without appearing woefully insecure.

CHAPTER ELEVEN

Beth Wheeler, the woman who abducted Gustavo Reynoso and dumped him on a street in San Diego, didn't have any problems talking her way past the ranch hands, driving up to the main house in a dented GMC ten-foot box truck, and getting a face-to-face with Eli Tanner on his front step. That was because she came across as one of them, a local girl. She had the walk, the Texas twang in her voice, and she dressed the part, from her Stetson down to her authentic snakeskin boots. She pulled it off effortlessly because she wasn't acting. This was who she was, except for the red hair, brown eyes, and freckles that she'd expertly applied to change her appearance.

Her parents had been Russian spies who had come to Texas to work as wildcatters and infiltrate the oil industry, which they did. Their final mission had been the sabotage of an oil rig in the Gulf of Mexico a decade ago. The rig exploded and sank, creating an environmental disaster that coated the Gulf states in 130 million gallons of raw crude oil and crippled a UK-based petroleum company that had been an obstacle to Russian energy interests worldwide. Beth's parents were killed in the blast but she was their legacy, a roving disaster agent, going anywhere the GRU felt her talent for death and destruction was needed. Today, that place was Dunn, Texas, and Eli Tanner's ranch.

Tanner stepped off his front porch and regarded her. It was different from the leering looks she got from the ranch hands when she came in. There was nothing sexual about his appraisal. He was judging her musculature, her endurance, and strength, as if she were a horse that he was thinking of buying. Finally, he said: "You told my boys that you had urgent business with me."

She got right to the point, knowing that men like him hated small talk and distrusted people who indulged in it. "I saw you on Dwight Edney's show. You're putting up a good fight against the illegals swarming over the border. But let's be honest, you're losing. Most of 'em are getting past you and laughing all the way to Houston."

"That isn't my problem," Tanner said. "I'm only interested in protecting my ranch."

"But that's exactly what you're losing. This hopeless fight is eating up your days and nights, time you aren't spending on your business. Keep this up much longer, and you won't have a ranch to protect."

"So you're some liberal do-gooder who came here to tell me to let 'em trample my land, vandalize my home, and kill my cattle?"

"C'mon, is that what I look like to you?" She stood up straight and took a step toward him. "I came here to help you fight."

He smiled and acknowledged her offer with a nod. "You look like a woman who can handle a horse, and probably a gun, too, but having you here isn't going to change anything, no offense intended."

"None taken. But what if you could get your hands on enough weapons, ammunition, thermal-imaging scopes, night-vision goggles, and other gear to equip, say, a hundred men? Could you put together a citizen militia to protect your piece of the border?"

"Sure I could, but those resources will never come."

"Why not?"

"Because Dunn, Texas, is a pimple on the state's scrawny ass. Most of the people here live hand to mouth. There isn't enough votes or money here to get any politician to do anything for us."

"Who needs politicians?"

Beth walked to the rear of her truck, unlatched the roll-up rear door, and lifted it to expose the contents of the cargo area. The interior was filled with wooden crates and cardboard boxes. "This is all yours, free and clear."

"What is it?"

"Everything I just talked about. All you have to do now is find some good men."

Tanner raised a bushy gray eyebrow and lifted the top off one of the crates to reveal it was full of AK-47s that were carefully packed in straw. "Why are you doing this?"

"Because you're a patriot and I've got child-bearing hips."

"That's mighty kind of you, but I'm a happily married man with more kids than I can feed."

Beth laughed, her amusement genuine. "I didn't bring you the guns so you'd fuck me."

"Well, that's a relief." Tanner scratched one of his leathery, stubbled cheeks. "But I don't understand what you're trying to say."

"What I'm saying is that I respect you, your wife, and your kids. I don't want you to sacrifice your ranch fighting a losing battle to protect the children I'm going to have someday from being raped by Mexican drug pushers or growing up poor because there won't be any jobs. A lot of God-fearing Texans feel the same way that I do."

"So why aren't they here to join the fight?"

"Because they're better at writing checks than shooting guns."

"What about you?" Tanner asked.

"I'm just a driver making a delivery."

"You look like a lot more than that."

"It's your imagination," she said. "In fact, I was never here."

It wasn't until after the truck was unloaded, and she was driving off, that Tanner realized she didn't tell him her name.

CHAPTER TWELVE

Ian Ludlow's House. Malibu, California. November 5. 8:26 a.m. Pacific Standard Time.

Since the night Mei seduced Ian, the two of them had only left his bed to eat, shower, and watch *Match Game*, though they'd never finished an episode without having sex again. He was terrified the show was now an erotic trigger for him, and that for the rest of his life he'd get an erection every time he heard the theme or saw Gene Rayburn.

Ian had no illusions about the meaning of all the sex they were having together. It wasn't love. It wasn't really lust, either, though there was a lot of that.

It was avoidance. For both of them. Sex kept him from writing and kept her from thinking about the future.

The sexcapades couldn't go on. That was what he'd decided in his postcoital stupor that morning, her naked body curled up against him, his head turned away from her so she wouldn't have to smell his bad breath when he spoke.

"We can't just stay in the house having sex all the time," he said. That was definitely something he never thought he'd hear himself say.

"Why not?" Mei said.

"Because we both need to work. I need to write and you need to act."

"I don't need to," she said. "I have enough money to do nothing but this for the rest of my life."

"You don't act for the money," Ian said, turning his head to face her. He wasn't feeling so bad about his breath now that he'd caught a whiff of hers. "You act for the same reason I write, because it's who you are, though I also need to do it to pay my bills. I have a book due in three months that I haven't started yet."

"At least you know that somebody wants your work," she said. "Nobody is going to cast me in anything until they see how *Straker* turns out."

Ian considered that fact for a moment. "How would you feel about doing a guest part on a television series?"

"It depends on the show," she said.

He hesitated, afraid he was about to unintentionally insult her. "How about *Hollywood & the Vine*?"

She sat up and began enthusiastically singing the theme song, which had a catchy tune that some years back a jury had determined, in a landmark, multimillion-dollar copyright infringement suit, was lifted from Marvin Gaye's "I Heard It Through the Grapevine."

"Oooh you heard about that cop Vine / a plant who can't stand crime / you get caught you're gonna do time / honey honey yeah."

Mei bursting into song wasn't the reaction Ian had expected. He'd also never imagined he'd have a naked woman in his bed singing the *Hollywood & the Vine* theme to him. So many things were happening in his life lately that were beyond belief that the unbelievable was becoming his new normal. That, too, was another reason he was having trouble writing. Nothing he put on the page seemed wilder than what he was experiencing.

"You know the show?" he asked.

"Are you kidding me?" She shifted to a deep announcer's voice. *"Half-man, half-plant, all-cop."* She laughed at her impersonation, then said: "It was the best thing on TV since the cop with the talking car. It was a big hit in China."

"And you liked it?"

"I loved it," she said. "It was brilliantly subversive."

"It was?"

"The subtext about the relationship between man and nature, with nature being an allegory for freedom, and how it transcends race, religion, or government, was explosive stuff that slipped right past the censors in China," she said. "Ronnie Mancuso's performance was incredibly nuanced."

Ronnie's hair and skin were dyed green, he wore green clothes, he drove a green car, and his character's name was Charlie Vine. There was nothing remotely nuanced about that. But that was not what Ian said.

"I never thought of the show that way." And that was true.

"His performance was one of the reasons I became an actress," Mei said. "Being on the show would be a dream come true, but it's been off the air for years."

"It's back again."

She broke into a big smile. "It is? And you can get me on it?"

"No problem," he said. "I was a writer-producer on the show the first time around and I'm good friends with Ronnie, who is the executive producer now."

After the end of the original series, Ronnie had retired from acting to live off the grid in an underground bunker in the Nevada desert to escape the government, which he fervently believed was listening to his thoughts and planning a global pandemic to usher in a new world order.

Ronnie would have still been in his bunker today, waiting for the apocalypse to arrive, if Ian and Margo hadn't come to him for help when they were on the run from assassins. The three of them ended up thwarting the kind of government conspiracy that everybody told Ronnie he was crazy to believe was real.

Ian hadn't spoken to Ronnie much since their adventure, or Ronnie's subsequent six-month commitment to the Corcoran mental hospital, or Ronnie's renewed stardom upon his release, but he wasn't worried about that. They'd both been busy, that was all.

"I'm sorry, Ian. I never paid any attention to the credits," Mei said. "I had no idea you worked on the show. Why didn't you ever tell me?"

"It's not something that I publicize."

"Why not?"

Because he was deeply ashamed of it, but since she liked the show so much, he said: "I don't like to brag."

She gave him a kiss with a lot of tongue action. If this went on, they'd never get out of bed.

"I should get up and give him a call," Ian said.

"You're already up," she said, reaching between his legs to emphasize her point. "Call him later."

He decided that was a good idea.

CHAPTER THIRTEEN

An excerpt from the script for the *Hollywood & the Vine* episode "The Bad Apple," written by Jackson Burley.

INT. BARN — DAY

Hollywood and Vine are sitting in the hayloft, watching a house.

> HOLLYWOOD
>
> I hate stakeouts.

> VINE
>
> I don't mind them. It's a chance to photosynthesize.

He's using a shiny piece of cardboard to shine sun on his face.

> HOLLYWOOD
>
> I have to sit for hours, eating lousy food, drinking lousy coffee, and willing myself not to pee.

As he's talking, Vine sets down the board, takes out a bottle of water, and pours it on his green-haired head.

HOLLYWOOD

And I've got to watch you water yourself.

VINE

I'm just trying to stay hydrated. It's no different than you drinking coffee.

HOLLYWOOD

I don't pour it on my head.

VINE

Maybe you should. It might improve your disposition.

Vine notices something.

VINE

Here they are.

A car rolls up. Two men get out and go to the WELL. They pull up a package.

HOLLYWOOD

They've got the ransom.

VINE

Let's go!

The two cops burst out of the barn.

HOLLYWOOD

LAPD. Freeze. You're under arrest.

A third man, hidden in the back seat of the car, pops up and opens fire with an automatic weapon. Hollywood and Vine take cover, returning fire. The other two men take out their guns. Hollywood shoots one man, who falls into the well. The other man RUNS out into the ORANGE GROVE. Hollywood fires at the gas tank of the car . . . and it BLOWS UP, sending the remaining man spiraling through the air. Vine darts into the orange grove.

EXT. ORANGE GROVE — DAY

Vine takes cover behind a JEEP. Hollywood joins him.

HOLLYWOOD

The shooter could be hiding behind any one of those trees.

VINE

We start a gunfight here and a lot of innocent trees will get hurt.

HOLLYWOOD

A bullet isn't going to hurt a tree.

VINE

Tell that to the tree. Actually, that's a great idea.

Vine goes to the base of the tree, puts his hand on the trunk, and closes his eyes.

HOLLYWOOD

What are you doing?

VINE

Asking my cousins a question. There is a vast root system under this field that's like a chat room.

HOLLYWOOD

What's the question?

VINE

Where's the shooter?

A moment later, a nearby tree shakes loose all of its ORANGES, the fruit RAINING DOWN hard on the shooter, who squeals and, the instant he breaks cover, Hollywood shoots him in the leg, taking him down, before the bad guy can get off a shot. Hollywood nods with approval.

HOLLYWOOD

Sweet.

Fillmore, California. November 5. 3:45 p.m. Pacific Standard Time.

The director yelled, "Cut!"

Ian and Mei stood behind the director, a shaggy-haired young man in an Aloha shirt and board shorts, who sat in a chair facing a bank of four camera monitors. The bad guy got up off the ground, his leg soaked in red corn syrup from the exploding "blood bag" that was under his pant leg. A group of special effects men ran out to the burning car and used fire extinguishers to put down the flames.

"I don't think you can blow up a car by shooting it," Mei whispered to Ian so the director wouldn't hear her.

"You can in a world where a cop can be half-man and half-plant," Ian said, not caring if he was heard or not. "A TV show creates its own reality."

They were in an orange grove in Fillmore, California, one of the last authentic small towns that still remained "in the zone," an area within a thirty-mile radius of the intersection of West Beverly Boulevard and North La Cienega Boulevard in Los Angeles, where shows could be shot without having to pay actors and crews a special fee for going out on location. But as authentic as Fillmore was, it was never itself on film. It doubled for countless fake towns across the country, and across time, its storefronts constantly being re-dressed to be someplace else, sometime else. Fillmore was real but it was also fictional. People who'd never been there before passed through the town with a disturbing sense of déjà vu.

"I get it," Mei said.

"Get what?" Ian asked.

"The series is a metaphor for what is happening in the world today," she said. "There are governments out there trying to create their own reality by controlling the media and censoring speech. It's amazing how many subversive political statements you can sneak into this show."

"It certainly is," Ian said, his eyes on Ronnie Mancuso and his costar, Jeff Dallas, who'd spent three years playing the goofy dad on a Disney Channel sitcom after the first run of *Hollywood & the Vine* ended and Ronnie went off to his bunker in the Nevada desert.

Now Jeff had to have his wardrobe tailored to hide his beer belly, but Ronnie had never looked better. It wasn't because the green makeup covered the creases on Ronnie's brow or the gray in his buzz cut. He stayed physically fit so he could survive the zombie apocalypse, which Ian was certain the actor still believed was coming any day now.

Ronnie spotted Ian, strode over, and pulled him into a bear hug. "Where have you been, stranger?"

"I've been busy saving the world," Ian said.

"I believe it." Ronnie let him go and smiled at Mei. "I saw the two of you on Edney talking about your escape from China. I'd love to hear what really happened."

"What makes you think you don't already know it?" she asked coyly.

"Because, honey, nobody tells the truth on TV and . . ." Ronnie pulled a mike off his shirt, removed the transmitter clipped to his belt on his lower back, and tossed the devices on an empty director's chair. "I know Ian's deep, dark secret."

"What's that?" Mei asked.

Ronnie put his arm around her and led her out of anybody's earshot except Ian's. "He *is* Clint Straker."

"What about you? Are you Charlie Vine?"

"Hell yes, baby. I can pollinate a rose garden with my smile," Ronnie said, flashing it at her. "Some women, too."

He walked them over to his trailer, which had three push-outs and a dozen antennae of different shapes and sizes along the roof. Once they were inside, Ronnie locked the door and faced them.

"It's safe to talk in here. All those antennas are creating a white-noise shield. They can't hear a word we say."

Mei looked up, though Ian wasn't sure what she expected to see besides the ceiling. "Who are *they*?"

"For starters, the people you ran away from. Every piece of electronic equipment made in China is a surveillance, data-mining, and tracking device, whether it's a TV set or a kid's talking dog toy."

Mei raised an eyebrow, expressing her skepticism, but Ian knew that what Ronnie said was absolutely true, though in her defense, it was hard to take someone seriously who was painted green.

"Uncle Sam also has his ear pressed against my wall," Ronnie added, opening the refrigerator and getting out some bottles of fruit-flavored waters for himself and his guests. "And so do a few Hollywood talent agencies, too."

"Why would they want to listen to you?" she asked.

Ronnie handed her a water. "Because they are out to get me. I fought shoulder to shoulder with Ian against the New World Order's attempted overthrow of our government and there are powerful people living in the shadows who still carry a grudge."

"You mean they're still upset about the hidden political messages you two snuck into the first run of this series?"

Ian spoke up before Ronnie could answer. "That's right. Every episode of this show is a blow against tyranny."

Ronnie shot Ian a look and read something in his expression that told him she didn't know about their battle against Blackthorn Global Security and their assassins.

"This show is more than a cop show about a plant," Ronnie said, following Ian's lead. "It's a political weapon."

"Believe me, I know it," Mei said.

"She's a big fan of yours, Ronnie," Ian said. "She'd love to work with you."

"Likewise," Ronnie said, pointing a finger at Mei. "I've seen every movie you've made. In fact, I think you're the perfect actress to play my archnemesis."

"I would love that," she said. "Tell me about her."

"Her name is Jade. She's half-woman, half–Venus flytrap."

"She's *what*?" Ian asked, opening his water bottle. "How would that work?"

"I don't know. You tell me," Ronnie said. "You're the one writing it."

It was a good thing Ian hadn't started drinking the water yet, or he might have choked on it. "No, no, no, no. I left TV a long time ago."

"Nobody writes this show better than you do," Ronnie said. "Don't you want Mei to have the best?"

Ronnie and Mei looked at him imploringly and Ian decided that he'd have to be certifiably insane to choose writing a *Hollywood & the Vine* over a life of constant sex.

"Okay," Ian said. "I'll do it."

CHAPTER FOURTEEN

Over the last few days, Gustavo Reynoso had thought a lot about the switchblade angel with a private jet for wings, especially when he fantasized about the beautiful women in the Pilates studio. The instant he got hard, he'd feel the angel's blade under his scrotum and the desire would pass. That was how he knew it wasn't a coincidence that the angel had dropped him off in front of that window. She was giving him a choice. Deliverance or damnation.

He wasn't a religious man and the experience hadn't turned him toward God, but it did make him think seriously about not repeating past mistakes. It was time for him to focus on making some money and finding a way of relating to women that didn't involve knives, strangulation, or blows to the head, though he had difficulty imagining what it might be.

The search for work had taken him to an industrial neighborhood in the north end of the city, east of the 805 freeway, and to a boulevard lined with stores selling tile, paint, hardwood flooring, kitchen cabinets, plumbing supplies, landscaping materials, and other businesses that were likely to attract contractors and do-it-yourselfers in immediate need of cheap manual labor.

He stood in a cul-de-sac off the boulevard, adjacent to some warehouses and auto repair garages, a spot where illegals like himself could mill around in denim and work boots, waiting for a job to come along, without getting in anybody's way or attracting too much attention. Most of the day laborers had already found gigs, leaving him almost by himself. There was something about Gustavo, an aura or smell, that made people leery about inviting him into their cars, their work sites, or their homes. Nobody had hired him yet.

There were a couple of food trucks parked in the cul-de-sac. Most of their customers were "foodies" and students from nearby University of California San Diego rather than hungry day laborers like Gustavo, who couldn't afford artisan shrimp tacos. The customers seemed to him to be more excited about taking pictures of their food than eating it.

A black Escalade pulled up beside Gustavo and the driver rolled down his window and leaned his head out. He was a white guy in his thirties wearing work gloves, a polo shirt, and a gold watch studded with diamonds. His face was pockmarked and his teeth as white as piano keys.

"I need someone to help me build a tree house for my kids," the guy said in lousy Spanish. "A hundred bucks for the day. Are you up for it?"

"Yes," Gustavo said, though he knew it meant that he'd be building the tree house by himself while the guy did something else.

"I'm Ted," the driver said. "What's your name?"

"Gustavo."

"As in *mucho gusto*?"

"Yes," he said, beginning to dislike this rich, lazy American. *"Mucho gusto."*

"Energy and enthusiasm, that's exactly what I'm looking for. Climb in."

Gustavo walked around to the passenger side, got into the huge car, and they drove off in silence. They headed west under the 805 freeway and into University City, where everything became a lot more upscale, a mix of gleaming office buildings, luxury hotels, and expensive condos. Ted pulled into a side street, beside a condo complex of several two-story buildings in a parklike setting of green grass and palm trees, and parked at the curb.

"I've got to run inside and pick up some things," he said. "Wait here."

The driver got out, leaving the keys in the ignition and the motor running, and disappeared among the condo buildings.

Gustavo sat there for a moment, enjoying the smell of the leather upholstery and marveling at how stupid the guy was to leave him alone with the keys to an $80,000 car. That was when he noticed that the key chain had an array of barcoded membership cards on it, including one with the logo of the Pilates studio Gustavo had seen his first night in town. It was an eerie and unsettling coincidence, coming right when he was thinking about stealing the car. It was like the angel was back, sticking a knife under his ball sack, reminding him of the consequences of bad decisions.

He opened the storage compartment under the central console armrest, just for the hell of it, and found a tube of women's skin moisturizer, hair ties, ChapStick, an eye shadow palette, a hairbrush, a makeup brush, breath mints, loose change, a nail file, a bottle of Purell, and a wrapped tampon.

The discovery made Gustavo pleasurably aware that he was in a woman's private space. The Escalade obviously belonged to the guy's wife and that made being there arousing, as if Gustavo had broken into her bedroom. He picked up the tampon, sniffed it like it was a fine cigar, and slipped it into his shirt pocket.

Gustavo opened the glove box, hoping for more feminine goodies, and was astonished to find a gun inside. He picked it up, just to make sure it was real, which it was, and then he wasn't sure what to do with it.

Put it back? Steal it?

While wrestling with the decision, he looked over his shoulder to see if anybody was around and noticed for the first time that the back seats were folded flat and that there were two shovels and a tarp over something. Curious now about what other secrets the car might hold, he reached back and lifted up the corner of the tarp.

Two women in leotards stared up at him with wide, dead eyes, a bullet hole in the center of each of their foreheads. He jerked away, choking back a little scream, and reached for the latch on his door to get out of the car.

But that was when he saw a reflection in the side-view mirror that stopped him: a black-and-white police car rolling up behind the Escalade. He looked over his shoulder to prove to himself that the police car wasn't an illusion created by his fear.

It wasn't.

Gustavo looked down at the tarp and the shovels, and then at the gun in his hand, and knew how it would go if he was caught with these bodies. There was only one thing he could possibly do.

Run.

He dropped the gun, jumped out of the car, and bolted into the condo complex. As he ran between buildings, around the pool, and across the parking lot, he wondered how the police happened to show up when they did.

Was the car parked in a red zone? Were they just planning on writing a ticket?

Gustavo risked a look over his shoulder and was relieved that he didn't see any officers on his tail yet. He kept on running, charging out into a street. And as he did, a Dodge Ram pickup truck came speeding around the corner in front of him. There was a woman at the wheel.

It was the switchblade angel and she was smiling.

He froze, convinced he was imagining it. He didn't get a chance to change his mind before the truck ran over him and kept on going.

Beth Wheeler left the stolen pickup truck, with its front grille smashed and blood spattered, in the same Walmart parking lot she stole it from two days earlier. Magar Orlov, the driver of the Escalade, drove up in a stolen Camry. She got inside and he sped off.

"How long did it take the police to respond to my anonymous tip?" Magar asked her in Russian. He'd left Gustavo and used a throwaway phone to call 911 and report that he'd seen a Mexican man covered in blood sitting in an Escalade. What Magar didn't tell the operator was that the Escalade belonged to one of the two women whom Magar and Beth abducted the previous night outside the Pilates studio and later executed.

"Two minutes," she replied. "But you cheated. You parked the Escalade a half mile away from the police station."

"I didn't want to leave anything to chance," Magar said. He wasn't an American sleeper agent like her. He was an experienced GRU operative who spoke multiple languages and traveled extensively doing covert work. But on this job, he was under her command.

"Neither do I," she said. "So we have some cleanup to do."

"Mucho Gusto survived?"

She'd heard the wet crunch of Gustavo's head under her thirty-seven-inch BFGoodrich Mud-Terrain tires and knew he wouldn't be talking to anyone.

"No," she said. "He's dead."

But she'd been at the cul-de-sac when Magar picked up Gustavo and she'd followed them until they parked to see if anybody noticed them along the way. Nobody did, but there was a chance that could change. That chance had to be removed.

"But you have more killing to do," Beth said.

CHAPTER FIFTEEN

Ian Ludlow's House. Malibu, California. November 6. 10:30 a.m. Pacific Standard Time.

Ian walked naked into his kitchen, opened the refrigerator, and idly scratched his belly while he surveyed the slim pickings for breakfast. He was about to reach for a slice of leftover Domino's pizza when he heard someone come in behind him.

"I thought only Jewish men were circumcised," Margo said.

Ian took cover behind the open refrigerator door and saw Margo standing in the doorway. "How did you get in here?"

"I'm a crack CIA agent, remember? And this isn't exactly the White House," she said, strolling in. "You don't have to hide. Naked men don't interest me."

Ian wished he could walk confidently around his kitchen naked, but he couldn't. He closed the refrigerator, turned his back to her, showing her his bare butt, and went through several drawers until he found an apron, draped it over his head, and tied it around his waist. He turned again to face her, hiding his naked backside against the counter. There was an enormous pig on the apron and the words *God, Country,* and *BBQ.*

"What do you want?" he asked.

"Something to do," she said. "An assignment that gets me out of LA and into the field."

She'd been renting an Airbnb apartment in West LA since they'd returned from New York. He wondered if she still had her apartment in Seattle or if she was living out of a suitcase now.

"You don't work for me," Ian said. "Talk to Healy."

"I did. That's why I'm here. He reminded me that I'm an off-the-books agent."

"What does that mean?"

"Only a few people at the CIA know I exist," Margo said, taking a seat on a stool at the kitchen island, the countertop and stove now between them. "I'm a *secret* secret agent."

"That sounds cool."

"It's not. It's a fucking bore. My job is to go where your stories take us, but you haven't written anything lately, so I'm stuck binge-watching TV shows, picking up girls at the gym, and going to the shooting range to stay sharp."

"Rough life," Ian said.

"You need to write something," she said. "If not for me, or for your country, then for your readers."

"No, I don't."

She gestured to the kitchen around them. "This house cost a fortune to rebuild."

"The insurance covered most of it."

"Not your deductible and all the extras."

The comment surprised Ian. The blueprints he'd submitted to the city for approval and permits didn't actually include all of his additions. He wondered how she knew about them or if she was just guessing, based on their past experiences together.

"I've got money coming in," Ian said. "I'm writing an episode of *Hollywood & the Vine.*"

She stared at him, more angry than incredulous. "Why the hell would you do that?"

"For me," Mei said as she came in, wearing only her silk bathrobe tied very loosely around her naked body. Ian couldn't remember if Mei knew that Margo was gay and if she was using that knowledge to toy with her now. "I'm guest starring on the show."

Ian looked back at Margo. "Ronnie says hello, by the way."

Margo ignored the comment. "What's the part?"

"A woman who is half-human, half–Venus flytrap," Mei said.

"You're perfect for it," Margo said.

"How can you say that without knowing anything about the character?" Mei took a tea kettle off the stove in front of Margo, gave Ian's exposed butt an affectionate pinch to get him to move, and went past him to the sink. The pinch didn't go unnoticed by Margo.

"Because I'm sure that she lures men into her clutches and eats them alive," she said. "You probably have lots of experience with that."

"Certainly more than you do," Mei said and started filling the kettle with water.

Margo looked at Ian. "Is she living here now?"

"Until she gets settled," Ian said, looking for a place to stand that kept his butt out of view of both women. He chose the end of the kitchen island.

Mei set the kettle on the stove, turned up the gas under it, then opened a cupboard to get a coffee mug while Ian and Margo watched her.

"She seems pretty settled to me," Margo said.

Mei set down the mug on the counter, opened a cabinet to get out a tea bag and packet of sugar, and then faced Margo across the island.

"Maybe you could help me with something," Mei said. "Ian and I were watching *Match Game* the other night and nobody could come up with a good answer for this: Because Lola was a spy, she kept a microphone hidden in her *blank*. Any ideas?"

Ian was afraid of the "C" word Margo might use, more to describe Mei than to answer the hiding place question, but she simply smiled, got off her stool, and turned to him.

"Could I talk with you privately?" Margo didn't wait for an answer. She grabbed him firmly by the arm and pulled him down the hall to his office. "Does Healy know about this living arrangement?"

"Only if he's listening to your microphone."

She pushed him hard into his office and slammed the door behind them. "I can't believe you're sleeping with her."

He faced her quickly to hide his butt. "You're just jealous because I got her into bed and you didn't."

"Of course not. I know you haven't had any action in a long, long, *long* time, but this whole situation is a bad mistake," she said. "You shouldn't get involved with the people in our missions."

"We don't have missions."

"We would if you'd write something," she said.

"You're overreacting. I'm just playing along with the romance cover story that Healy gave us."

"Like hell you are," Margo said. "Mei is taking advantage of you and you're going along with it for the sex."

"And that's a bad thing?"

"Yes!"

"It seems like a fair deal to me," he said.

"You're selling yourself short, Ian. You can do better than her."

"She's a young, wealthy, beautiful movie star. It doesn't get much better than that," Ian said. "Do you know how many men would kill to be in my situation?"

"I know there are lots of men who want to kill her."

"Because she defied government oppression."

"Don't give me that crap. I was there, remember? Mei did what she did for her own selfish reasons," Margo said. "It's also why she's sleeping with you. She's already got you doing something for her that you can't stand and that will fill you with self-loathing."

Ian couldn't argue with Margo's last point. "Don't worry, this relationship isn't going to last."

"How do you know?"

"Because it never does with me and actresses," Ian said. "I wish I could help you, but I've got writer's block."

"You're writing a *Hollywood & the Vine* script."

"That's not writing," Ian said.

"That's true," Margo said. "I'm not asking you to write a Straker novel, only the *idea* for one. Think about it."

He had been. For weeks. And it was destroying him. "I will."

"Thank you," she opened the door and started to go, then looked back at him with a smile. "Nice ass, cowboy."

CHAPTER SIXTEEN

Nocello Restaurant. West Fifty-Fifth Street, New York, New York. November 6. 1:45 p.m. Eastern Standard Time.

Dwight Edney met his mother, Cloris, for lunch at Nocello, a tiny Italian restaurant in midtown Manhattan that mostly catered to the theater crowd. The food was good, but he knew that wasn't why his mother had picked the spot. It was for the location, across the street from Spyscape, a tourist trap that charged people forty dollars a ticket for an interactive espionage experience, whatever the hell that was. For him, that experience was watching his mother drink half a bottle of wine while slurping up angel hair pasta, and it was about the same price.

She let him finish his rigatoni with sausage before she told him the reason for insisting that he meet her for lunch. "I have big news for your show tonight. The bodies of two women were found by San Diego police this morning. They were in a stolen SUV driven by their killer, an illegal alien who has been kicked out of the US five times before."

Edney looked at his watch. "You got this news awfully fast. Almost as if you knew about it before it happened. But I've already done dozens of stories about illegal aliens committing crimes in this country. It's becoming monotonous."

"This one has a twist. The killer was a convicted rapist, recently released from a Mexican prison," she said. "And he killed them with a gun that came from the Guns & Roses sting."

Guns & Roses was the code name for an infamously stupid sting operation mounted by the Bureau of Alcohol, Tobacco, Firearms, and Explosives. Over the course of four years, undercover ATF agents in Arizona and Texas sold two thousand marked weapons to Mexican drug cartels. The idea was to eventually expose the network of illegal arms sellers and buyers by tracking the market weapons. Instead, the ATF simply provided weapons to drug lords, specifically the Vibora cartel led by Arturo Giron. The scheme was exposed when gang members gunned down two LAPD patrolmen in South Los Angeles with AK-47s that came from the ATF's Guns & Roses operation. There were Senate hearings, and lots of angry editorials, but the only people who were jailed were the gang members and the gun merchant who'd sold them the weapons. The ATF director resigned and the government paid $25 million to the families of the dead officers. That was two or three years ago.

"Those guns are the gift that doesn't stop giving," Edney said. "If it's true the killer's gun really came from that cache."

His mother handed him a thumb drive, making no effort of any kind to be subtle about it. "The documents to back it up are all on here, along with the killer's deportation and jail records. Nobody else has it yet. Not even the FBI."

Edney pocketed the thumb drive. "Are the documents authentic?"

"Absolutely," she said.

There was no question that somehow the Kitchen had engineered these killings and his estimation of their skills rose considerably. It made him wonder what their long game was. It had to be more than just reviving the old Guns & Roses scandal. But there was no time for him to give the matter real consideration. His mother was right: this was big news, and if he was the first to break it, he would become the story, too.

His face would be on every network. Dwight Edney would be leading the news cycle for at least the next twenty-four hours, maybe longer.

"What is the killer saying?" Edney asked.

"Hello to Satan," Cloris said, laughing at her own joke. "He ran away from the police and got hit by a truck."

"That's convenient and tidy." Edney signaled the waiter for the check. He had to get out of here and put his staff to work on the story for tonight's broadcast.

"What is your angle going to be?"

Edney thought for a moment, then faced his mother as if she were a television camera. "Mexico is a deadly threat to our country. What's our government doing about it? They're giving out guns like breath mints to Mexican psychopaths and inviting them into our homes to rape and murder our wives, our sisters, and our daughters."

"It's a good start. The Kitchen wants you to go to Los Angeles as soon as possible and shoot your show from there for a while."

That took a lot of the joy out of the story she'd just given him. "What's the point of that? LA is an asphalt wasteland, a giant parking lot devoid of anything that gives life meaning. It's the American Siberia."

"They want you closer to the border," she said. "A lot is going to be happening there and you're going to make it your crusade."

A man needed to be passionate about something to make it his crusade, and he wasn't feeling it. Maybe he would if the Kitchen would share the big picture with him. If they wouldn't, he'd have to start finding his own crusades, whether they liked it or not.

The one upside to being in Los Angeles was that he'd be thousands of miles away from his mother and that made him smile.

"I can't wait." Edney rose from his seat. "You can pick up the check."

CHAPTER SEVENTEEN

The White House. The President's Study. November 6.
11:40 p.m. Eastern Standard Time.

The president of the United States watched CNN's report on Dwight
Edney's revelations on a small orange TV, the kind with an actual
picture tube in it, that must have been a gift from Elvis to Nixon or
bought by Ronald Reagan because the White House curators wouldn't
throw the damn thing out and install a flat screen for him. He was mad
enough to smash the TV and solve the problem right now.

The president wore pajamas and a bathrobe, both with the presidential seal embroidered on them, because he'd come to the study
straight from the residence, where he'd been watching Edney's program
in bed. Now Edney and his scoop about Gustavo Reynoso were on
every Goddamned channel.

He was joined in his cramped inner sanctum by his chief of staff,
Loretta Jones, a statuesque African American who'd once served as
White House counsel and, long before that, was an exceptional long-
distance runner who'd chosen Yale law school over a potential Olympic
medal. Standing beside her was Attorney General Ritchfield Douglas
III, the slim vegan grandson of the fat meat-eating segregationist, KKK

grand dragon, and former Alabama governor. Their awkwardness standing beside one another would have amused the president if he wasn't so angry about what he'd seen on Edney's show. He'd called them moments after Edney's show was over and demanded to see them in his study immediately.

"Is what Edney said true?" the president asked, turning off the TV. "Did a Mexican we've deported five times slip back into our country and kill two women with a gun that the ATF sold to the Vibora cartel?"

"Yes," Jones said. "I confirmed it with the directors of ICE and the ATF."

The president turned to Douglas. "I want all of the ATF morons who were responsible for this scheme sent to prison."

"The sting was an incredibly stupid idea," Douglas said, "but the people involved in it are no longer in the ATF and it wasn't a crime."

"It became one when the guns they sold the cartels started being used to kill Americans," the president said. "Those ATF assholes are accessories after the fact."

"I share your anger and frustration, Mr. President," Douglas said. "But we'll lose the case and the Justice Department will be ridiculed."

"That's already happening," the president said, pointing at the TV. "This is how you save face. I want to make it absolutely clear to the nation that these murders are a consequence of the last administration's monumental fuckups, not ours."

"I wish that were true, sir," Jones said. "But the killer slipped back into the country on our watch. I agree with the attorney general. If you set a precedent for prosecuting past officials for their mistakes, the next administration could decide to prosecute us for ours."

The president wasn't worried about that. He was worried about getting a second term. That wouldn't happen if he was seen as ignorant and feckless, which is how he felt right now. "How did Edney know all the details about the killer before I did?"

"It was news to me, too, Mr. President," Douglas said. "None of the details had worked their way up to me yet. In fact, I wasn't able to officially confirm the killer's criminal record in Mexico until a few minutes before this meeting."

"Then how the hell was Edney able to do it? How did he get all the incriminating documents so fast from the ATF, ICE, and the Mexicans?"

"I don't know, sir," Douglas said.

The president glared at him. "So you're telling me that you're inept."

Douglas took a deep breath. "Someone on the ground level of law enforcement or ICE in San Diego must have passed the information to Edney before it moved up the chain of command."

"Or there are people against you at ICE and the ATF who leaked the material to Edney," Jones said.

That seemed like the most likely explanation to the president. "I have to show the public that I am more outraged by this than they are. Call the director of ICE. It's his fault the killer got back in the country. I want his resignation on my desk in an hour or I will fire him."

"Yes, sir," Jones said.

The president looked at Douglas. "I want you to announce in the morning that you are initiating a new investigation of the ATF agents in charge of the Guns & Roses sting."

"I can't," Douglas said. "That case has already been fully adjudicated."

"Not for the ATF's complicity in the murder of these two women," the president said. "You're going after them for that."

"But there's no legal basis for an investigation on those charges," Douglas said. "We'd be laughed out of court."

"I don't care if it ever gets to that point. All I care about now is taking decisive action and humiliating the bastards who put me in this position," the president said. "And if you're unwilling to do it, you have five minutes to either resign or be fired. I'm sure the deputy attorney general will be glad to step up and do the right thing. He's had his eye on your chair from day one."

"You're putting me in an untenable situation," Douglas said.

That was stating the obvious. The president knew that Douglas was screwed no matter what choice he made. If he resigned, or was fired, for refusing to investigate the ATF agents, he'd be castigated as a weak, cowardly politician trying to cover up the government's mistakes rather than seeking justice for two murdered women. But if he pursued the charges, he'd be ridiculed as a presidential puppet abusing the justice system for political theater.

But the president didn't care about Douglas' predicament and tapped his watch. "Tick-tock, Ritchy. What's it going to be?"

Douglas made the political calculations, considered the historical burden of his grandfather's racism that he already carried, and made the decision that was best for his future ambitions.

"I'll launch the investigation," he said.

CHAPTER EIGHTEEN

The final scenes from the first draft of Hollywood & the Vine script "The Bad Seed" by Ian Ludlow.

INT. FBI GULFSTREAM JET — DAY

Hollywood is kissing Jade. They share two adjoining seats on the private jet.

                    JADE

          I could just eat you up.

                    HOLLYWOOD

          Don't let me stop you.

                    JADE

          I won't.

They embrace. He doesn't see her FANGS. She's about to bite his neck when Vine bursts out of the restroom, holding a gun.

FAKE TRUTH

VINE

Back off, you miserable weed.

HOLLYWOOD

What's the matter with you?

VINE

She's going to devour you.

She closes her mouth, hiding her fangs.

HOLLYWOOD

I'm counting on it. Go away.

VINE

You don't understand — she's the serial killer we've been hunting.

HOLLYWOOD

Don't be ridiculous. She couldn't hurt a fly.

VINE

She eats them — she's only half-human. The other half is Venus flytrap.

JADE

Don't listen to him, Hollywood. He's insane.

VINE

Am I?

Vine tosses a ball of raw hamburger at her. She instinctively catches it in her mouth and eats it. Hollywood rears back in horror.

HOLLYWOOD

You're . . . a plant?

JADE

You say that as if we're something inferior. There are trees that have seen human civilizations rise and fall while they've stood tall, laughing at your brief, pitiful existences. It was easy to make you love me.

HOLLYWOOD

Don't flatter yourself, baby. You're just another lettuce leaf in the salad bar to me.

She raises her arm to slap him and he slips a pair of cuffs on her wrists.

HOLLYWOOD

You're under arrest on twelve counts of murder.

FAKE TRUTH

JADE

I'm just a woman with a healthy appetite.

HOLLYWOOD

Tell it to the judge.

Hollywood gets up and joins his partner.

HOLLYWOOD

The FBI's top serial killer hunter is a serial killer. And to think I was about to fly back to Quantico with her. I was just going to be her in-flight meal.

VINE

Her mistake was forgetting that she's half-woman. Every time she ate a man, she devoured another piece of her own humanity.

HOLLYWOOD

I think that was the idea.

VINE

But it was also her downfall . . . as her humanity diminished, more and more of her mindless, carnivorous nature revealed itself.

HOLLYWOOD

Not to me . . . you were the only one who saw it.

VINE

Because I'm half-plant, too.

HOLLYWOOD

But you've got more humanity than most people I know.

VINE

And there aren't many plants who are as deeply rooted in justice as you are.

HOLLYWOOD

I guess that's what makes us great partners . . . I just wish you weren't so full of fertilizer.

And on their smiles, we FREEZE FRAME.

CHAPTER NINETEEN

Ian Ludlow's House. Malibu, California. November 9. 12:30 p.m. Pacific Standard Time.

Ian typed THE END on his *Hollywood & the Vine* script, emailed it to Ronnie, and for the first time in his life truly felt like a hack. He'd written the script in two days of nearly marathon writing and hated every word. At least when he'd written for the show, he'd been able to convince himself that he cared, that he was writing the best possible *Hollywood & the Vine* that he could within the framework of what the show was: a horrendous piece of shit.

But this time, what he was doing was not much more than typing, relying on pure, almost instinctive craft, the muscle memory of TV writing, and hitting every clichéd beat of a *Hollywood & the Vine* story by rote, hoping his utter disdain for the material didn't come through.

Even so, he'd underestimated the emotional and psychological toll that writing the script would have on him. He'd had to revisit a past, and a former self, he'd thought he'd left far behind. To get into the right frame of mind, he'd had to get into character and feel as unhappy and creatively unfulfilled as he had when he was writing and producing the show. That feeling still lingered, like the aftertaste of vomiting, when Margo drove up outside the gate in her Mini Cooper.

He buzzed her in and met her at the door. She was carrying a Costco pizza. "Are you doing pizza delivery now?" he asked.

"It probably pays better than being a superspy," Margo said as she came in and went past him to the kitchen. "I don't know how Bond can afford an Aston Martin."

"What are you doing here?" he asked, following her into the kitchen.

"I came by to see how you're doing on your Straker story."

"I've been busy working on my *Hollywood & the Vine* script."

"You aren't going to save the world with that." Margo set the pizza box on top of the *Los Angeles Times* that was on the kitchen island and then helped herself to a slice of pepperoni and cheese. "How long until you're done?"

Ian handed out napkins and took a slice. "I just finished it and sent it to Ronnie."

"Is it awful?"

He nodded as he chewed, then: "It redefines the word."

"Congratulations," she said. "Now we can get to work on your new Straker novel."

"I told you before, I've got nothing." Ian went to the refrigerator, took out two cans of Coke, and brought them to the island.

Margo glanced over each shoulder. "Since you're dressed, I guess that means Mei isn't around."

"She's at Pinnacle Studios, doing some publicity shots for the movie."

"Good. She won't get in our way while we work."

"I write alone," Ian said.

Margo took a drink of Coke. "Who said anything about writing? We're just kicking around ideas. How do you usually come up with a Straker story?"

"By myself."

"Do you enjoy the self-loathing you feel right now?" Margo picked a piece of burned pepperoni off her pizza and tossed it into the sink. "Isn't writing soul-sucking shit for *Hollywood & the Vine* what drove you to write a Straker novel in the first place?"

Yes, it is, he thought, and I can do it again. She'd said exactly what he needed to hear. He could have kissed her, and might have, too, if he wasn't afraid she'd take it the wrong way and knee him in the groin.

"I need two things to get started," he said. "The big idea—that's the bad guy plot—and the small, personal angle into it for Clint Straker."

"So Straker starts out fighting for the little guy and ends up taking down a vast conspiracy."

"That's the formula." Ian started in on a second slice of pizza. "It's what invests the reader emotionally in what's happening."

Margo followed his lead and took a second slice. "Where do you get your inspirations for the big idea and the personal story?"

"From the TV news and what I read in the paper. I just absorb stuff and, after a while, a story percolates up from my subconscious." Usually while he was in the car, or in the shower, or on the toilet, or lying in bed late at night, times when he wasn't particularly *trying* to come up with a story. Maybe, he thought, he should go to the bathroom right now.

"And what news have you been watching lately?"

"Honestly?" Ian said. "I've been obsessed with Dwight Edney ever since we did his show."

Margo grimaced as if she'd just taken a bite of something sour instead of finishing her pizza slice. "Why?"

"Because he's insane, rattling off one conspiracy theory after another," Ian said. "Actually, it's more than that. He twists the news to fit his own agenda. It's sort of like what I do with the news in my books."

"What's his agenda?"

Ian said the first thing that popped into his mind: "Whip up American fury against illegal immigrants and start a war with Mexico."

"Why would he want to do that?"

"I don't know," Ian said. "Maybe the same reason William Randolph Hearst got us into the Spanish-American War."

"Hearst did it to sell newspapers," Margo said.

"So maybe Edney is doing it for ratings. Ever since he broke the Gustavo Reynoso story, his numbers have been way up. He hasn't stopped milking it. He's doing his show from here in LA now and ranting that armed, drug-dealing, plague-carrying Mexican rapists and murderers are swarming over our border."

In fact, every time Ian turned on Fox now, all he saw was news about Gustavo Reynoso, his "Deathscalade" (the Escalade with the two dead women inside), and his "ATF gun" (one of the weapons sold to the Vibora cartel in the Guns & Roses debacle). It was almost as bad on CNN, MSNBC, and the three legacy TV networks, all of them eager to capitalize on the same ratings bounce that Edney was enjoying.

"That's not much of a bad guy plot," Margo said.

Ian held up his hands in surrender. "I told you I had nothing."

"What about the personal story?" she asked. "Where does that come from?"

"That's easy." Ian pulled the *Los Angeles Times* out from underneath the pizza box. "I could take almost anything from here and run with it. Like this one . . ."

He pointed to an article he'd read that morning.

COUPLE KILLED TAKING SELFIE

PORTO, PORTUGAL—A San Diego couple, Stan Rolfe and Briana Clemens, fell to their deaths yesterday while taking a selfie at a scenic overlook popular with tourists.

Authorities believe that Rolfe, 28, and Clemens, 26, were on a morning jog shortly after dawn in this steep, hillside city and stopped at the Miradouro da Vitória to take an impromptu selfie while standing atop a rocky wall with views of the Porto Cathedral, Ponte Luís I bridge, and the Douro River behind them.

"The evidence suggests that Rolfe, with one arm around Clemens, dropped his phone while trying to take a selfie, reflexively reached to catch it, and they both lost their footing, falling thirty feet to their deaths," said Tito Sampaio, a spokesman for the Polícia de Segurança Pública.

The bodies of the couple, and their shattered phone, were found several hours later on Rua da Vitória by a local resident driving on the narrow, cobblestone street below the high overlook. The resident thought at first that they were sleeping, but as she got closer, she saw their "horrifically broken bodies" and alerted authorities, Sampaio said. The couple was found with their passports and hotel room card keys still in their pockets. Foul play is not suspected.

Rolfe, an executive with a San Diego wine and spirits importer, was in Porto to visit vineyards in the Douro Valley and brought along Clemens, his longtime girlfriend and a graduate student in geology at the University of California San Diego. Photos on their Facebook and Instagram accounts show they were avid hikers and rock climbers, taking selfies together on peaks in Yosemite, Joshua Tree, the Grand Canyon, and the Alps.

Serious injuries and deaths caused by people taking selfies from precarious locations are on the rise.
According to a recent report, nearly 200 people worldwide were injured or killed in the last 24 months attempting to photograph themselves.

The Miradouro da Vitória, high above the city, offers
unobstructed views of most of Porto and its most icon-
ic landmarks. There are no security measures in place
preventing anyone from standing along the top of the
retaining wall that creates the edge of the overlook
and is approximately 30 feet tall at its highest point
above Rua da Vitória.

Authorities declined to say if other tourists or locals
have been injured or killed while taking selfies from
the same spot.

"How is that a Straker story?" Margo asked.

"What if Straker knew the guy who was killed?" Ian said. "What
if Straker and Rolfe free-climbed mountains together in Switzerland?"

"Free-climbed?"

"No ropes. They only used their bare hands."

Margo gestured to the newspaper. "Were these two free climbers?"

"I have no idea. But they would be in my story, which is why
Straker doesn't buy Rolfe's accidental death," Ian said. He also wondered
how an experienced rock climber could make such a stupid mistake,
which is why the article had stuck with him. But to make it a Straker
story, his hero had to have personal knowledge that gave him strong
reasons to question the facts. "A guy who can climb mountains with his
bare hands isn't going to fall off a wall taking a selfie. He's not that dumb

or careless. Straker knows it has to be murder. So Straker investigates . . . and it leads him right into the bad guy plot."

"Okay." Margo slapped the counter. "Then that's what we'll do."

Ian was confused. "Do what?"

"We'll investigate this selfie death and see where it takes us."

What she was suggesting was ludicrous. Ian pointed to the article. "Did you read the story? This wasn't murder."

"How do you know?"

"Because I just made that part up," he said. "But even if this was murder, it's a job for Jessica Fletcher, not Jason Bourne."

"I don't understand."

"It's a whodunit, not a spy story," Ian said. "It's not something the CIA is going to be interested in."

Margo shrugged. "We won't know that until we investigate. Think of it as an all-expenses-paid research trip."

"You just want to go on a trip to Portugal."

"You picked the article, not me," she said. "It will be fun."

"Healy will never clear this," he said.

"He already has. Getting you to walk through how you create a story was his idea." She carefully tore the selfie-death article out of the newspaper. "I'll have the Agency get us the entire life stories on these two, their full travel itineraries, and whatever pictures were on their phones. Be ready to go in the morning."

Margo got up and headed for the door. Ian hurried after her.

"This is ridiculous, Margo. I'm not going to Portugal tomorrow. It's a total waste of time."

She opened the door and turned back to him. "You're probably right. But look at it this way—if you're out of the country, you can't be called to the set of *Hollywood & the Vine* to do rewrites. It will all be over when you get back."

"I'll start packing," he said.

CHAPTER TWENTY

CIA Headquarters. Langley, Virginia. November 9. 4:04 p.m. Eastern Standard Time.

Healy entered his office after a long lunch with the vice president, under the pretext of briefing him for his state visit to the tiny nation of Tuvalu, a collection of islands in the Pacific that comprised barely ten square miles of landmass. The president liked to send Penny on pointless and humiliating diplomatic trips as far from Washington, DC, as possible. Penny's mission was to reaffirm the island's support for a tuna-fishing treaty.

During the lunch, Penny told Healy that the Chinese wanted him to urge the president to take aggressive action against illegal immigration from Mexico. They also wanted Penny to do his best behind the scenes to whip up anti-Mexico sentiment in Congress.

Why, Healy wondered, would the Chinese want that? He was still puzzling over that question when his personal cell phone rang. The caller ID read FRENCH.

"Margo," Healy said. "What plot has Ian come up with?"

"He's in the research stage, sir. We're going to Portugal tomorrow to investigate the death of an American couple who fell off a wall while taking a selfie."

"That doesn't sound like it's going to lead to anything involving national security."

"We don't know that. This is Ian's process, the same one that led him to create two other Straker plots that came true and would have fucked our country if they weren't stopped."

Healy couldn't deny Ian's past foresight, but this felt like a stretch. "What else has he got?"

"Dwight Edney is trying to start a war with Mexico."

That was the second time Mexico had come up today, but Healy didn't see how Edney and China could be involved in a plot together or that it would present much of a threat if they were.

"Ian really does have nothing," Healy said.

"He's as creative as he's always been, but reality is getting in the way of his fiction. The solution is to get him to live more in his imagination and less on cable news."

"And you think going off to Portugal on the CIA's dime will do that."

"It couldn't hurt," she said.

"Why do I get the feeling that I'm being conned?"

"Creative people are emotional and psychological basket cases, sir. That's where their stories come from. If you want to use Ian's imagination, you're going to have to spark it."

She made a good argument. "Fine. Go to Portugal. What do you need?"

Margo told him she needed to know everything about a San Diego couple and their itinerary in Portugal, including access to their credit card statements and all the photos they took on their trip.

"That's no problem," he said. "You'll have access to all that information and much more in an hour."

"Thank you, sir," she said. "I'll keep you informed."

After she hung up, his secretary informed him that Glen Talbot, his liaison with the Pentagon, was there to see him. Healy invited him in. Glen had been recruited a decade ago prior to his graduation from Harvard and he still dressed like a tweedy academic heading to a lecture class.

"What's up, Glen?" Healy asked.

Glen passed a file folder to him that contained satellite photos. "We got this from the Pentagon. Russia is moving troops and equipment to their borders with Belarus and Georgia."

This didn't surprise Healy. Ever since the Russians took Crimea and went to war with Ukraine, Belarus had cozied up even more toward the West, hoping for the protective and economic embrace of the NATO countries that lined its western border. This jacked up the trade and political tensions with Russia and provoked the Russian military to regularly increase the number of troops by the thousands that they sent to their western border for their annual "military drills."

As for Georgia, the country was fiercely independent, Western leaning, and desperately courting NATO membership and protection, which was something Russia couldn't allow. The Russians invaded Georgia in 2008 but after a few devastating days agreed to a French-brokered cease-fire and pulled out. However, Russia essentially held on to the northern Georgia regions of Abkhazia and South Ossetia, by recognizing the separatists there as "independent republics," to use as future bases of operation. It wouldn't take much to finish the job of taking Georgia. All the Russians needed was the right provocation and the perfect global political climate.

"It's just the usual intimidation," Healy said, "reminding their former republics of what will happen if they get too far out of line."

Glen adjusted his tortoiseshell trifocals. "How do we know that it's not what's happening now?"

"Because launching an unprovoked invasion of Belarus or Georgia now would instigate an immediate military response from the United States and our allies and probably spark a third world war."

"We let them take Crimea," Glen said.

"That was different. They've got no political cover or provocation for this."

"Yet."

Glen was beginning to irritate him. "Do we have any intelligence that suggests the Russians are destabilizing Belarus or Georgia by covertly inciting devastating social, political, and economic unrest as an excuse to march in and establish order for the sake of protecting the Russians who live there?"

"Nothing beyond their usual meddling and their ongoing fake news campaigns."

Healy handed the file back to Glen. "Then I'm not going to worry about their training exercises any more than North Korea should worry about our annual military exercises with the South Koreans."

Glen gave him a look and Healy gestured for him to give him back the file. "Okay, perhaps that was a bad example. Is the Pentagon brass worried?"

"Irritated is more like it," Glen said. "They never like it when they see major enemy troop movements near NATO's borders."

"Have our assets in Russia reported anything unusual?"

Glen smiled with amusement. "Kirk Cannon was seen in the halls at GDR headquarters. Maybe he's advising them on intelligence matters now. Imagine being that desperate for ideas that you'd turn to a burned-out action movie star."

They shared a laugh, though Healy wondered what his counterparts at the GDR would think if they knew he'd recruited author Ian Ludlow as a consultant. Hell, what would his own agents think?

"Keep your eye on those troops and have our assets look into it, too," Healy said. "Just in case."

"Yes, sir," Glen said and walked out.

CHAPTER TWENTY-ONE

Ian Ludlow's House. Malibu, California. November 9. 3:45 p.m. Pacific Standard Time.

While Ian packed his suitcase in his bedroom, he stole glances out the window to the backyard, where Ronnie and Mei were stretched out on chaise lounges by the pool, reading his *Hollywood & the Vine* script. Mei was in a bikini and wearing a huge sun hat and sunglasses. Ronnie wore Ray-Bans, a floral Aloha shirt, cargo shorts, and a baseball cap covered with aluminum foil.

He finished packing and went out to the backyard just as Ronnie finished the script.

"How bad is it?" Ian asked.

"It's like you never left the show," Ronnie said.

"That bad?"

Mei laid the script on her lap. "The script is terrific. There is so much provocative subtext."

"I have to be honest with you," Ian said. "There isn't any subtext. The stupid stuff is just stupid."

Mei wagged a finger at him. "You're not fooling anybody, Ian."

"Apparently I'm fooling you," Ian said. He had to put a hand over his eyes to shield himself from the light reflecting in his face from Ronnie's aluminum foil hat.

"The script is a master class in television writing," Ronnie said. "It works on so many levels—as a police procedural, as a comedy, as a drama, and as an allegory. Emmy material, buddy."

Ian gave up. What was the point of arguing? Why talk them out of loving it? He just wanted to be punished for writing crap. "You're right. It's full of hidden meaning. It's about so much more than an FBI profiler who is actually a plant that eats men."

"She's the government," Mei said, "devouring humanity and ultimately justice, as represented by Detective Hollywood, who himself is an allegory for popular culture."

Ronnie added, "And Vine is nature, which is purity, integrity, and innocence, the enduring virtues that will always expose deceit."

"That's exactly what I was going for," Ian said.

"I don't know why you put so much effort into trying to pretend otherwise," Ronnie said. "The complexity underlying the banality is why *Hollywood & the Vine* endures."

It was amazing to Ian how some people could delude themselves, and Ronnie, being both an actor and someone who was certifiably insane, was better at it than most.

"I wanted you to read it now because I'm going to Portugal tomorrow to research my next novel," Ian said. "After today, I won't be able to do any rewrites."

Ronnie set the script aside on the small table between the two chaise lounges. "This script doesn't need any revisions. It's perfect."

Mei leaned forward and slid her glasses down her nose. "You never mentioned to me that you were going on a trip."

"I didn't know I was going until this morning," he said. "I got a great idea and I wanted to jump on it while it's still fresh."

"It feels like you're running away," she said.

"From what?" Ian asked.

"Me? The show? Both?"

She was right, because there was certainly no Straker story waiting for him in Portugal. But what he said was: "Don't be silly. This is just how I work. I'll be back in a week."

Ronnie took off his hat and held it out to Ian. "Take this with you."

"Why would I want to do that?"

Ronnie gestured to the sky. "So nobody knows what you're thinking."

"Nobody cares what I'm thinking," Ian said.

"Are you kidding me?" Ronnie tipped his head toward Mei. "She's a Chinese defector and you're the guy who got her out. I guaran-fucking-tee you that sophisticated spy satellites from the US and China are positioned over us right now, watching and listening with microscopic intensity." Ian and Mei, almost by reflex, both looked up to the sky. "There's probably someone in Beijing at this moment who can tell you with one hundred percent accuracy the percentage of hydrogen sulfide in my last fart."

Mei lowered her head, picked up her script, and got to her feet. "I think I'll read the script again inside."

"I'll be right there, honey," Ronnie said. "We can run lines together."

Mei smiled. "I'd really like that."

She walked past the two men and into the house. As soon as she was out of earshot, Ronnie pulled Ian aside, took a device out of his pocket that resembled a digital voice recorder, and held it between the two of them.

"What is that?" Ian asked.

"A sonic scrambler. Totally distorts our voices to the ears in orbit. All they are hearing now is gibberish."

"They'd be hearing gibberish without that machine."

"Has it occurred to you, amigo, that Mei only pretended to defect and that she's actually a double agent?"

Ian laughed. "No, it has not."

"She could be here to spy on us for Red China."

"I'm not doing anything they'd care about," Ian said. "Are you?"

Ronnie shrugged. "I dabble."

"What does *that* mean?"

"The assault on our freedom didn't end when we took down Blackthorn, buddy. The New World Order, funded by the military industrial complex, is still out there watching, listening, preparing . . . waiting for their chance to strike. We both know that."

Ian narrowed his eyes at him. "What are you up to?"

Ronnie narrowed his eyes, too. "What are *you* up to?"

"Nothing," Ian said, breaking the stare. "I'm just a writer trying to put words on the page."

"And I'm just an actor who plays a crime-solving plant on TV. Who'd want to watch or listen to us?" Ronnie gave Ian a big wink, put his white-noise device back in his pocket, lifted his face to the sky, and yelled: "One percent, motherfuckers!"

Ian resisted the urge to look up, too. "One percent? What's that?"

"The amount of hydrogen sulfide in my farts."

"How do you know that?"

"Because I like to analyze them in my gas chromatograph."

Ian searched Ronnie's face for a hint of humor and saw none. "You have one?"

"Of course."

"And you fart into it regularly."

"You say that like it's unusual," Ronnie said.

"Why would you do that?"

"Why do dogs sniff butts? Think about that." Ronnie patted him on the back and went inside to rehearse with Mei.

CHAPTER TWENTY-TWO

In a crumbling wooden barn on a weedy ranch just a few miles south of the Rio Grande, two dozen men and women with sad eyes and dark skin sat on fruit and vegetable crates, listening to a pitch from Caesar Orona, a human smuggler in khakis. Four of his men were evenly spread out around the barn.

"We know the best routes and we have paid off the Border Patrol agents, so there's no danger of capture," Orona said with a reassuring smile. "Once you cross the river, you'll be led by experienced guides on a five-mile walk to an air-conditioned bus, which will take you to Houston, where jobs will be waiting. You can pick and choose what you like. The cost is only three thousand dollars per person, which you will earn back in your first month in America."

A woman stood up and addressed the crowd. "Don't listen to this lying bastard. We paid him every penny we had and he left my husband to die in the desert."

"It is not my fault if your man was fat, weak, and unprepared," Orona said. "This is a journey for the strong in mind and body."

"You're a liar and a vulture," the widow said. "We never hear from half of the families you send across. Men, women, children, they all just disappear."

"That's because they are rich and happy and want to forget the pitiful lives they left behind."

Two of Orona's men rushed up and grabbed her.

"Thief! Murderer!" she screamed as the men dragged her away.

"Can you blame her husband for wanting to escape from that drunken shrew?" Orona said.

The two men opened the back door of the barn to find a woman in black standing there holding a gun with a suppressor. It was Beth Wheeler, her hair dyed black, and with a ferocious scar across her throat, as if she'd survived a near beheading. She smiled and promptly shot the two men in their knees. The men collapsed with shrieks of agony, releasing the widow, who backed away in terror.

Orona's two other men went for their guns, but Beth shot them both in the forehead before their weapons cleared their holsters. They dropped like sacks of fertilizer, which is exactly how they smelled, the sphincters in their bladders and bowels opening wide in death.

She marched up the aisle to Orona and aimed her gun at him. He stood stock-still. Everyone else was still as well.

"I want you to tell these people what's really going to happen if they pay you to smuggle them over the border," she said to Orona in perfect Spanish, but her voice was raw, a nice theatrical touch to underscore the scar on her throat. "How far will they actually have to walk?"

"Ten miles," Orona said.

Beth shot him in the left knee. It exploded like a water balloon filled with blood. He screamed and dropped to the floor. She aimed her gun at his crotch. In her experience, threatening a man's genitalia always got his complete attention. "The truth this time, Caesar, or your balls are next."

"Fifty miles," Orona said through gritted teeth, holding his bleeding knee with both of his hands, blood seeping between his fingers.

"Do they have a guide?"

"We give them a map," he said. There were tears of pain filling his furious eyes.

"And if they survive the walk, what happens then?"

"We give them a ride into Houston," Orona said.

"On an air-conditioned bus?"

Orona hesitated. She jammed the gun in his crotch. "I asked you a question."

"In a truck," he said.

"When the truck shows up, how many people are jammed into the back of the windowless, airless trailer?"

"Thirty."

Beth turned now to the people in the barn, their faces etched with anger. "More like fifty, locked inside with nothing to eat or drink, shitting and vomiting on each other. And the people who manage to survive, and make it to Houston, are told that you'll kill them and their families if they ever tell the truth about their ordeal." She let that sink in with the audience, then looked back at Orona. "Isn't that right, Caesar?"

He didn't answer and just glared at her, but that in itself was a confession. She faced the room again.

"Last month, Caesar's driver got spooked by a cop car and left a truck full of people in a parking lot of an abandoned Kmart. It wasn't until people in town smelled the stench of a ton of rotting flesh that the bodies were finally discovered." There were gasps of horror throughout the barn. Beth glanced down at Orona. "How many died?"

He didn't answer. She tapped his forehead with the muzzle of her compressor.

"Forty-one," he said.

"I hear confession is good for the soul. You'd better hope so." Beth shot him in the head and he toppled over.

There was a long moment of silence, which was broken when the widow began to clap. The applause began to spread through the room. Beth held up her hand to quiet everyone down.

"I will get you to America, but you won't have to pay me to do it," she said. "I will pay you. One thousand dollars to each of your families today, plus five hundred dollars in your pockets now, another five hundred dollars when you get there. We'll give you good shoes and plenty of food and water for the journey."

One of the men in the audience spoke up. "What do we have to do in return?"

"You'll be delivering heroin and cocaine for the Vibora cartel."

Her blunt honesty was almost as startling as the murders. There was another moment of silence before another man said: "You want us to be drug mules."

A third man added, "I'm not sticking drugs up my ass or swallowing a bag of pills to shit out later."

Beth laughed. "That won't be necessary. We'll strap the bags to your bodies. Once you cross the river, you'll be going across the land of a rancher who works for us. You will deliver the drugs to him, get your five hundred dollars, and then you'll be taken by van to Houston, where you will be on your own."

"What happens if we get caught on the way?" another man asked.

"You'll go to prison and get deported upon your release."

"What happens if someone tries to take the drugs from us before we get to your people?" someone else asked.

"We'll give you a gun to protect yourself and our product," she said. "You can keep it as our gift."

The first man spoke up again, a cocky grin on his face. "What's to stop me from running off with your drugs and your money and using your gun to shoot anyone who gets in my way?"

"We'll kill you, massacre your entire family, slaughter your pets, and desecrate the graves of your ancestors," Beth said, then smiled. "Who'd like to sign up?"

A dozen men and one widow raised their hands.

CHAPTER TWENTY-THREE

There were no direct flights to Portugal from Los Angeles, so Ian and Margo took an 8:00 p.m. flight to Paris. They would arrive at Charles de Gaulle airport in midafternoon the next day and catch a two-hour flight to Porto, getting there in time for dinner.

Margo had convinced Healy to buy them first-class tickets because, she argued, that was how *New York Times* bestselling authors traveled when they were researching their books. The truth was that Ian only flew first class when someone else, like a publisher, a movie studio, or an intelligence agency, was paying the bill.

Once they were in flight in their side-by-side, first-class pods, Margo settled in by ordering champagne, putting on her airline-supplied slippers, and listening to music on the airline's complimentary noise-canceling Bose headphones.

Ian ordered a Diet Coke and got to work. He opened up his laptop and reviewed the astonishing amount of data that the CIA had given them on Rolfe's and Clemens' activities in Porto. He could precisely follow the couple's footsteps, in easy-to-read spreadsheets, from their arrival in Porto to the moment they'd died. Or if he really wanted to be nosy, he could trace their movements, minute by minute, going back years.

That was possible because whenever Rolfe and Clemens had their phones powered on, their carriers, operating system, and dozens of apps were secretly watching them and saving the information. Even when the couple disabled "location history" or "location services" in an app, their wishes were ignored. The couple was more closely monitored than a paroled child molester with a tamperproof GPS tracker around his ankle. And so are all of us, Ian thought.

He also had all the photos that Rolfe and Clemens had taken over the last four weeks. But if he really wanted to pry into their private lives, he could access their pictures going back years, since they'd been automatically backed up to the cloud, which was less secure than an actual cloud and wide open to the CIA and now, by extension, to him.

He browsed through some of their pictures, most of them selfies. Stan Rolfe and Briana Clemens were both young, slim, and tan, often wearing tank tops or short-sleeve shirts to show off their strong shoulders and arms. Rolfe had a carefully manicured shadow of a beard that took the edges off his angular face and somehow softened his sharp nose. Clemens had an endearingly goofy smile and a slightly chubby face that, combined with all the pictures she took of food, suggested to Ian that their hiking and climbing was the only thing that kept her from blimping out.

He closed the photo app, went back to the spreadsheet of the couple's timeline, then reached into his bag for a pen and a Porto guidebook by Rick Steves. He opened the book to the city map and spent the next hour or so marking all the places the couple went and the exact times they visited, so that he and Margo could follow the same path. When he was done, he reached across the partition separating his pod from Margo's and nudged her. She lifted off her headphones.

"What?" she asked.

"Doesn't it bother you that it was so easy for the CIA to get all of this information on Rolfe and Clemens?"

"Why should it?"

"Because it proves we have absolutely no privacy anymore."

"Privacy is so last century," she said. "Even my mother has a Twitter account now."

"What does she tweet about?"

"Everything and anything. What she eats, the pills she takes, what she's watching on television, and whether my dad has left the toilet seat up or down," she said. "News flash, it's always up. Nobody wants privacy, Ian. TMI is the new normal."

"TMI?"

"Too much information," she said. "Do you live in a cave?"

"Sometimes I wish I did. I don't like the government watching me."

"You're beginning to sound like Ronnie."

"Maybe he isn't the one who is crazy," Ian said. "Maybe it's the rest of us."

"Does he still wear aluminum foil on his head?"

"Yes," Ian said.

"Have you ever met a sane person who does that?"

"No," Ian said.

"I rest my case." Margo put her headphones back on and raised the partition between the pods.

There was no more work he could do until they got to Porto. So he closed his laptop, stowed it away with the guidebook, then put on his headphones and browsed through the airplane's entertainment options.

The satellite feeds from CNN, Fox News, and MSNBC were available, so he chose Dwight Edney's show to see if it might provide any inspiration. Edney was on location in San Diego, standing on the shoulder of Interstate 5 with the twenty-five-lane border checkpoint with Mexico as his backdrop.

"This is the border crossing between California and Mexico, where each day tens of thousands of immigrants from Mexico, South America, and scores of other impoverished countries try to enter the United States legally. But this is a trickle compared to the hordes of sex-crazed, bloodthirsty rapists and killers who rampage into our country from Mexico over our unprotected borders in Arizona and Texas. I'm talking about animals like convicted rapist and five-time deportee Gustavo Reynoso, who prowled the streets of San Diego in his stolen Escalade of Death, looking for women to defile and kill—"

At this point, Edney cut briefly to an old ICE booking photo of Reynoso, presumably taken during one of his deportations from the United States, and Fox News footage of the Escalade he was driving with two dead women in the back.

"I applaud Attorney General Douglas' announcement today that he intends to prosecute the ATF agents behind the Guns & Roses sting who sold weapons to Arturo Giron, the Vibora cartel leader who recently 'escaped'"—Edney used his fingers to put air quotes around the word—"from a maximum-security Mexican prison. It makes you wonder, doesn't it? What if Arturo Giron owned those ATF agents just like he owned the guards at that prison? What if the Guns & Roses sting was just a ruse to get United States taxpayers to give the Viboras the firepower to massacre their rival cartels and take complete control of the corrupt Mexican government? Think about that."

Edney stared at the camera to let that sink in.

"We know Arturo Giron owns the Mexican government. Does he own ours now, too? What is his insidious endgame? And are we the suckers who are paying for it?"

This wasn't a conspiracy theory that Ian found compelling or creatively inspiring, so he switched over to the airline's movie offerings. He was delighted to discover they had all the vintage Bond movies, from Sean Connery to Pierce Brosnan. They were his favorite movies and he couldn't resist picking one to watch, even though he owned them all and he'd seen them maybe a hundred times each.

He selected *You Only Live Twice* because it was the first 007 film that truly went over the top, more so than he'd ever dared with his fiction. The bad guy had a spaceship that he launched into orbit to swallow American and Soviet space capsules and bring them back down to his secret lair in a dormant volcano in Japan. The intention of the scheme was to provoke the Americans and Soviets into a nuclear war. Ian didn't follow the logic, and wasn't sure how the bad guy would benefit, but he didn't care. It was just what he needed to see right now, a movie made in the good old days when it was still possible to separate fiction from reality.

It comforted him to know that this was one spy thriller that would never come true.

CHAPTER TWENTY-FOUR

Porto, Portugal. November 11. 8:08 p.m. Western European Time.

The medieval center of Porto is a densely packed maze of stone buildings with red terra-cotta rooftops, theatrically baroque churches, and cobbled streets with limestone-mosaic sidewalks that ramble down the steep granite hills on the northern bank of the Rio Douro.

Porto's defining image, logo, and perhaps even its registered trademark is the Ponte Dom Luís I, a 146-foot-tall wrought iron bridge that spans the Douro with one quarter-mile-long deck atop its dramatic central arch and another 565-foot-long deck below it. The bridge joins Porto with Vila Nova de Gaia, where port, the sweet fortified wine that gave the city its name, ages in oak casks in the dozens of centuries-old stone wine cellars that line the southern riverbank.

Ian and Margo took a taxi from the airport to their hotel on Rua do Almada in central Porto. The narrow cobblestone street was one way, with a single southbound lane and a long row of cars parked bumper to bumper on the east side. The stone buildings, none taller than four stories, were packed so tightly together that they formed an unbroken wall of rusting wrought iron, faded paint, dirt-caked glass, and grime-coated tiles.

The Almada Regent Hotel was at the corner of Rua do Almada and Rua do Dr. Ricardo Jorge in a three-story building that had recently been completely gutted and renovated on the inside, while retaining the original yellow-tiled facade and wrought iron balconies.

Ian and Margo wheeled their bags into the lobby, which was decorated with minimalist, almost industrial furniture amid wood paneling, polished concrete floors, and cleverly exposed sections of the original distressed stone archways and columns. They approached the marble check-in counter, where a young woman was helping an elderly couple. The desk clerk was olive skinned with doe eyes and long black hair pulled into a ponytail.

While Ian waited, he imagined how he'd write what happened next if it were a Straker novel . . .

The desk clerk had more dangerous curves than Nürburgring, but Straker had driven that course once blindfolded, at 100 miles per hour, with a lunatic in the passenger seat jamming a gun into his kidney, so he figured he could handle her just fine. He strode up to the counter with the lethal grace of a cougar. She greeted him with a warm smile and moist lips.

"I'm Clint Straker," he said. "I'm checking in for two nights. Room 302."

"May I see your passport and credit card?" she asked. He gave them to her and she typed something into her computer. "Are you in Porto for business or pleasure, Mr. Straker?"

"I'm here for business, but I'm always hard up for pleasure."

Amusement flickered in her eyes. "I'm sure you are, Mr. Straker. Would you like one key or two?"

"Two."

She put the card keys on the counter in front of him and then picked up a bottle of port from the table behind her. "May I offer you a glass of port?"

The hotel was known for this courtesy and it was one of the incentives for tourists to book a room here.

"Only if you join me," he said. "I never drink alone."

"I'm not allowed to drink on the job."

Straker smiled and looked her in the eye. "I can wait."

"I get off at midnight," she said, holding his gaze.

"You'll get off a lot later than that. I don't like to rush."

He took one of the two keys and walked away.

She came to his room shortly after midnight carrying a bottle of port. They never got to the wine. Sometime after her fourth orgasm, he asked her if she knew Rolfe and Clemens, the former occupants of his room.

"It's so sad what happened to them," she said, still breathing hard, her skin glistening with sweat that tasted like salted caramel. "Were they friends of yours?"

"Yes, they were. You must have been on duty when they checked in."

"I was. They seemed like a nice couple. I never spoke to them again."

"Did anyone ask about them before they fell?"

"No."

"Did anything unusual happen in the neighborhood before or after their deaths?"

"Like what?"

"A bank robbery, a kidnapping, a murder . . ." Straker let his voice trail off.

"You mean, did they see something they shouldn't have and were they killed to keep them quiet?"

"Yes," he said.

"Nothing that I know of," she said. "You certainly have a vivid imagination."

"Let me show you how vivid," he said and rolled her on her side.

She staggered out of Straker's room at dawn, more spent than she ever imagined it was possible to be without losing consciousness. But she was still clearheaded enough to know that he'd leave in two days and she'd still have to live here. She had to consider her future. She took out her cell phone and made a call, whispering in Portuguese.

"You told me to tell you if anyone ever came asking about the dead Americans. Someone just did. His name is Clint Straker."

The elderly couple left the counter and the clerk greeted Ian and Margo with a big customer service smile. Not quite as alluring as the sensual smile that Ian had imagined, but he could live with it.

"Welcome to the Almada Regent," she said in English. Her name tag read BEATRIZ. "Do you have a reservation?"

"Yes, for Ian Ludlow," he said, wondering if her sweat really did taste like salted caramel. "I've reserved room 302 for me and 304 for my associate, Margo French." He tipped his head toward Margo, who stood beside him.

"Yes, you have, and they are available. You're lucky it's off-season for us. I rarely see guests succeed in reserving specific rooms. May I see your passports and credit card, please?" Beatriz asked. Ian and Margo complied and she entered some information in her computer. "I see you will be with us for two nights."

"Possibly longer. It depends on what we learn," Ian said. "We're investigating what happened to Stan Rolfe and Briana Clemens, your two American guests who fell to their deaths at Miradouro da Vitória while taking a selfie."

Beatriz glanced at her computer screen, then back to Ian, her customer service smile vanishing, her expression turning cold. "You've booked the same room they were in."

"I want to experience Porto the same way they did," Ian said, immediately regretting his choice of words.

"By sleeping in the same bed?"

"It's not as creepy as it sounds," Ian said, knowing that it absolutely was. "I'm a writer doing a story about them and Margo is my research assistant. I'm following in their footsteps to understand how and why they died."

He looked to Margo for some support, since it was her fault he was here, but she was busy pretending to check her email on her phone.

"The police said it was an accident," Beatriz said.

"The police aren't always right," he said. "Did anything unusual happen during their stay?"

She handed Ian his credit card and their passports. "Not until they died."

"How about afterward?"

"Not until a writer showed up and asked to stay in their room so he could experience what they did."

Margo laughed hard and it brought back Beatriz's smile, a real one this time, and she started laughing, too. Ian felt left out.

"You're sassy," Margo said, matching Beatriz's smile with her own. "I love it."

"That's a relief," Beatriz said. "Sometimes my mouth gets me in trouble."

"Mine too," Margo said. "I wonder what else we have in common."

Beatriz's smile didn't waver. Were they flirting with each other, Ian wondered, or was the clerk just being polite? Regardless, this wasn't going the way he'd imagined it at all, which wasn't saying much for the awesome predictive powers of his creativity.

"Did you ever talk with the couple?" he asked Beatriz.

"I checked them in the night they arrived," Beatriz said, which seemed to remind her that she still had work to do. She passed their card keys over to them. "They asked me about a good place to eat, so I recommended éLeBê, right up the street."

"We're going there tonight, too," Ian said. He knew they'd eaten there from their credit card receipts, which had also been supplied to him by the CIA.

"Do you have time for a complimentary glass of port?" Beatriz asked.

"Hell yes," Margo said, and that made the clerk smile again.

Beatriz placed two small, crystal port glasses on the counter and filled them up from a Graham's bottle that she had under the counter.

Ian took a sip. It was strong and sweet with a woodsy taste. He wasn't sure if he liked it or not. Margo tossed hers back like it was a shot of Redheaded Slut.

"That's nice," Margo said, though Ian didn't see how she could have tasted anything. The wine must have flown right over her tongue and straight down her throat. "I've never been offered a drink at check-in before. I think I'm going to like Porto."

"I hope so," Beatriz said. "You two aren't planning to take a selfie on the same wall the couple did, are you?"

Margo shook her head. "We aren't going to follow every step they took."

"That's good," Beatriz said, taking their empty glasses. "I'd hate for you to suffer the same fate."

CHAPTER TWENTY-FIVE

éLeBê was a small, upscale restaurant a couple of blocks west of the hotel. Ian chose their table based on the photos that Rolfe and Clemens had taken during their dinner. Instead of asking for a menu, Ian showed their waiter the couple's pictures of their entrées and asked him what they were.

The baffled waiter, who had a nose so large it looked like he'd grown a thick mustache to help support its weight, identified the dishes as codfish prawn risotto and grouper with clams, so that was what they ordered, along with a pitcher of cold sangria, which he brought for them while they were waiting for their entrées. The sangria wasn't what Rolfe and Clemens ordered, but Ian couldn't resist.

Their table was beside a saltwater tank where two enormous lobsters, their claws banded shut, were engaged in an epic battle, stepping on sluggish crabs and startling the anxious fish. It was hard for Ian to tear his eyes away from the bout as he nursed his sangria.

"At least we have live entertainment," Margo said. "You can't watch your dinner kick ass before you eat it at Denny's."

"The true measure of fine dining," Ian said.

The waiter dropped off some hot bread and butter, topped off their glasses from the pitcher of sangria, and walked away.

"What's our game plan?" Margo asked.

"What we're doing right now. Using the GPS info and photos from the couple's phones to go to the same places at the same times and do the same things that they did."

"What are we looking for?"

"I'm not sure. We'll look around, compare what we see to what's in their photos, and maybe we'll notice something that's changed or is out of place. Then we can find out if anything happened in Porto, like a kidnapping or a car bombing, since they were killed that might be related in some way to what they saw, what they did, or who they met."

"Then we follow the clue trail to the bigger plot."

"That's what Straker would do," Ian said.

"There's just one problem," she said. "There haven't been any assassinations, kidnappings, or major heists since the couple died."

"How do you know?"

"Because I asked the Agency to check on that before we left Los Angeles," she said.

"You *did*?"

"I'm not stupid," she said. "It seemed like the obvious thing to do."

"Why didn't you tell me this before?"

"I was afraid you'd cancel the trip," she said.

"You were right, because now this whole exercise is pointless."

"No, it's not. Just because there wasn't some major crime that happened after they died doesn't mean they weren't murdered," she said. "What if what they stumbled upon wasn't quite so obvious? It would make a better story, wouldn't it?"

Yes, it would, and a new approach occurred to him that he immediately liked better. "What if whatever it is hasn't happened yet?"

That would add a ticking clock, he thought, something that was always good for a thriller.

"That could be your bad guy plot," Margo said. "Straker would have to figure out what it is and then prevent it. It wouldn't be the first time he's done that. Or that we have."

She was right, but there was another way to go. "What if nothing happened or is going to happen? What if they unknowingly took a picture of a wanted fugitive, or a missing person, or someone who is supposed to be dead but isn't and that is what got them killed?"

"Good idea. I'll have the Agency run a facial recognition scan of all the people in the couple's photos and cross-check them against our facial databases of known terrorists and major criminals, alive or dead."

"Can the Agency really do that?"

Margo shrugged. "How the hell would I know?"

"Because you're a CIA agent."

Margo leaned across the table to him. "A little louder, Ian. I don't think the other diners or the kitchen staff heard you."

"As if they care," he said.

"Maybe they do. Maybe one of them is the terrorist who killed Rolfe and Clemens. Maybe it's even our waiter. Maybe he killed them for taking his picture and endangering his plot to . . ." She looked around, as if the answer was in the fish tank, or out on the street, or hanging on the wall, but then she found it and faced Ian again. ". . . to poison the world's supply of port wine."

"I can't believe you don't know what resources the CIA has for you to use. Didn't they give you any training before they put you in the field?"

She narrowed her eyes at him. "I was trained how to use anything on this table as a weapon."

"Oh really." Ian gestured to the pat of butter. "Can you kill me with that?"

"I'm really tempted to try," she said.

The waiter arrived with their dinner, saving Ian from immediate death by butter. After the waiter set down the plates and asked them if he could get them anything else, Ian held up his phone with a picture of Rolfe and Clemens on the screen.

"Do you remember our friends Stan and Briana? They told us we had to eat here. They sat at this table a few nights ago."

"Yes, very nice couple," the waiter said. "It's so sad what happened to them."

"Yes, it is," Ian said. "Do you remember anything else about them?"

"They asked me why the lobsters were fighting."

Ian glanced at the tank, then back at the waiter. "What did you tell them?"

The waiter stared at him for a moment. "They are lobsters. It is what lobsters do. It's why they have claws."

"Of course," Ian said. "Thank you."

The waiter walked away. Margo leaned toward Ian.

"He's definitely a terrorist," she whispered. "A real waiter would have known the psychological motivations of all the crustaceans on the menu."

They finished their dinner at 9:45 p.m., the same time Rolfe and Clemens did, and took the same short walk down Rua do Dr. Ricardo Jorge, a high stone embankment on one side of the street and empty storefronts along the other, back to the hotel.

Before Ian unpacked, he thoroughly searched his room, opening drawers, lifting the mattress and box spring, and checking behind the framed photographs of Porto street life, though he had no idea what he was looking for and felt stupid for even making the effort.

Rolfe and Clemens weren't spies, detectives, or reporters. He knew that they weren't killed because they had stolen gems, or a thumb drive containing North Korean launch codes, or a vial of a deadly virus, or anything else that they might have hidden somewhere in the room. They were just a couple of tourists who fell taking a selfie, that was it.

But Ian was here in Porto, and as long as he was, he would go through the motions of pretending the couple was killed for some nefarious reason and see if it led to a Straker plot, though he didn't believe it would expose a real plot in the real world. That was Margo's delusion, not his.

It was also one of the reasons why he went right to bed and didn't stay up until midnight to see if Beatriz would knock at his door with a bottle of tawny port to claim her four orgasms.

CHAPTER TWENTY-SIX

Eli Tanner's Ranch. Dunn, Texas. November 11. 1:33 a.m. Central Standard Time.

Christmas came in November for Jim-Bob Sanderson. That was when Eli Tanner gave him desert-camouflage tactical clothing and boots, a Kevlar vest, a walkie-talkie, Bushnell 260501 Night Vision 4x50 Equinox Z digital binoculars, a Sightmark SM15070 Ghost Hunter Night Vision Goggles binoculars kit, a 700-lumen waterproof flashlight, a bag of zip ties, a Glock, and an AK-47.

Jim-Bob was the team leader of a six-man patrol covering the southwestern corner of Tanner's property, the part closest to the Rio Grande. He felt like Rambo even though he was built like Dumbo and had never served a day in the military. His job was to stop Mexicans from sneaking over the border and onto Tanner's property. But the truth was, he hoped they failed and that the illegals never stopped coming. This was a lot more fun than feeding cows and shoveling their shit, his usual vocation. And even that, he was told, was a job these Mexicans wanted to take from him. They could have it.

He was hiding behind some rocks and scanning the darkness for any sign of movement. The infrared goggles and binoculars were so good, he could see a lizard taking a crap from a hundred yards away. So when four men suddenly loomed up out of the river, they looked like giants and he almost screamed.

He used his walkie-talkie to alert his men that four "bogeys" were approaching and to surround them once they'd cleared the river, though he had no idea what a "bogey" was besides a cool word that professionals used in situations like this. As soon as one of the bogeys was ten yards away, Jim-Bob popped up and revealed himself, pointing his AK-47 in front of him.

"Hold right there."

The soaking-wet Mexican stopped and said in broken English, "It's okay, we're amigos."

"You're no friend of mine," Jim-Bob said as the rest of his boys surrounded the four jittery, shivering illegals.

"We have a delivery for you." The Mexican smiled and reached under his shirt.

Beth was in a sniper's nest that resembled a shallow grave, twenty yards behind the Mexicans, and stared at Jim-Bob through the infrared scope of her rifle. She aimed between the legs of one of the Mexicans, at the ground in front of Jim-Bob's feet, and fired.

The gunshot startled Jim-Bob and he reflexively pulled the trigger of his AK-47, blasting the Mexican in front of him, who fell backward. Another illegal to Jim-Bob's left whipped out a gun from under his waistband. Jim-Bob whirled and shot him, too, again and again and again, screaming as he did it, and then all his men opened up on the illegals, squeezing off as many shots as they could, the flashes like fireworks, blinding him.

When it was over, the four Mexican men were dead on the ground, and not one of Jim-Bob's boys was hurt.

Jim-Bob's ears were ringing, he was shaking all over, and he desperately wanted to pee as he looked around at his shell-shocked men.

"He had a gun," Jim-Bob said.

"They all had guns," one of the boys said.

"It was us or them," another one agreed, nodding as if to reassure himself and the others that what they'd done was right.

Jim-Bob looked down at the body of the Mexican who'd spoken to him.

It's okay, we're amigos.

The dead man's face was covered with white powder, which made no sense. He took out his flashlight and lit up the corpse. The bullets had torn open the Mexican's shirt, revealing a shredded vest made up of transparent plastic packets filled with white powder that was rapidly soaking with blood.

Jim-Bob aimed his beam at the other bodies. All the Mexicans were splattered with blood and white powder. He hadn't graduated from high school, and he fed cows and shoveled shit for a living, but he knew he wasn't looking at baking soda, sugar, or flour.

"Oh shit," Jim-Bob said.

CHAPTER TWENTY-SEVEN

Porto, Portugal. November 12. 6:30 a.m. Western European Time.

Thanks to jet lag, Ian had been up for two hours before he met Margo in the lobby. Rolfe and Clemens had begun their first morning in Porto with a robust two-mile jog. Ian knew he couldn't jog a block without needing CPR. So they decided that Margo would replicate the jog while Ian walked the same route and took a closer look at the neighborhood.

The route took them west, then south into the Clérigos quarter, named after the 246-foot-tall baroque clock and bell tower that could be seen from everywhere in Porto. It was also the neighborhood with the best bars and nightlife, which Ian figured was why Rolfe and Clemens had chosen a hotel that was so close by.

The only people Ian saw on the street were students in black capes and cloaks who, if they'd had magic wands in their hands, might have been heading to class at Hogwarts instead of the nearby University of Porto. The similarity of the students to J. K. Rowling's young magicians wasn't a coincidence. She'd lived in Porto and supposedly the art nouveau interior of the hundred-year-old Lello & Irmão bookstore, which Ian quickly walked past, was the inspiration for Hogwarts Castle. That was why five thousand people a day now bought tickets just to step inside the shop.

The devotion J. K. Rowling inspired in her readers astonished him. He was sure that nobody would ever buy tickets to visit Hot Dog on a Stick on the Santa Monica Pier because that was where Ian got the idea to have Clint Straker use two corn dogs to beat up three ninja assassins.

Ian crossed through Lisboa Park, which was the grass-topped roof of an underground parking structure, and then crossed the wide intersection of four streets in front of the Clérigos Tower to reach the top of Rua de São Bento da Vitória, a single tight cobblestone lane that tumbled down to the dead end where Rolfe and Clemens had tumbled to their own.

But Ian didn't have the time this morning to see where they'd died, not if he and Margo wanted to stick to the couple's timetable, because the walk back to the hotel was mostly uphill and he guessed it would take him almost twice as long as it had taken to get where he was. He turned around and headed the way he came.

It was a wise decision. Margo got to the hotel thirty minutes before he did, but that was fine. It gave her time to shower and change before they had to be at the historic Café Majestic for breakfast.

On the way to the restaurant, as they crossed the Praça da Liberdade in front of the grimacing, muscle-bound statues holding up city hall and, presumably, the weight of liberty, Margo told him she hadn't seen anything unusual on her jog and that, when she got to her room, she'd received an encrypted email from the CIA informing her that nobody in the couple's Portugal photos matched the faces of known terrorists, spies, or wanted fugitives.

"So we have nothing," Ian said.

"Stop whining," Margo said. "The day has just started. Clint Straker never whines."

"I'm not Clint Straker."

"You are when you want to be," Margo said.

Not in bed, Ian thought. Or in a fistfight. But he did think like Straker, or rather vice versa, and lately that had served him and his country well. There was no harm in taking that approach now.

Briana Clemens had taken a clever selfie of herself and Stan Rolfe sitting together in the ornate art nouveau café by photographing their reflection in one of the mirrors directly across the crowded dining room. Above the mirror, a sculpture of two naked, chubby cupids looked mischievously down on them.

"It's unsanitary to have naked babies floating over the food," Margo said, picking at her croissant. "I seriously doubt they are toilet trained."

"Those are angels," Ian said, comparing the couple's photo on his phone, taken days ago from the same seat at the same moment, to the scene in the dining room around them this morning. He didn't see anything that had changed since Clemens' picture was taken besides the faces of the customers. "You have no appreciation for fine art."

"It's creepy kiddie porn. If you put that up in a restaurant in Los Angeles, you'd be arrested. But in Porto, it's fine art."

"If this offends you, then it's a good thing there are no museums on our itinerary today."

What did await them was a walking tour that seemed designed to cram as many Porto landmarks as possible into a single day, pausing only to take a selfie or a postcard shot at each one to prove they'd hit everything.

It was an ambitious tour, but achievable, since the city was relatively compact, though it meant going up and down many steep cobbled streets. Ian wasn't in the same great physical shape as the couple, and within the first hour of their walk, his polo shirt was sweat soaked, his legs ached, and he had serious doubts that he could keep up the pace necessary to follow their timetable to the minute.

Almost everywhere that the couple took a selfie—whether it was in front of the tiled mural of a historic battle on the wall inside the São Bento train station, or the old trolley cars winding through the medieval streets, or the piles of salted cod outside a grocer's stall—there were dozens of other tourists taking the same shots at the same time.

That fact raised an issue for Ian to consider. If Rolfe and Clemens were killed over a picture they took, then presumably anybody else who took the same shot at the same time had to be killed, too. But he was pretty sure that hadn't happened. Surely someone would have noticed by now if a hundred people who'd visited Porto on a particular day ended up dead, accidentally or otherwise.

But that speculation gave Ian an idea, which he shared with Margo as they stood on the plaza of the Se Cathedral, atop a cliff facing west, and admired the spectacular view of the city, the Douro River, and the port wine warehouses of Vila Nova de Gaia.

"Everyone here is taking pictures with their phones," Ian said, gesturing at the people striking poses with their selfie sticks all over the plaza, "which means they are constantly being tracked by their devices the same way that Rolfe and Clemens were and that we are now."

"That's true," Margo said.

"And probably most of these people are automatically saving their photos to the cloud the same way that Rolfe and Clemens did."

"Most likely," she said. "What's your point?"

He lowered his voice to a whisper. "The CIA should be able to get us the photos taken by anyone who was here, or anyplace else, at the same time as Rolfe or Clemens."

"That's a lot of photos," she said, glancing at the tourists posing for selfies or taking pictures of the view. "Not many of these tourists look like Americans to me. I don't know if the Agency can get the same data from foreigners."

"What kind of intelligence agency is the CIA if they can only steal secrets from Americans?"

"I'm just saying it may not be as easy as you think," she said. "Or get us everybody's pictures."

"Even so, whatever we are able to get would still show us more of what was going on around Rolfe and Clemens at each spot than the selfies we've got."

Margo took out her phone and started texting. "Can't hurt to ask. At least it shows Healy that we're working and aren't just blowing the government's money on a vacation."

"You can text the CIA?"

She gave him a look. "That surprises you? Anybody can tweet directly to the president of the United States and he might even reply during a cabinet meeting or a bathroom break. Why does a text shock you?"

It wasn't something he'd ever seen James Bond do. Then again, he'd never seen anybody climb out of an airplane in flight and have a fistfight atop the fuselage, either.

"Sending a text just doesn't seem very covert to me."

"Who is watching us?"

"Everybody," he said.

"They can watch us, but it doesn't mean they are, right this second. Why would they? We aren't doing anything. We aren't on a dangerous mission."

"We are if Rolfe and Clemens were killed instead of having died from being clumsy," Ian said.

"I'll take that chance," she said.

She was taking it for both of them, Ian thought. But she was also right. What were the odds that the couple had been killed or, if they were, that anybody would be watching a thriller writer and his research assistant go sightseeing?

They made their way down to the Cais da Ribeira, Porto's vibrant riverfront promenade that seemed designed to keep postcard makers in business. The picturesque riverfront was lined with tightly packed old buildings with red rooftops and facades comprised of brightly glazed tiles in shades of blue, red, and yellow. Lines of drying laundry were strung across the wrought iron balconies, adding even more color, the clothes fluttering in the breeze like flags. The first-floor storefronts were occupied by souvenir shops and bistros with outdoor seating where diners were entertained by street performers of all kinds hustling for spare change.

But the sidewalk hustle that had drawn the attention of Stan Rolfe and Briana Clemens, and another crowd today, was the kids jumping off the lower level of the Dom Luís bridge into the Douro River.

Ian and Margo joined the people who were standing at the edge of the high stone embankments along the river and aiming their phones at the divers on the bridge, waiting for the perfect shot of their jump.

There were four boys, perhaps in their twenties, standing nervously on the bridge railing in their bathing suits, gathering up their courage to jump, while their friends with hats in hand worked the crowds for donations for the high divers. A pair of *barcos rabelos*, the Nordic-style, flat-bottomed barges once used for ferrying casks of wine and now for tourists, passed beneath the bridge, buying the jittery divers some time.

But two younger boys in bathing suits, no older than ten or twelve, grew impatient with the show, climbed up onto the railing, crossed themselves, and jumped, undercutting the older boys and generating applause, and probably dozens of Instagram posts, among the crowd.

Ian heard a scream of pain behind him. He whirled around to see Margo twisting the wrist of a man holding a wallet. The man was in his twenties, wearing a baseball cap, dark sunglasses, an oversize T-shirt, and loose-fitting sweatpants and he was down on one knee, his face contorted in pain.

"Drop the wallet," Margo said.

"*É minha carteira,*" the man protested in Portuguese.

"Drop it or I will break your wrist," Margo said. "I won't ask again."

"Foda-se vadia." From the way he hissed the words, Ian assumed they were a Portuguese curse.

Margo broke his wrist. Ian wasn't sure whether he heard the bone snap or if he'd imagined it.

But the man's scream of pain was real and he involuntarily released the wallet, which Margo caught and tossed to Ian, who caught it out of reflex. He immediately recognized the wallet as his own.

"He's a pickpocket." Margo tipped her head to the man writhing on the ground, then she turned and snatched a big shoulder bag from the startled young woman beside her. "And she's his accomplice."

The woman swung a fist at Margo, who ducked the blow and shoved her off the embankment, sending the pickpocket's accomplice squealing ten feet down into the river below, where she hit the cold water with a big splash.

Margo held open the shoulder bag so Ian and everybody else around him could see what was inside: it was full of wallets of all sizes.

"The pickpocket lifted the wallets and dropped them into her purse," she said.

The crowd broke into spontaneous applause. Margo took an elaborate bow.

Ian looked back and saw two police officers approaching from the plaza to investigate the scream and the commotion.

The pickpocket saw the officers, too, so he snatched up something from the ground and ran off, clutching his broken wrist to his chest. Ian glanced at the river and saw the pickpocket's accomplice pulling herself up onto a dock. She glared furiously back at him, then hurried up the gangway to make her escape.

Ian turned back to Margo. "We have to get out of here. We don't have time to explain ourselves to the police."

Now the men in the crowd were patting their pockets and the women were checking their purses and gasping as they discovered their wallets were missing.

Margo handed the shoulder bag to one of the victims so they could sort through it and then she and Ian hurried away, losing themselves in the throngs of people on the busy riverfront.

"You need to be more careful with your wallet," Margo said to Ian once they were safely away. "There are pickpockets everywhere."

"You didn't have to break the guy's wrist and toss his accomplice into the river."

"It's what Clint Straker would have done."

That was true. "Not because it's smart, but because I think it will entertain the audience."

"The audience seemed entertained to me," she said. "Or did you miss the applause?"

"We aren't here to be Clint Straker," he said as they reached the bridge. "We're here to be Rolfe and Clemens."

"What's next?" Margo asked.

Ian looked back and didn't see any police officers pursuing them. He checked the time on the phone. Remarkably, they were still on schedule.

"Port tasting," Ian said. "Think you can do that without breaking anyone's bones?"

"I can try," she said.

CHAPTER TWENTY-EIGHT

The White House. Oval Office. November 12. 9:30 a.m. Eastern Standard Time.

The president paced in front of his desk. Healy sat on a couch across from Attorney General Ritchfield Douglas, who sat on the matching couch opposite him and looked to be in considerable discomfort, as if he'd eaten something that violently disagreed with him.

"I called you both here because this border situation is getting out of control," the president said. "First that illegal in San Diego murdered two women with a gun the ATF sold to a drug cartel. Now a bunch of Mexicans with bags of cocaine taped to their bodies crossed the border in Texas and got into a gunfight with a citizen militia patrolling a ranch down there."

Healy frowned. "With all due respect, sir, this is a law-enforcement and immigration problem. I don't understand what I am doing here."

The president glanced at Douglas. "Tell Mike what you told me."

The attorney general cleared his throat. "No Americans got hurt last night, but the Mexicans were killed. The dead men were carrying guns that the ATF sold to the Vibora cartel, which is run by Arturo Giron, who escaped from a Mexican prison into a quarter-mile-long tunnel that was lit, air-conditioned, and had an electric-powered rail system. It was well engineered and must have cost millions."

"I've followed the story in the news," Healy said.

"Then you know that Giron is a rich, smart, calculating son of a bitch who has half of the Mexican government in his pocket," Douglas said. "He's smuggled hundreds of millions of dollars' worth of heroin and cocaine into the United States using elaborate tunnels, homemade submarines, tricked-out speedboats, and private jets. He's trucked his heroin directly across our border as frozen orange juice and shipped cocaine into our ports disguised as bathtubs and ceramic tiles."

The president faced Healy. "What Ritchy is saying is that the Frito Bandito wouldn't tape kilos of cocaine to illegals running into Texas."

"It's amateurish and makes no financial sense for him," Douglas said. "The quantities are too small and the odds of his drug mules getting ripped off or caught or dying on the journey are too high."

"Maybe it's not Giron," Healy said. "Maybe it's some small-time operator."

Douglas shook his head. "The Viboras own that corner of Mexico. Anybody who crosses them would end up with their head on a spike. And there's more that doesn't fit. Giron's stuff is pure. It doesn't get recut until it hits his dealers. Those bags were mostly baking soda and flour with a bit of coke. You'd get a bigger high snorting crushed Cap'n Crunch."

"You're saying it's a setup," Healy said.

"I'm saying it's not about drugs. All I know is that someone is going to a lot of trouble to humiliate the Justice Department, the Border Patrol, the ATF, and this president," Douglas said and looked at the president, who looked at Healy.

"It's a hostile act against our country by a foreign agitator," the president said.

Now Healy understood why Douglas seemed uncomfortable. It was Healy who was being set up now. The attorney general knew the president's logic was an outrageous stretch and that the CIA had no business getting involved in this. But the attorney general couldn't really go to the FBI or DEA for help, not after declaring war on the ATF by announcing that he was going to prosecute the agents for being accessories to murder in the San Diego homicides. Healy hated politics. Espionage seemed so much more ethical and bloodless by comparison.

"I don't see what Mexico has to gain from this," Healy said. "It's more likely that someone in the United States is trying to inflame tensions at the border for their own nationalist, political agenda. That makes it a problem for the FBI to deal with."

"I disagree," the president said. "Whoever is behind it, the problem came from the Mexico side of the border and that makes this a national security matter involving foreign agitators. That's CIA territory. I want your spies in Mexico to find out who is shaking the maracas on this. And while you're at it, the DEA hasn't been able to pinpoint exactly where the Frito Bandito is. I'd like your boys on that, too."

"To what end?" Healy asked.

"You give the info to Ritchy, who passes it along to the DEA," the president said. "And then they use it to apprehend or kill Giron and shut down his operation."

Healy nodded. "Even if we can locate Giron for you, the DEA is going to have to work with local law enforcement, or even the Mexican military, to make a move on him. What are the odds you can do it without someone in Mexican law enforcement tipping him off hours before you get there?"

"The odds are against us," Douglas said. "But that doesn't mean we shouldn't try."

Healy turned back to the president. "I'm not a politician, but in the likely event that the operation goes wrong and Giron gets away, how is that failure going to improve the situation?"

"It changes the narrative," the president said. "The story will be about us taking decisive, righteous action and being undermined by the corrupt Mexican government. It's better than the story that's being told now."

But that was all they were, just stories, Healy thought, that were about as real as the ones Ian Ludlow told, only a lot less fun to read.

CHAPTER TWENTY-NINE

Porto, Portugal. November 12. 6:00 p.m. Western European Time.

After spending an hour or so sampling port served with nuts, cheese, and chocolate at one of the wineries, Ian and Margo had spent the rest of the day on a whirlwind tour of the sights of Porto. They didn't see anything unusual, but Ian took pictures along the way to compare to the couple's shots in case they missed something in their haste to keep to the schedule. Ian felt it was important to be where Rolfe and Clemens were, at the same time they were, in case whatever the couple might have seen or heard that got them killed was based on something that occurred each day.

Thankfully, Stan Rolfe and Briana Clemens returned to the hotel for an hour and a half before going out again for dinner. That would give Ian time to take a long, soothing shower and change out of his sweat-soaked clothes. But when he reached the door to his room, he discovered that he'd lost his key. He figured it must have fallen out of his pocket when his wallet was lifted at the river.

Ian went back down to the lobby and was pleased to see Beatriz working the desk. It meant he wouldn't have to go through the effort of proving he was a guest.

"I've lost my key," he said as he stepped up to the counter.

"Really?" she said with a raised eyebrow.

"Yes, I did," Ian said, not sure why she doubted him. "I can't get into my room."

She pulled a blank card key from a drawer and set it on the counter while she typed something on her computer. "You really are following every step that poor couple made."

"Why do you say that?"

Beatriz slid the card through a reader on her keyboard and then handed it to him. "Because the gentleman lost his key, too."

That was interesting, but Ian wasn't sure what to make of the coincidence. He checked his card. The only information it had on it was the name and address of the hotel, but no room number, so it was useless to anybody but him.

"I'm sure people lose their keys all the time," he said.

"They certainly do," Beatriz said. "Would you like a glass of port?"

She held up the bottle and a glass. Perhaps his Straker scene could still play out in real life.

Ian smiled. "I would, but I never drink alone."

"No problem." She set down the bottle and the glass. "It will still be here if you want to return with someone."

He might be able to accurately imagine global espionage plots, but foretelling the behavior of a woman was obviously well beyond his creative powers. Ian went back to his room and took a cold shower.

Porto's signature dish is the Francesinha, sliced pork, steak, *linguiça*, and ham jammed between two thick pieces of peasant bread that was pressed, covered with cheese, grilled until it was a gooey brick, then topped with a fried egg and slathered with a sauce of tomato, beer, wine, and anything else that happens to be handy. It was cheap, hearty, industrious, and proudly working class. It was the character of the city and its people distilled onto a plate.

So Ian was looking forward to trying the Francesinha for dinner, and that was what he was thinking about as he and Margo left the hotel and headed single file up the steep, alley-like Rua do Dr. Ricardo Jorge on their way to the restaurant.

He didn't notice how dark the street was, or that they were all alone, until a huge man dressed in black stepped out in front of Margo from between two parked cars. The big man held a fourteen-inch hunting knife and he towered over her like a grizzly bear. Ian's stomach cramped with terror.

Something moved behind him and Ian whirled around to see a woman marching up the street, holding a claw hammer at her side. It was the woman Margo had pushed in the river and her eyes blazed with fury.

There was a fight coming. Margo was unarmed but at least she had some self-defense training. All Ian had was prayer and the Rick Steves Portugal guidebook in his hand. Ian was sure that he was going to get very badly hurt, assuming that he even survived. He wondered if begging for mercy was a viable strategy.

The big man lunged at Margo with his knife out in front of him and Ian jumped aside with a yelp of fear, slamming his back into a wall.

Margo smoothly sidestepped the knife, grabbed the man's wrist, and pulled him past her, using his height, weight, and the steepness of the hill against him, and stuck out her leg in front of his ankles. As he tripped on her leg and fell, she slammed her elbow hard into the spot where his skull met his spine and that was that. He hit the sidewalk facedown and out cold, his knife skittering to a stop at Ian's feet.

Ian kicked the knife between two parked cars, and that was when the woman swung her claw hammer at his head. He ducked, the hammer's iron claw scratching the granite wall, and then he came up swinging, slapping the woman's face with the Portugal guidebook. She staggered back, lost her footing, and tumbled head over heels down the street before coming to rest unconscious against a lamppost.

"This has not been her day," Ian said, stunned by the way the fight had played out and that he'd emerged without even a scratch.

He turned to see Margo smiling. "That's a Clint Straker line."

"It's mine now," he said, though the line would have come off a lot cooler if he wasn't trembling.

Margo pretended not to notice. They stepped around the big man on the ground and continued walking up the street.

"How did they find us?" she asked.

"My room key," he said, remembering the pickpocket scooping something up from the ground at the river before he fled. "I think it fell out of my pocket when they took my wallet."

Margo stopped abruptly beside a parked car and peered inside. Ian stepped up beside her and saw the pickpocket cowering in the back seat, his wrist in a cast.

She gestured to the Portugal guidebook in Ian's hand. "Can I borrow that for a sec?"

He gave the book to her. Margo placed the book against the car window and then punched the book. The window cracked, but it held together. She punched the book a few more times, then used it to clear away the pebbled glass, which fell on the pickpocket like snowflakes. She reached inside the car, opened the door, and leaned over the wide-eyed man.

Margo spoke evenly, her face tight, as if she was fighting to control herself. "I am in Portugal because it's all I dreamed about while I was in prison. They put me away for breaking my boyfriend's arms and legs, setting his house on fire, and eating his puppy for dinner. I did it because he irritated me." She grimaced, took a deep breath, and let it out slowly. "But now *you* are irritating me. If I ever see you or your friends again, I will kill you all. Understood?"

He nodded frantically.

"Good." She straightened up, closed the door, and shook some bits of glass off the guidebook before handing it to Ian. "What a practical book."

"I'll be sure to let Rick Steves know," Ian said and they resumed their walk to the restaurant. His hands were still shaking. "You didn't check if the car door was unlocked before you broke the window."

She shrugged. "I wanted to make an impact."

"You certainly did," Ian said. "That was quite a story you told him."

"I wasn't sure whether to go with the boyfriend thing or that I gouged out a woman's eyes in a bar fight."

"Did you eat her cat afterward?"

Margo gave him a look. "Why would I eat her cat?"

"You ate your boyfriend's dog," Ian said.

"The two stories aren't related," she said. "She doesn't have a pet."

"Sorry, I thought you had a theme going."

"What are you trying to say?"

"I thought you went a bit over the top."

"What part?"

Now Ian gave her a look. "Isn't it obvious? The eating-the-dog part."

"I thought it added character," she said. "And twisted menace."

"You almost blew the whole thing," Ian said. "You're lucky he didn't start laughing."

She nodded. "I'll keep that in mind next time."

"Next time?" Ian said, but she let his question go unanswered.

CHAPTER THIRTY

Ian and Margo sat at an outdoor table at Café Luso, facing Carlos Alberto Park, a triangular plaza of limestone and basalt tile mosaics and patches of shrubs over an underground parking structure. It seemed to Ian that every park was just a parking lot with a lawn on top.

They devoured their Francesinhas, which tasted delicious despite looking like sandwiches that someone had vomited their breakfast on. For dessert, they had dark chocolate cake and port.

"I haven't beaten up anybody in months," Margo said, licking some chocolate off her lips. "It felt good."

"You beat up some muggers the first time we visited a foreign country together."

"I remember," she said. "I still miss that dildo."

"They turned out to be Chinese intelligence agents."

"That's true," she said, her eyes sparkling with mischief. "Maybe these pickpockets are actually assassins from Portuguese intelligence."

They looked at each other for a moment and then burst into laughter. When their laughter ebbed into shared smiles, Ian took a sip of his port and sighed. "Can you believe how our lives have changed since the day we met?"

"No, I really can't."

"We're secret agents," he said.

"On assignment in Portugal," she said.

"Investigating whether two idiots who got killed taking a selfie were actually assassinated because they discovered a plot that threatens our national security."

She shook her head. "It's unreal."

"Everything is lately. I'm not sure whether I'm losing my grip on reality," he said. "Or if reality is losing its grip on us."

"That makes absolutely no sense."

Ian finished his port and set the glass down. "Nonsense is the new sense. To truly understand the world we are in today, you have to be a writer, or an actor, or a lunatic."

He signaled the waiter for their check, paid it, and they took the same walk around the neighborhood that Rolfe and Clemens did after their dinner at Café Luso. But as they walked past the many bars and cafés, all of them bustling and crowded with students who spilled out into the streets, Ian and Margo kept their eyes open for anybody who might be following them.

There was no sign of their attackers and nobody was waiting to ambush them when they walked down Rua do Dr. Ricardo Jorge on their way back to their hotel, though Ian noticed Margo had stolen her knife and fork from the café and had them in her hands, ready to use as weapons. She noticed him noticing and pocketed the cutlery again.

"Souvenirs," she said.

When Ian got to his room, he turned on the TV and clicked through the stations until he found CNN, where he learned about a gunfight in Dunn, Texas, between a citizens militia and a group of drug smugglers armed with weapons tracked back to the scandalous Guns & Roses sting operation.

This led an obviously outraged Chris Cuomo, the CNN host, to launch into a blistering recap of "the ineptly conceived" Guns & Roses scandal from its earliest days on up to Gustavo Reynoso murdering two women in San Diego with one of those ATF guns.

"The only good news out of Dunn, Texas, is that this time no Americans were killed with guns that cops sold to a Mexican drug cartel," Cuomo said, taking a dramatic pause before staring into the camera and saying again: *"This time."*

Cuomo switched to a related story about the hunt for Arturo Giron, the Vibora cartel leader, who'd vanished after his escape from a Mexican prison.

Ian turned off the TV and went to bed. As he was drifting off to sleep, he thought it would make a great Straker story if Arturo Giron was hiding in Porto, and what got the couple killed was unknowingly capturing his face in the background of one of their selfies. But the CIA's facial recognition scan for terrorists and fugitives in the photos had already ruled out that possibility in reality.

Okay, he thought, what if it was Giron's bodyguard or his girlfriend in the picture? And what if Giron *was* in the shot, too, but with his *new* face? This could pit Straker against an international drug cartel trying to spark a war between the United States and Mexico.

But why? What could the cartel possibly gain from that?

Ian had no idea. Yet. All he knew was that he might have found the concept for his next Straker novel. He fell asleep satisfied that the trip wasn't a complete waste of time after all.

CHAPTER THIRTY-ONE

Somewhere in Nuevo León, Mexico. November 12. 4:00 p.m. Central Standard Time.

Arturo Giron was pumped full of Vicodin and lying in his king-size bed, recuperating from the brutal beating he'd allowed a plastic surgeon to inflict on his face. Bones were broken and shaved, implants inserted, skin stretched, fillers injected, and hair implanted so that when everything healed, he wouldn't look like Arturo Giron anymore but he might be mistaken for one of the Hemsworth brothers, either Thor or the one who'd been married to Miley Cyrus for a few months before she decided she liked women more than men. Or was that the same Hemsworth? It was hard for Arturo to tell the movie stars apart.

He was in his bedroom in a compound made up of two houses, a six-car garage, a swimming pool, a tennis court, a putting green, and a helipad all atop a graded butte that was surrounded by a high wall topped with shards of broken glass and coils of razor wire that he could see from his bedroom window. When the sunlight hit the glass shards just right, they glimmered like diamonds, and he thought it gave the wall a magical quality, or perhaps that was just the opioids talking.

And while he recuperated, he watched Fox News and Dwight Edney, and couldn't believe what they were saying about him. Edney was on the TV now, accusing Arturo, "the escaped drug lord and de facto leader of Mexico," of sending "legions of drug mules armed by the ATF" across the border wearing vests filled with cocaine underclothes.

Coraline lifted her head from his crotch. "You're a legend."

She was naked, bleary eyed from her own liberal snacking on his Vicodin, and tired from working on his flaccid cock with hands, mouth, and cleavage for the last twenty minutes, doing her part in his pain-killing regimen. He wasn't sure whether she was praising him as part of her therapeutic efforts or because she was genuinely impressed to be in the company of greatness. Either way, she would be executed and dumped in a ravine as soon as the bandages on his face came off.

While he was pleased to be acknowledged as such a powerful, fearsome, and influential figure in Mexico by the American media, he was also deeply insulted to have his name associated with the drug mule story. It made him seem like an idiot, especially among the Mexican public and his rival cartel leaders, all of whom he controlled through fear and respect. That was dangerous, because if they thought he'd lost his mind, he could face an uprising or an attack.

"Nobody is more powerful than you," Coraline said, wrapping her hand around his limp dick and giving it a few more tugs of encouragement.

Was she making fun of him?

Arturo was considering whether or not to strangle her when there was a knock at his door. He pushed her off him and pulled the sheets up over his crotch.

"Come in," he said.

Mateo, his second-in-command, strode into the room, stroking his black goatee, something the thirty-year-old killer did when he was anxious or perplexed about something. His gold-capped teeth, and the gold-plated knife he used to slice the throats of Arturo's enemies, made him the monster in the horror stories that Mexican parents used to frighten their children into doing what they were told.

Do your chores or the Golden Devil will slice your throat!

"Go away," Arturo said to Coraline and used his remote to mute the TV. She scampered naked past Mateo, who ignored her. "What have you learned, Mateo?"

"Two days ago, Caesar Orona and his men were executed in a barn in Guardados de Abajo."

"Why should I care about the murder of a greedy coyote?"

"They were all killed by a black-haired woman with a scar across her throat," Mateo said. "She saved Orona for last. She tortured and killed him in the middle of his sales pitch to some peasants."

Impressive, Arturo thought. This was a woman his dick would wake up for. This might even be a woman he could marry, though he already had two wives, one in Mexico and another about to give birth to his child in Portland, Oregon, so he could be an American citizen.

"Who is she?"

"I don't know," Mateo said. "But she offered the peasants five hundred dollars up front to carry her cocaine across the border and another five hundred dollars when they arrived. She even gave them guns, apparently from the crate that was stolen from us a few months ago."

Arturo raised his eyebrows, or at least he imagined that he did. He wasn't feeling much on his face besides pain and his head was wrapped up like a mummy, so it was hard to actually tell.

"That makes no fucking sense," he said.

"It gets even stranger," Mateo said. "Our sources in Texas tell me the product that was confiscated was mostly flour and baking soda."

"This is too stupid to be a real smuggling operation," Arturo said. "I can't believe even the DEA would think I was responsible."

But they do, he thought. Or at least they *want* others to believe it. But why? What do they gain from embarrassing him and their own ATF?

"The operation may be stupid, but this woman isn't," Mateo said. "Anyone who can kill like that is a professional. There's something else going on here."

"We need to know what it is," Arturo said. "Find her and bring her to me."

"Alive or dead?"

Arturo gave him a withering stare, but the impact was ruined by his bandages. "What fun can I have with a corpse?"

CHAPTER THIRTY-TWO

Porto, Portugal. November 13. 6:30 a.m. Western European Time.

The Miradouro da Vitória was a vacant dirt lot wedged between Our Lady of Vitória church and an old abandoned building covered with layers of graffiti. But the unobstructed southeast view from the weedy, trash-strewn promontory was truly spectacular, sweeping out over the steepled red rooftops to the Se Cathedral and the Dom Luís bridge to the east, all the way down to the Cais da Ribeira, the Douro River, and across to the wine lodges of Vila Nova de Gaia to the south.

In any other city, Ian thought, a view like this would be monetized and commercialized, with rich landscaping, a snack bar, a souvenir shop, bleacher seating facing the city, and coin-operated telescopes along the edge of the plaza with illustrated plaques mounted on the protective railings that described all of the landmarks within view.

But there wasn't even a bench to sit on. Just a single, forlorn tree and a couple of tree stumps in the dry, hard dirt and a graffiti-covered, two-foot-high stone pony wall that ran along the far edge of the lot. There wasn't a railing or fence on the pony wall, so it offered an irresistible spot to sit or stand for a selfie, despite the sheer thirty-foot drop on one side to the winding, cobbled road below. He doubted that Rolfe and Clemens were the first people to fall, though perhaps they were among the few who'd died.

Ian was alone in the empty, roughly triangular lot, which felt strangely secluded, even though it was out in the open. There were no cameras around and it was unlikely that anybody was watching him now unless there were squatters peeking through holes in the boarded windows of the crumbling, derelict building, or clergy peeking between the slats of shuttered windows of the church, or a tourist looking through binoculars at the Se Cathedral.

Margo came running up to him. "I didn't see anything suspicious on my jog. How about you on your leisurely walk?"

"Nope, but this would definitely be a great place to set a killing in a novel. I can see the couple here, trying to get just the right angle for a selfie, when a friendly stranger comes up and offers to take the perfect picture for them. He suggests they stand on the wall with that fabulous view of Porto in the background. So they get up on the wall, and the moment they do, he pushes them off, then tosses the phone after them."

She peered over the edge and frowned. "You could fall from here and survive. He might have had to go down there with a rock to finish them off."

"We can imagine lots of ways they might have been killed here, but we don't have any evidence that's what happened. We don't even have a reason why anybody would want them dead."

"We just haven't found it yet."

"I don't see how we can stretch this trip out another day," Ian said. "At least not if we want to maintain the charade that we're doing an investigation."

"I do," she said. "I got a text from Langley while I was jogging. The photos you asked for came in, the ones from tourists who were at the same spots at the same time the couple were. Maybe there's something there."

Ian sighed. "Going through them all will be tedious, but I suppose it will buy us another day."

"There are worse places to be," Margo said. "Like in your office, staring at a blank screen."

"Actually, I think I may have my Straker story."

"Any chance it could become a mission for us?"

"Not unless the CIA is interested in taking down a notorious Mexican drug lord."

She glowered at him. "We're in Portugal, not Mexico. How did our trip here send your imagination there?"

"Creativity doesn't follow a straight line," Ian said. "But don't worry, I'll keep taking this exercise seriously, at least for another day. I'm enjoying the city. Let's look at those photos."

They returned to the hotel, where Margo showered and changed while Ian went to his room and opened up his laptop, downloaded the files from a link that Margo had forwarded to him, and unpacked the pictures on his hard drive.

There were hundreds of shots, perhaps as many as a thousand, in directories separated by date and location. But the CIA had helpfully narrowed things down for him by using facial recognition technology to isolate the shots that included any angles on Rolfe and Clemens. Those photos were in a separate subdirectory. He opened up another window so he could compare the tourist shots with the ones that the couple had taken.

That was when Margo knocked on his door, her hair still wet and her laptop tucked under her arm. "Let's get out of here. We're in Porto. I don't want to stay in a hotel all day."

"We have a lot of pictures to look at. Where do you suggest we go?"

"Up to the university square," she said. "We're more likely to find a café there that caters to students and that will let us hang out and use their Wi-Fi as long as we keep ordering pastries and coffee."

And that was exactly what they did, settling down at a café that faced the severely baroque Carmo Church, which was known for the blue-and-white-tiled mural on one outside wall and was topped in front with statues of four saints, who stood on the roof's edge as if they were contemplating suicide.

Ian and Margo sipped coffees and gobbled down *pastéis de nata*, addictive little egg tarts, and Pão de Deus, deliciously sweet, streusel-topped rolls while they browsed through the photos, looking for something without having the slightest idea what it might be.

In each photo, a person, couple, or family were usually in the foreground, or sometimes it was a shot of a Porto landmark like a church, a statue, or a bridge, with Rolfe and Clemens somewhere in the background, walking by or taking a picture themselves, usually a selfie.

After an hour or so, Ian began to feel a strange variation of déjà vu while he looked at the photos. At first, he thought it was the cumulative effect of seeing the same couple, over and over, from different angles in places that he'd visited before. But this sensation was something else, persistent and nagging, on top of creepy and disorienting.

So he started over, but this time looking at everything in the photos *except* Rolfe and Clemens. The feeling was getting stronger, but whatever it meant felt just beyond his grasp, like a name he couldn't remember.

Margo yawned and stretched in her seat. "This is like *Where's Waldo?* without knowing what Waldo looks like or even if it's Waldo that you're looking for."

That was it.

Her words were like a trigger. The instant the words were out of her mouth, he knew what he was looking for, what he saw but didn't see.

"You're right," he said.

"Right about what?"

He pulled up four pictures at once, taken in four different locations the couple had visited by four different tourists, and began zooming in on the other faces in the crowds besides Rolfe and Clemens.

And then he saw it.

Or rather, *him*.

Ian felt a jolt of excitement, like getting a blackjack at a casino, and turned the laptop so Margo could see his screen. "Meet Waldo."

The man's face was pockmarked, as if he shaved with a cheese grater, and his teeth were so white Ian suspected they'd either been capped or replaced. Waldo wore a short-sleeved, tan panama shirt, white linen slacks and loafers, and a gold watch studded with diamonds.

"Waldo is in all four of these photos," Ian said, "trailing behind Rolfe and Clemens."

"Maybe he's just a tourist on the same walking tour out of the same guidebook."

"They weren't on a walking tour," he said.

"We don't know that," she said. "In a few of these photos, they are looking at a map. Maybe the map had a suggested route on it."

Ian shook his head. He knew that wasn't it. "Waldo was following them. He's always looking at them, not at the sights."

"Because Rolfe and Clemens were standing right in front of what everybody wants to see," she said. "These are only four pictures. You may be reading more into it than there is."

"Let's go back to the beginning and see if Waldo is there," Ian said, turned the laptop back to him, and began scanning through photos. "The first place the couple took pictures after breakfast at Café Majestic was outside the Santo Ildefonso Church."

Ian pulled up the photos that Rolfe and Clemens took outside the elaborately tiled church and those taken by other tourists who were there at the same time.

Waldo was there, too.

He turned the laptop toward Margo again so she could see for herself.

"Okay," Margo said. "Now it's getting creepy."

"Maybe this wasn't the beginning," he said, taking the laptop back.

He closed the photos from the other tourists and pulled up Briana Clemens' first selfie, the picture she took of the couple's reflection in the mirror at the Café Majestic.

Boom.

Waldo was in the reflection, too. He was seated at another table, his back to the couple, staring into the mirror.

Staring right at them.

And staring at Ian, too, or so it seemed. Waldo's gaze was intense, utterly focused, a hunter targeting his prey.

"Waldo was already watching them at breakfast," Ian said, turning the laptop to face Margo again.

"Why do you think he was so interested in them?"

"I don't know, but look at the expression on his face. It certainly wasn't to surprise them with a check from Publishers Clearing House."

"What is Publishers Clearing House?"

"Never mind," Ian said, suddenly feeling a hundred years older than Margo. He copied the Café Majestic photo, cropped the duplicate into a close-up of Waldo's face, and sent the new picture to his phone. "The point is I don't believe that his intentions were friendly."

Margo scooted her chair over beside him. "Let's check the pictures they took at the restaurant the first night they were here."

Ian pulled up the pictures. There were shots of their food, and a few of the couple, but there were no other faces visible in the background.

"If Waldo is there," Ian said. "We can't see him."

"Or he didn't start following them until he saw them at breakfast," Margo said.

"What if the surveillance is related to something that happened *before* they got to Porto?"

"Like what?"

"I don't know," Ian said. "Let's look at the photos that they took on their way here."

He brought them up on his laptop, but there were only three shots—one a selfie Rolfe had taken of the two of them at the departure gate at LAX, one that Clemens had taken of Rolfe sleeping on the plane, and another she'd taken of a decadent Ladurée chocolate pastry that they'd shared at Charles de Gaulle Airport in Paris during their layover before their Porto flight.

"These are all tight shots," Margo said. "You can't see anyone or anything happening in the background."

He swiped backward again, intending to reexamine the three shots, but went too far back, calling up a photo taken the day before their trip in San Diego. It was a selfie of Briana Clemens eating a taco at a food truck in a cul-de-sac in what appeared to be an industrial area. The picture sent a chill down Ian's spine that made him shiver.

"Holy shit," Ian said, looking up at Margo. "They *were* murdered."

CHAPTER THIRTY-THREE

Margo studied the photo on Ian's laptop. "I don't understand. Someone killed them over a taco?"

"It's what's happening behind her that got them killed." He zoomed in on a black Escalade in the cul-de-sac and a man standing outside the driver's-side window, talking to the man behind the wheel. "This is San Diego and the driver of that Escalade is Waldo."

She narrowed her eyes, as if that would bring the faces into even sharper focus. "Holy shit, you're right."

"We have to find something else to say besides 'holy shit' when we have a holy shit moment."

"Why?"

"Because it's repetitive. I just said it before you said it."

"If it's a holy shit moment, that's what you say, not 'exalted vomit.'"

"Nobody says 'exalted vomit,'" Ian said.

"Exactly, because you say 'holy shit' in a holy shit moment."

"We could say 'my God,' or 'hot damn,' or 'holy smoke.'"

"Only a cartoon character would say 'holy smoke.' Why are we even having this conversation?" Margo said. "You aren't *writing* this. We're *living* it."

"That's not how it feels to me."

"Focus," Margo pointed to Waldo. "Why would he follow them all the way to Porto?"

"Because the man Waldo is talking to is Gustavo Reynoso."

Margo gave him a blank look. "Who is that and why do you know his name?"

"Don't you ever watch the news?"

"Not if I can avoid it," she said. "It makes me too angry."

"Gustavo Reynoso is an illegal immigrant and convicted rapist who killed two women in San Diego with a gun from the Guns & Roses sting." Ian tapped the screen with his finger. "And that's the Deathscalade with the bodies in the back."

"The Deathscalade?"

"That's what Dwight Edney is calling the stolen SUV that Reynoso was in when he was spotted by the police," Ian said. "Reynoso fled, ran across a street, and was killed by a hit-and-run driver. It happened the day before Rolfe and Clemens came here. The story is that Reynoso acted alone in the killings. But this photo changes everything."

"It means the story is bullshit," Margo said.

"It means there's a conspiracy," Ian said.

"How do you figure that?"

"Because there had to be other people involved in this besides Waldo. Someone was out there watching these two men meet and spotted Briana Clemens taking a selfie that might have captured it going down. Someone was worried that once the news broke about the murders, there was a slim chance that Clemens would recognize Reynoso in the photo and go to the police. She had to die before the murders hit the national news. That means they knew when the bodies would be discovered and Reynoso would be killed. There's only one way that's possible."

"If it's all a setup," Margo said.

"It has to be or they wouldn't have killed her on the remote possibility she could become a risk," Ian said. "And we're talking about people who have the resources to learn who she was, get her travel itinerary, and send Waldo after her. I think this is more than a setup. It's part of a much bigger scheme."

"What is there to gain from murdering two women in San Diego and making the fall guy a convicted rapist from Mexico?"

"I don't know, but the answers aren't here. They're at home."

"I'll get us on the first flight back tonight," Margo said, gathering up her stuff, a smile on her face. "In the meantime, I'll send Waldo's picture to the Agency and see if they can ID him."

"Why are you smiling?" Ian asked, closing up his laptop.

"Because you did it again, just like I knew you would. You started working on a Straker story and uncovered a real-life conspiracy along the way."

She was right and it made him both proud of himself and frightened. Once again, he was the spoiler of a deadly conspiracy, which meant he could soon become a target himself if he wasn't one already. He glanced up at the sky and wondered if maybe he should have brought Ronnie's aluminum hat and white-noise device after all.

Then again, maybe he was exaggerating the significance of whatever this conspiracy was. Maybe it wasn't as big or as dangerous or as global as what he'd uncovered before.

"Just because I've discovered a conspiracy, it doesn't mean that it's a job for the CIA," Ian said as they got up and started walking back across the plaza toward their hotel. "It could be tawdry and domestic."

"Who else besides a rival intelligence agency has the resources to mount this kind of operation and send a professional assassin here to kill the couple and make it look like an accident?"

"I can think of all kinds of possible bad guys. It could be some billionaire who either murdered his cheating wife or a mistress who was blackmailing him or both and framed an illegal alien for it."

"That's a stretch," she said.

"I'm just getting started. It could be American nationalists trying to create a crisis on the Mexican border to force the US government into taking harsher measures on immigration. Or it could be Dwight Edney trying to start a war with Mexico to jack up his ratings. Or it could be Ernst Stavro Blofeld in a secret base in a dormant volcano, stroking his white cat and plotting world domination."

"Let's go with Blofeld in the volcano," Margo said. "Out of all of those plots, it sounds like the most fun."

CHAPTER THIRTY-FOUR

When Ian and Margo got back to the hotel, Beatriz was at the front desk along with the bellman, a ferret-faced, skinny man in a pillbox hat, bow tie, and a red, oversize waistcoat that made him look like a child playing dress-up. His name tag read DUDA.

On impulse, Ian approached Beatriz and showed her the photo of Waldo that he'd sent to his phone. "Have you seen this man before?"

She glanced at the photo. "Yes, I have."

Ian and Margo shared a look.

"When and where?" Ian asked.

"He checked in the same night as the couple you're interested in," Beatriz said and began typing something on her computer.

"I'm surprised you remember it so clearly," Ian said.

"We don't often have guests who get killed. I'll probably always remember everything about them, from the day they arrived until the day they fell, including the other guests who checked in." She looked from the screen to Margo. "This is an odd coincidence."

"What is?" Margo asked.

"The gentleman you're asking about was booked in your room."

The room right next door to the one Clemens and Rolfe were staying in. And Waldo had their key.

It wasn't a coincidence. Now Ian was certain that Rolfe hadn't lost his room key. Waldo had lifted it from his pocket at some point during their walking tour of Porto.

Waldo came to Porto to kill the couple. He was following them until he saw an opportunity to do the deed and make it look accidental. And if that failed, Waldo had their room key. He could murder them in their bed if he had to, then make it look like they'd OD'd or something.

"When did the man check out?" Ian asked.

"The day the couple died," Beatriz said.

"Can you tell us his name?"

"No," Beatriz said, glancing uncomfortably at the bellman before looking back at them. "I've probably told you too much as it is. Why do you ask?"

"Because he killed them," Margo said.

Ian gave Margo a sharp look, then smiled at Beatriz. "Margo is joking, of course. We just thought he might have befriended them while they were here and could tell us more about how they spent their time."

"Before he killed them," Margo said.

"Sorry I can't help you," Beatriz said. "Perhaps you should speak to the police."

"Good idea," Margo said. "Did the detective leave a card?"

"Yes, he did." Beatriz opened a drawer, pulled out a card, and placed it on the counter.

Margo took a picture of it. "Thanks!"

Beatriz put the card back in the drawer and slammed it shut with her hip. "Will there be anything else?"

"No, thank you," Ian said. "We'll be checking out today."

Beatriz flashed her customer service smile, but Ian thought she also looked relieved that they were leaving. "I hope you had a pleasant stay."

"It was delightful." Ian smiled and headed to the elevators with Margo, asking her in a near whisper: "Why did you tell the clerk that he killed them?"

"I wanted to see how she'd react."

"Are you planning to call the police?"

"Of course not. I just wanted to see how far she'd go with it," she said. "She's clean. She wouldn't have given me the cop's card if she'd been involved with Waldo."

The elevator doors opened.

"That's ridiculous," Ian said as they stepped inside. "Why would she have been involved with Waldo?"

Margo shrugged. "You never know."

That was when he remembered that Beatriz ratting out Straker to the couple's killer was how he'd ended his imaginary scene, but he didn't tell Margo that.

The elevator doors closed and they went up to their rooms.

Duda the bellman waited until the couple was gone, then turned to Beatriz and told her that he was stepping outside for a smoke.

He walked out of the hotel and around the corner onto Rua do Dr. Ricardo Jorge, where Beatriz couldn't see him. But Duda didn't really want a cigarette. He took out his phone, then opened his wallet for the slip of paper the man in the photograph had given him with half of a torn hundred-euro bill clipped to it. The bellman dialed the number on the paper. The call was answered after a few rings.

"Yes?" The man sounded drowsy, clearly awakened from sleep, his reply escaping through barely opened lips and articulated with a heavy, dry tongue.

"This is the bellman at the Almada Regent in Porto," Duda said in English. "Do you remember me?"

"Yes." This time the response was sharp, firmly articulated. The man was alert now.

"You gave me half of a hundred-euro note. You said you'd give me the other half if anybody ever came asking about you and I called to tell you about it. Do you remember this?"

"Yes." Now he sounded irritated. It was interesting to Duda how a single word, spoken in different ways, could convey so much.

"Someone came."

"Who?"

"An American writer named Ian Ludlow and a woman named Margo French. They were asking about the American couple who were staying here, the ones who died in a fall off the Miradouro da Vitória. They showed us your picture and asked if we knew you," Duda said. "The woman said you killed them."

"You said *us*. Who else was with you?"

The bellman thought it was odd the man had nothing to say about the woman's accusation. "Beatriz, the desk clerk."

"What did Beatriz tell them?"

"That you stayed here, but nothing else. She let the woman take a picture of the business card the police left with us and that was it," Duda said. "Do I get the other half of the note?"

"I'll send a friend to you soon with the other half and another hundred to forget we ever spoke."

"It's already forgotten." The bellman disconnected the call. Duda didn't ask if the man killed the couple because he was afraid of the answer.

Nice Nite Motel. Rio Grande City, Texas. November 13. 5:15 a.m. Central Standard Time.

Magar Orlov sat up shirtless in bed, his back against the headboard, and removed the SIM card from his burner phone immediately after finishing the call with the bellman.

"Who was that?" Beth Wheeler asked.

She was lying on her side, staring at him from the other double bed. The two feet of space between their beds might as well have been the Grand Canyon. She'd made it very clear she had no interest in sleeping with him.

They were in a cinder block motel room that reeked of industrial-strength disinfectant. The TV was bolted to the wall and the lamps were glued to the nightstands. He'd been in prison cells with more charm and thicker mattresses.

"The bellman at the hotel in Porto," Magar said and he gave her the details as he got up in his boxer shorts, went into the bathroom, and flushed the SIM card down the toilet along with his future as a field agent. He stood in the bathroom doorway and faced her when he was done talking.

Her eyes were cold and her face was rigid. She definitely would never sleep with him now. This was a simple kill and somehow, inexplicably, he'd failed. He'd be working a desk somewhere very cold for the rest of his career.

She threw off the thin sandpaper sheets and got out of bed in her tank top and panties. "How did they get on to you?"

"I have no idea," he said.

It was an honest answer. Magar couldn't think of a single mistake that he'd made. He'd been meticulous and professional in Porto, constantly checking whether he was under any surveillance or if the couple was aware that they were. He was certain the couple had never suspected they were in any danger. He'd always remember the look of bewilderment and fear in the woman's eyes after her fall and right before he smashed her skull in with a rock to finish her off.

Was he equally clueless? Did he have that look in his eyes now?

Beth went to her knapsack and pulled out one of her burner phones. "You must have fucked up in a big way."

"No," he said emphatically. "Something else is at work here. I didn't make any mistakes."

"Obviously you're wrong or two civilians wouldn't have discovered that you murdered Clemens and her boyfriend."

"We don't know that Ludlow and French are civilians," Magar said. "They could be CIA agents."

Beth laughed and somehow it was as emasculating to him as a knife swipe to his scrotum, something he knew Beth enjoyed doing to her male adversaries.

"Ian Ludlow is a famous author. He writes spy novels, but he's definitely not a spy himself."

"How can you be sure?" He was afraid that he'd heard a squeal in his voice, that he was already a soprano.

"It's clear from the idiotic shit that he writes."

"You've read his books?"

"I picked up one of his Straker novels to blend in on a train ride once and to keep anyone from engaging me in a conversation. The book was a stupid male fantasy that had no relation to actual spy craft and represented everything that's wrong with American popular culture."

"Maybe his books are intentionally unrealistic so nobody will question his cover as a bestselling novelist."

"Or you screwed up big-time. Which explanation do you think is the most likely to be true?" Beth said, then held up her phone. "I have to notify Moscow about this."

Magar knew what explanation the Kitchen would pick. He just hoped their solution to the problem wouldn't be to order Beth to put a bullet in his skull. If it was, he would see it in her eyes and kill her first. He was devoted to his country, but even more to self-preservation.

CHAPTER THIRTY-FIVE

Top Chef Catering. Khimki, Moscow Oblast. November 13. 3:06 p.m. Moscow Standard Time.

Kirk Cannon sat in a fourth-floor editing room, watching footage on a computer screen of the president of the United States being interviewed by Anderson Cooper on *60 Minutes* and thought about unintended consequences.

"The balance of world power will be changed forever because actors hate to loop," Cannon said.

"Loop?" asked Viktor, who sat beside him, manning the keyboard while the software analyzed the presidential footage.

"It's Hollywood slang for rerecording dialogue after the film has been shot," Cannon said.

As a tremendously gifted and tragically unappreciated actor himself, Cannon understood why his fellow thespians hated looping. They had to stand in a recording booth and repeat their lines while watching the film, re-creating the emotion of the scene, staying in character, and exactly matching the timing of how they delivered their dialogue the first time to match up with their flapping lips on-screen.

Or they had to record entirely new dialogue, usually heard in the final cut on the back of their heads or on someone else's close-up to avoid lip-synch problems. This kind of looping was done to cover chunks of a scene that were edited out to make the film move faster, or to correct continuity errors, or to make up for a bad performance.

Looping was miserable, difficult work but it was a necessary part of filmmaking. It could also be inconvenient and costly for the studio if the actor was in some far-flung location, shooting another movie or on a vacation, when they were needed to record new dialogue. The producers had to either bring the actor back to Los Angeles for a day or two of recording or fly the director to the actor, book a recording studio, and hire audio engineers wherever that place might be.

"I don't record any audio in my movies while I'm shooting," Viktor said. "I record all the sound and dialogue later, like the great Italian director Sergio Leone did."

But the audio in Viktor's movies, amateur skin flicks uploaded to Pornhub, were mostly moans and groans of fake ecstasy. There wasn't much dialogue and acting certainly wasn't an issue. Cannon knew this because Viktor had screened some of his awful porn for him, eager for advice from a renowned master of the cinematic arts. Viktor's skill was altering existing video content for fake news, not creating films of his own. But Cannon took pity on him and said he had a "unique artistic vision," which wasn't exactly a lie. His vision just happened to be shit.

"I still don't see why the actors have a problem with recording the audio later," Viktor said. "It's easy. They don't have to memorize their lines, get naked, or put their hand up in anyone's ass. They can just read their lines off the script and concentrate on the words."

"It's hard to recapture a character, and an emotional moment, that you shot weeks or months ago, especially if you're already in the middle of filming a new role," Cannon said, trying to sound wise and not condescending to his disciple. "On top of that, there are the technical problems of trying to match your performance to the footage. There are actors who can't do both."

Viktor nodded toward the screen. "That won't be an issue anymore."

No, it wouldn't.

A few days earlier, Cannon had read an article about how the company behind the most popular film-editing software in Hollywood had developed a new audio feature that eliminated the need for looping. All a director needed was twenty minutes of an actor talking and the software could flawlessly re-create his dialogue or put new words in his mouth, and could even match the performance.

The company had secretly tested the software to loop the audio of a famous actor who'd died of a drug overdose shortly after he'd completed filming his part in a $100 million science fiction movie. Nobody noticed the tinkering.

But the software company didn't consider the real-world security and ethical implications of their postproduction breakthrough until word leaked about their work. Now they were indefinitely delaying release of the software until they could come up with safeguards against misuse or at least until their lawyers could compose a half-assed "ethical statement" to put on the box.

The Kitchen wasn't waiting. At Cannon's insistence, their hackers had broken into the company's computers and stolen the program. Now they were inputting the US president's voice into the software to use for their own diabolical purposes. And that was what prompted Cannon's musing on unintentional consequences.

"It's done," Viktor said. "All you have to do is type what you want the president to say and he will say it."

He slid the keyboard over to Cannon and turned up the volume on the speakers. If it worked, he believed this technological innovation could speed up their operation in America by weeks.

Cannon was about to type a sentence for the president to speak when Leonid Morzeny burst into the editing room like Kramer coming into Seinfeld's apartment and almost tripped over his untied sneakers in the process.

"Here you are," Morzeny said, catching his breath. "I've been looking all over the building for you. What are you doing down here?"

"Working on a new plot twist for our border operation," Cannon said.

"I've already got one for you," Morzeny said. "And it could ruin everything."

Morzeny told Cannon about the call Magar Orlov received from the bellman at the hotel in Porto. Ian Ludlow, an American thriller author, had discovered that the San Diego tourists who appeared to have died in a selfie accident were actually murdered.

"Ludlow even has a photo of Orlov," Morzeny said. "He showed it to the desk clerk at the hotel."

Cannon was shocked, but he was also an actor who could improvise on the spot. He shrugged off the concern. "It's an unwelcome complication, but it doesn't mean that Ludlow will tumble onto our entire plot."

But Ludlow was a writer, and Cannon believed that made him far more likely than a trained intelligence operative to discover their scheme. That was because Cannon knew writers instinctively tried to generate plots from events around them as a means of survival, the way a pigeon is always searching for food, pecking at everything in sight. A spy lacked the imagination or the drive for that kind of free-association creativity.

Cannon knew he should be worried and upset by this startling development, but instead he found it exciting. Now there was someone out there opposing him, someone who saw the world the same way he did. A doppelgänger. It somehow made the whole operation electrifying in a way that it hadn't been before.

What he was feeling must have shown on his face, because Morzeny said: "Why the fuck are you smiling?"

It always amused Cannon when foreigners used American profanity. The swear words always seemed too big to fit in their mouths and were spit out rather than spoken, like a glob of tough meat they couldn't chew and didn't dare try to swallow.

"Because I always appreciate a twist I never saw coming," Cannon said. "And in my own story no less."

"You don't seem to realize how serious this is," Morzeny said. "How did he get on to us so fast? Is he a spy? Does this mean that US intelligence already knows what we are doing?"

Cannon held up a hand in a halting gesture. "Calm down. Ludlow isn't a spy. There's a simple explanation for this."

"Really? Because I don't see it." Morzeny glanced at Viktor. "Do you?"

Viktor wisely didn't answer.

Cannon sighed. "Ludlow is a novelist who started in television, where the hacks churn out twenty-two episodes a season. They are so desperate for stories to feed the machine that they steal ideas from the news for inspiration. They use the term 'ripped from the headlines' for their stories because it sounds a lot better than 'plagiarized from the *New York Times* because we have no imagination.' Now Ludlow is obviously doing the same thing for his books."

Morzeny's smirk told Cannon that he wasn't buying it, though it was what Cannon honestly believed was at work here. "How can you possibly know that?"

"First off, because I did my time in television, doing guest shots on shows written by guys just like Ian Ludlow. I know how the game is played. But you don't need to have my Hollywood experience to know that I'm right. The proof is right in front of you," Cannon said. "All you have to do is look at the timing. Ludlow went to Porto the same day the news broke about the two Americans getting killed taking a selfie. That tells me he was a desperate novelist staring at a blank screen who saw a hook for his next story and used it as an excuse for a trip to Portugal, probably at his publisher's expense."

"But you're forgetting something," Morzeny said. "Ludlow is the same guy who got Wang Mei to defect from China. That sounds like the work of a spy to me, not some hack novelist."

"Because you don't know any writers besides me. Your man Edney got it right when Ludlow and Wang Mei were guests on his show. He said that Mei was a rich, spoiled actress in deep legal and financial trouble in China who seduced a horny, visiting American writer into helping her escape prosecution. Ludlow was a dupe. The fact that it's Ludlow who stumbled onto the murder in Porto is a fluke, but an understandable one."

"Then how did he get Orlov's picture?"

"I don't know. The obvious answer is that your agent was sloppy and left a trail even an amateur could follow," Cannon said. "But lucky for us, Ludlow is a novelist, not an investigative reporter. He makes stuff up for a living. Our operation isn't in any immediate danger."

"It will be if he knows Gustavo Reynoso was framed."

"He'd need the dead woman's photos for that, and that's assuming she actually took a picture that shows Reynoso and Orlov together," Cannon said. "But Ludlow won't see her pictures because her phone was destroyed in Porto."

"Did you erase her photos in the cloud?" Viktor asked Morzeny, startling both men, who'd forgotten he was there.

The bewildered expression on Morzeny's face told Cannon and Viktor that the answer was no, the cloud backup wasn't hacked and deleted. But Morzeny was quick with an explanation.

"Of course not. Her death was accidental. There was no reason to think that anybody would go looking through her archived photos in the cloud. And besides, if anybody did access her archive for some reason, and discovered that some photos were deleted after her fatal death, that would have raised immediate, unwanted suspicion. We took a calculated risk that it was better not to touch her cloud archive."

Cannon was sure the truth was that it never occurred to Morzeny to hack her cloud backup, but his improvised excuse was impressive and actually made a lot of sense. The skillful ass-covering demonstrated to Cannon how Morzeny had risen so far within the dark realm of Soviet politics.

"It doesn't matter," Cannon said, letting Morzeny off the hook. "Ludlow is a novelist. He doesn't have the resources to hack her cloud account anyway, so it's a nonissue. Where is Ludlow now?"

"He and his assistant are on their way to the airport for a flight back to Los Angeles," Morzeny said. "They are flying from Porto to Lisbon, Lisbon to New York, and finally New York to Los Angeles. With layovers between flights, they will be in transit for nearly twenty-four hours."

"Perfect," Cannon said. "That gives us plenty of time to deal with the problem. I don't see any reason to rewrite our script. The operation in Texas can continue on schedule tonight. But you should send a cleaning crew to Porto now."

"That's already in motion. This isn't my first rodeo," Morzeny said and it made Cannon cringe. He hated clichés, but even more so when they were repeated by foreigners who thought they were being clever. "What do we do about Ludlow and his assistant?"

Cannon typed his answer on the keyboard and an instant later the president of the United States spoke for him in his distinctive, and unmistakably crass, voice as if he'd been listening to their conversation on a speakerphone all along.

"Kill them both and make it look like an accident," the president said. "But don't fuck it up this time."

CHAPTER THIRTY-SIX

Almada Regent Hotel. Porto, Portugal. November 13. 5:37 p.m. Western European Time.

The man wearing a wide-brimmed hat, long overcoat, and black leather gloves dragged a large roller bag behind him as he crossed the empty lobby and approached the front desk, where Beatriz and Duda were waiting to greet him with their customer service smiles. His head was slightly lowered, and shadowed by his hat, so it was hard for either Beatriz or Duda to get a good look at his face, not that the man was worried about being recognized or remembered by them. It was force of habit to keep his face obscured from security cameras.

"I'd like to check in," the man said in Spanish.

Beatriz answered in Spanish. "Do you have a reservation?"

"That depends," he said. "Are you Beatriz and is he Duda?"

He gestured first to her, then to the bellman.

She smiled and touched her engraved plastic name tag. "Yes, we are, just like it says on our name tags."

"Do you ever wear another person's name tag or one with a false name?"

Duda shared a bemused look with Beatriz. "Why would we do that?"

The man shrugged. "To maintain your anonymity or as a joke."

"We'd be fired if we ever did that," Beatriz said.

"How would the boss know?" the man asked.

Beatriz pointed to the security cameras on the walls. "The cameras would give us away if one of the guests didn't first."

"Then I have no reservations about this." The man reached into his jacket, took out a gun equipped with a long suppressor, and shot Duda between the eyes, then Beatriz in her mouth, which was wide open, preparing for a scream that never came. Their bodies dropped to the floor like clothes that had slipped off their hangers.

The assassin bent down and unzipped his suitcase, removed the gasoline can that was inside, unscrewed the lid, and began pouring out its contents on the floor as he stepped behind the counter and into the back office, where the DVR and security monitors were.

The hackers in the Kitchen would be wiping clean the hotel's guest records and their online archive of security footage, but he splashed gasoline over the DVR and the computers just to be on the safe side and continued pouring as he walked back to his suitcase. None of this cleanup would have been necessary, he thought, if the Kitchen had sent him to handle the American tourists rather than having Orlov follow them from the United States. But what do caterers and bureaucrats know about spy craft?

An elderly couple emerged from the elevator. The assassin reflexively shot them both as they stepped out and continued his work, not bothering to see if they were dead because it didn't matter.

He snatched a souvenir matchbook from a dish full of them on the counter, packed the gasoline can back in the roller bag, and dragged it with him to the front door.

The assassin took one more look back, just to make sure he hadn't forgotten anything, then struck a match, lit the matchbook with it, and tossed the burning matches into the gasoline on the floor.

The gasoline ignited instantly with an audible whoosh, flames washing over the entire front desk area. As he stepped out onto the street, his back to the hotel, the fire alarms went off and the sprinklers sprang on, but the water only spread the gasoline-fed inferno further through the lobby, setting the furniture and wood paneling ablaze.

He checked his watch while he strolled toward the Praça da Liberdade, the sound of alarms and sirens and screams behind him, and decided he had time to treat himself to a Francesinha and a glass of port before his flight back to Madrid.

Somewhere over the Atlantic Ocean. November 13. 10:11 p.m. Greenwich Mean Time.

Ian was seated beside Margo in first class on the second stage of their journey home, a flight from Lisbon to JFK airport in New York, arriving at 8:00 p.m., which would give them a two-hour layover before their flight to Los Angeles.

Shortly after takeoff, Margo put on her noise-canceling headphones and began listening to music.

Ian watched the satellite news on the in-flight entertainment system to see if there were any new developments in the Gustavo Reynoso killings, but all he saw was a report about a buildup in the number of troops participating in Russia's annual military exercises on its borders with Belarus and Georgia. Some pundits were worried that it was a cover for a possible invasion by Soviet leaders emboldened by the lack of meaningful international opposition to Russia's annexation of Crimea.

Ian turned off the TV, took out a legal pad and a pen, and began to list the things he knew about the San Diego couple's murder, and the story about Reynoso's killings, in chronological order to see if a potential plot would emerge that tied the events together into something more. He wrote down the first item:

1. Illegal immigrant and convicted rapist Gustavo Reynoso meets Waldo in San Diego. Waldo is driving the Escalade, presumably with the bodies inside. Briana Clemens captures them in a selfie. Someone else is watching. Who? Why?

Ian tapped Margo on the shoulder to get her attention.

She opened her eyes and took off her headphones. "What?"

"Can you ask your friends in Langley to look at the metadata on the picture Briana Clemens took of Waldo and Reynoso talking and get the time it was taken? Then can you ask your friends to find out what time Gustavo Reynoso was stopped by the cops? I'd like to know how close the two events were. Oh, and can you also have them get us detailed information on the two women who were killed?"

"Would you like me to do it now?"

"Can you?"

She gave him a look. "No, I can't. We're on an airplane over the Atlantic."

"We have Wi-Fi," Ian said.

"The only thing less secure than airplane Wi-Fi is running naked through Compton holding all of your money, jewelry, and credit cards in a baggie. You, of all people, should know that."

"I thought you might have a device from Q Branch that gives you added protection or encryption."

"Of course I do. I just forgot to pack it, along with my tampon flamethrower," she said. "Make me a list of what you need and I'll do it as soon as we get back."

She put her headphones back on and Ian went back to his list. He added the two questions he'd asked Margo to item #1 and then continued.

2. Gustavo Reynoso is sitting alone in the parked Escalade with the two dead women and a gun from the Vibora/ATF sting when he's stopped by the police. Why was Gustavo parked there? Where was Waldo? Who killed the women? Who were the women?

3. Gustavo flees and is killed by a car in a hit-and-run. That was convenient. Was it an accident—or was he run down intentionally? If so, by whom? Was it whoever was watching before? And what were they doing there? Did they follow Gustavo or were they already in place? Do the police have any information on the hit-and-run driver?

4. Dwight Edney reveals Gustavo snuck into the country before, is a convicted rapist, and used a gun from the Guns & Roses sting. Media goes crazy and the Guns & Roses scandal is resurrected. The president, Homeland Security, and ICE are trashed for ineptitude and weak border enforcement. Fingers are pointed at Arturo Giron and his Vibora cartel. Is this just noise or is it part of why Gustavo was set up?

5. Waldo follows Clemens and Rolfe to Porto and kills them. Who is Waldo and who sent him? Did Waldo kill the women in San Diego, too? Was he protecting himself or someone else by killing Clemens and

Rolfe? Is Waldo in charge or working for someone else?

6. The media, led by Dwight Edney, say Gustavo is just the beginning of the problem at the border. Justice Dept. announces its intention to prosecute the ATF agents involved in the G&R sting years ago.

7. Drug mules are killed in Texas carrying drugs and Guns & Roses weapons. Edney and Cuomo and the rest of the media, still amped up by the killings in San Diego, tie the two events together . . . but are they actually related? If so, how? Or is this all smoke, a big distraction? Is this really all about one or both of the dead women?

8. Bottom line: Four people are dead. Rolfe and Clemens were killed to cover up the murders of the women in San Diego . . . but why were the women killed? Who is Waldo? Who is he working for? How many people are involved in this conspiracy and what is their endgame?

Ian stared at his list, added more notes and questions and doodles in the margins, but it wasn't long before it was all just a jumble. He needed to clear his mind, so he set the notepad aside, fired up the airline's entertainment system, and found another Bond movie to watch.

He chose *The Spy Who Loved Me*, his favorite 007 flick from the lighthearted, quippy Roger Moore era. It was basically a remake of *You Only Live Twice*. This time a megalomaniac bad guy, hiding in a secret base underwater, uses a supertanker to gobble up submarines equipped with nuclear warheads from the British and the Soviets. His evil plan is to obliterate New York and Moscow with missiles fired from the two submarines, sparking a nuclear war between the superpowers that will destroy the surface of the planet, all so he can rule a new, undersea civilization. As the action unfolds, Bond skis off a cliff with a Union Jack parachute hidden in his pack, drives a sports car that turns into a missile-firing submarine, and battles Jaws, a seven-foot-tall assassin with serrated steel teeth.

The movie was exactly what Ian needed, an action-packed spy story that was far removed from reality and too ridiculous to ever come true. When it was over, his mind was clear and he drifted off into a peaceful sleep.

CHAPTER THIRTY-SEVEN

Eli Tanner's Ranch. Dunn, Texas. November 14. 2:22 a.m. Central Standard Time.

Beth Wheeler and Magar Orlov peeled out of the night unnoticed behind the four-man patrol that was searching for illegals. The militia men were expecting any threats to come from the Mexican border somewhere in front of them, not from the darkness of Texas behind their backs.

The two Russian spies were each armed with an AK-47 and a Glock equipped with a suppressor and were dressed entirely in black, from the balaclavas that covered their faces and the night-vision goggles over their eyes, to the Kevlar vests and utility belts that held their extra ammo, hand grenades, and knives, down to their boots.

Beth shot two of the men in the back with her Glock, and Magar shot the two others. They were virtually silent kills. The spies wordlessly climbed into the patrol's Jeep and Beth drove them toward Tanner's compound, which was comprised of the ranch house, stables, barns, water tank, equipment shed, bunkhouse, and other structures.

When they were about a hundred yards away from the compound, another militia Jeep came bouncing across the desert toward them.

Magar took careful aim as they closed in on the oncoming vehicle and fired three shots at it in rapid succession with his silenced Glock. Two shots went into the other Jeep's windshield and the third blew out the front right tire.

The other Jeep spun, flipped over, and rolled into the desert brush, landing upside down. Beth slowed to a stop beside the smoking, crumpled vehicle and could hear moans of agony from inside.

Beth waited with the motor running while Magar got out to finish off the survivors. She heard three muffled pops from his Glock and then he got back into the Jeep.

She pulled away, her headlight beams sweeping the desert and briefly illuminating a man on the ground, trying to get to his feet. He'd obviously been thrown from the Jeep when it flipped.

Beth floored the gas pedal and hit him, the Jeep rocking as it rolled over his body. It sounded like she'd driven over a pile of melons and dry branches, which was nearly the equivalent of what the man's life meant to her.

Jim-Bob Sanderson felt that he'd been treated very unfairly. Because he'd killed a drug mule who'd pulled a gun on him, Eli Tanner had benched him from the militia, taken away all his cool weapons and battle tech, and sent him back to the barns to shovel horse shit.

That was plain wrong. Wasn't stopping drug dealers, rapists, and murderers from sneaking into the United States what Jim-Bob was supposed to do? Shouldn't he be put back on the front lines of the fight for border security and American virtue as an example of how to do the job right?

Tanner assured him that the benching was only temporary, until the cops officially cleared him, but Jim-Bob knew in his flabby gut that he'd never get back on the line, protecting America from the invasion.

On the plus side, the shooting got him on the Edney show and his picture in the newspapers, which impressed his mom, but that fifteen minutes of fame didn't mean much once he was up to his ankles in steaming piles of fresh crap and horse-piss-soaked sawdust. The horses weren't wowed and, so far, neither were any of the local women.

So while all the other able-bodied men in town were out patrolling the border, getting to wear camo, carry guns, and talk on the radio about bogeys, Jim-Bob was back at the bunkhouse with a dozen old farmhands who'd been around cattle so long they smelled like them and chewed tobacco like it was cud.

Jim-Bob drowned his disappointment in six-packs of cheap beer, which kept him up at night pissing, which he was doing right now, watering a cactus out in the desert, twenty yards from the bunkhouse, where nobody could see him in the darkness. He much preferred doing his business outdoors rather than in the stinking, cramped, fly-infested outhouse. Pissing on a bush or crapping in the dirt made him feel like a true cowboy and that he was one with nature, like Grizzly Adams or Jeremiah Johnson. Every man has peed outdoors, that was for sure, but he knew there were men who'd never taken a natural shit in the wild and he pitied them.

These were the issues that Jim-Bob was pondering, his pants open and his dick in his hand, when a Jeep charged up to the bunkhouse. The driver slowed down, the passenger tossed what looked like a rock through one of the bunkhouse windows, and the Jeep sped off again toward the main house.

What the hell? Were they drunk?

An instant later, the bunkhouse exploded, startling Jim-Bob so much that his pants fell to his ankles without him even noticing.

That wasn't a rock . . . *It was a fucking grenade!*

The blast brought Eli Tanner and his two eldest sons charging out of the big house with their guns, but before they even cleared their front door, the two figures in the Jeep mowed them down with their AK-47s, spraying the front porch with bullets. Then the two shooters lobbed a couple of grenades into the house. An instant later, the house blew up, fire and glass belching out the doors and windows.

Jim-Bob turned and ran, immediately tripped over the pants around his ankles, and fell into the cactus, arms outstretched, like he wanted to give it a hug. He screamed in blinding agony as the needles skewered his body, miraculously missing his eyes but piercing his nose, lips, nipples, hands, and dick.

He peeled himself off the cactus, screaming again as some of the needles came out of his flesh, and he hit the ground flat on his back, arms and legs extended, looking like an enormous porcupine wanting a tummy rub.

Jim-Bob was so overwhelmed with pain and humiliation that he wanted to die, and when he saw a dark figure looming over him, he feared that his wish was about to come true.

The figure was a man, dressed in black from head to toe. He aimed a gun with a silencer on it at Jim-Bob's head, but instead of pulling the trigger, he started laughing instead.

"You're pathetic. Letting you live is more brutal than killing you."

The man had a Mexican accent. He lowered his gun, lifted the balaclava from his face, and squatted down close to Jim-Bob. He had a black goatee and breath like a rotting corpse, but then Jim-Bob realized what he smelled was himself. His bowels had sung "Born Free" when he saw the gun aimed at him.

"Tell your friends that this is what happens when you oppose the Viboras." He smiled and Jim-Bob wanted to scream again but couldn't find his breath.

The man's teeth were capped with gold.

The horror stories Jim-Bob had heard some Mexicans tell their children was real.

This was the Golden Devil.

The man lowered the balaclava over his face, rose to his feet, and stepped back until he was enveloped in darkness.

Jim-Bob began to cry.

Beth drove the Jeep with the headlights off to the spot where they'd stashed her pickup truck. Along the way, Magar peeled off his goatee, removed the gold-colored caps that he'd placed over his front teeth, and tossed them all in the desert.

There was a plane waiting in Rio Grande City to take them to Los Angeles. They had two more people to kill.

CHAPTER THIRTY-EIGHT

Ian Ludlow's House. Malibu, California. November 14. 3:30 a.m. Pacific Standard Time.

Ian took an Uber home from LAX, undressed, and went straight to bed without bothering to shower. The house was dark and quiet, so he had no idea if Mei was there or not. But that question was answered some time later—Ian didn't know whether it was minutes or hours—when Mei awoke him. She slid naked and warm into his bed, pressed her body against his back, nuzzled his neck, and slipped her hand between his legs, quickly making him achingly hard. They made love without speaking, with desperate, sweaty urgency. He drifted back to sleep, still entwined with her.

CIA Headquarters. Langley, Virginia. November 14. 9:18 a.m. Eastern Standard Time.

The president called Healy from Air Force One. "Are you up to speed on what happened last night in Texas?"

"The attorney general called and briefed me," Healy said, though it made him very uncomfortable to be participating in a domestic law-enforcement issue that was clearly outside of the CIA's mandate. It could be very damaging, for him personally and for the Agency, if word ever leaked out about the assistance he was providing to the Justice Department at the president's urging.

"I'm on my way now to Shithole, Texas, to be consoler-in-chief to the widows of those damn fools who were playing army on the border," the president said. "Did you find out where Arturo Giron is hiding?"

"Yes, we have and I gave the location to the AG."

"Good. This bastard needs to be put down fast."

Healy could, and probably should, have ended the call at this point, for political as well as legal reasons. But he didn't, partly out of his devotion to his country and to the office of the president, and mostly because he couldn't keep his mouth shut if something felt wrong to him. Not morally, ethically, or politically, he was quite capable of living with those wrongs. It was preventable, operational mistakes that bothered him.

"Nothing about this attack in Texas makes sense," Healy said. "The AG told us in the Oval Office that the smuggling operation was too amateurish, and the product that was being carried was too low grade, for the Viboras."

"Clearly Ritchy was wrong," the president said.

"But the DEA and US Customs have confiscated tens of millions of dollars' worth of high-grade cocaine that Giron has tried to smuggle into the United States before and he didn't retaliate. So why kill dozens of people in Texas for stopping a small shipment of low-grade, penny-ante garbage?"

"Perhaps because this time it was civilians who screwed up his operation, and not a government agency, so it was possible to make them pay for what they did to him. Who knows?" the president said. "The *whys* and *what-fors* don't matter. We can't let some lunatic drug lords send death squads into Texas like we're just another part of Mexico."

The president might as well have been quoting one of Dwight Edney's rants and that concerned Healy. The CIA chief made his decisions based on solid facts, not emotion or politics. The intel on this just didn't support the conclusions that were being made.

"I'm not arguing that Giron shouldn't be apprehended. He obviously should be. But I do question the basis for the urgency for you to act. We don't know that he's responsible for the smuggling or the killings."

"Yes, we do. His top killer, the Golden Goose or something like that, led the death squad," the president said. "We have a witness who positively identified him."

That bothered Healy, too. "Why did the killer let himself be seen?"

"A guy doesn't cap his teeth with gold if he wants to be discreet. He wanted the world to know he did this."

"So why did the killers cover their faces at all if they didn't care about being identified?"

"I don't know and I don't care," the president said, irritated. "Arturo Giron and his cartel have killed hundreds of people, *thousands* if you count the people who've died using his dope. And what has the Mexican government done about it? Not one thing. All the Mexican politicians and cops are in his pocket. That leaves the responsibility to us. We need to take action. Nobody is going to complain if we take this drug lord off the field, regardless of whether or not he was guilty of the killings in Texas. Hell, when we do it, there will probably be celebrations on both sides of the border. Afterward I could run for reelection here, and for the presidency of Mexico, and win both seats by a landslide."

In other words, Healy thought, the president couldn't see any possible negative political blowback from going after Giron, so why not do it? The only risk for the president was if something went wrong—if any DEA or FBI agents, women, children, or puppies were killed in the operation. Even so, Healy couldn't shake the feeling that they were being played somehow.

The president added: "I hope you will continue to provide Ritchy and his people with any operational assistance they might need to bring this asshole down."

"Of course," Healy said, though it went against his better judgment.

The president let him go and a moment later Healy got a call from Norman Kelton, the CIA veteran who ran the operations desk. Kelton asked if he could see him and Healy told him to come right up.

Kelton hated leaving the operations room, where they tracked all the active field operations worldwide, for anything. He only left to go to the toilet, and even then, he'd often stay in constant communication by cell phone, which led to some embarrassing and uncomfortable moments for everybody except Kelton. That meant this had to be important news for Kelton to leave his seat.

A few minutes later, Kelton came into Healy's office, his ever-present pipe in his mouth and clutching a folder in his hand.

"What's up, Norm?" Healy asked.

"Your apprentice may have stumbled into something big." Kelton was one of the few people in the Agency who knew about Margo French's activities, though even he had no idea that Ian Ludlow was a spy, too. As far as Kelton knew, working as Ian's research assistant was simply Margo's cover. "Was it her idea or yours to investigate the deaths of those two Americans in Porto?"

"Neither one of us," Healy said, not seeing any reason to lie. "It was Ludlow's."

"He's got great instincts. You should recruit him next," Kelton said, and for an instant Healy wondered if the old pro suspected that Ian was already in the fold. "Before the American couple died taking a selfie, they were being followed by this man."

Kelton pulled a photo out of the folder and handed it to Healy.

"Where did she get this?" Healy asked.

"Margo asked us to pull the sightseeing photos taken by people who were at the same spots at the same time as the couple who were killed. She picked his face out of the crowd in every location."

"Clever idea," Healy said.

"It paid off. We've ID'd him. His name is Magar Orlov. He's a GRU hatchet man."

Healy looked up at Kelton. "The American tourists were killed by a Russian assassin?"

"It gets better. Margo found a selfie one of the two Americans took in San Diego the same day they left for Porto. These two men were in the background." He handed Healy another photograph. It was a blowup of Orlov in the driver's seat of a black Escalade and leaning out the window to talk to someone. "That's Orlov talking to Gustavo Reynoso, an illegal immigrant and convicted rapist from Mexico. Thirty minutes after this photo was shot, the police rolled up behind that Escalade outside of a condo complex. Reynoso was in it alone with two dead women and a gun from the Guns & Roses sting. If you've been watching the news lately, you know what happened next."

He did and he found it especially troubling given recent events and the conversation he'd just had with the president about the Vibora cartel. "Have you shared this information with Margo?"

"I thought you'd want to hear it first, considering that your apprentice has discovered that there's a Russian spy running around killing American civilians."

"Did she ask you for anything else?"

"Detailed background information on the two women that Reynoso supposedly kidnapped and killed with that ATF gun," Kelton said, shaking his head. "I don't blame the attorney general for wanting to prosecute the idiots who came up with that sting. How many different ways can that monumental fuckup come back to screw us?"

"Apparently more than we can imagine." But not, he hoped, for Ian Ludlow. Healy passed the photos back to Kelton. "Give Margo what you've found right away. But otherwise, let's keep this between us for the time being."

"That's why I'm here and not calling you from my desk."

"Thanks, Norm."

Kelton nodded and walked out, but the old pro was no fool. He knew there was probably a lot more that his boss wasn't telling him. But, Healy thought, it wasn't as much as Kelton might think.

Healy knew that the killings of Americans in San Diego, Texas, and Porto were all connected somehow with illegal immigration, the Viboras, an ATF gun sting gone wrong, and a Russian assassin. But he didn't see how it all fit together.

All Healy knew for sure was that the president of the United States was on Air Force One right now, flying straight into the center of whatever the hell it was.

CHAPTER THIRTY-NINE

Margo French's apartment. West Los Angeles, California. November 14. 5:08 a.m. Pacific Standard Time.

Margo was jet lagged and couldn't sleep, but since she didn't have a nine-to-five job or any place she had to be, she didn't worry about it. She'd sleep when she felt like sleeping. So she got out of bed, put on her sweats, and made herself a cup of instant coffee and a scrambled egg in a cast-iron pan while she waited for dawn to break.

She stood and ate at the counter of her galley kitchen, which was directly across from the front door and looked out over her tiny living room, which was furnished with a futon and a flat-screen TV. It was fine for her needs, which was just a place to sleep, eat, and bring home an occasional lover.

Margo waited until she saw a hint of sunlight seeping through the slats of the blinds. She left the pan on the stove, and her dirty dishes on the counter, and grabbed her phone, earbuds, and house keys, stuffed them into her waist pack, and headed out for an easygoing jog around the neighborhood. She wanted to get her blood pumping, and loosen up her muscles, after her long journey home from Portugal.

There was a chill in the air when she stepped outside onto her "Welcome" mat and locked up her second-floor apartment at 6:15 a.m. The building was a 1960s-era square doughnut around a concrete courtyard with a couple of picnic tables and two sickly palm trees in the center that the tenants used as hitching posts to chain-lock their bikes and scooters. The tenants were primarily cash-strapped UCLA students, which was why she'd picked the building. She liked the vibe of university neighborhoods and she was still young enough that she could pass for a graduate student herself. Nobody paid any attention to her or her sometimes odd hours.

She put on her earbuds, cranked up Laura Nyro's 1967 album *More Than a New Discovery* on her phone, and dashed down the stairs and out the building. She took the cracked walkway to the street rather than cross the lawn, which every dog owner in the building, and many on the block, used as their pet toilet.

Margo jogged around the corner, oblivious to the white Camry parked up the street and the man inside who was watching her building.

Magar Orlov watched Margo jog away and smiled to himself. It was a perfect setup for her "accidental" death. Nobody would question how a woman exhausted after a twenty-four-hour flight, a sleepless night, and a run around the neighborhood at the crack of dawn managed to slip in the shower and break her neck. Who wouldn't be dazed, and clumsy, after all of that?

It was also considerate of her, he thought, to go out for her jog before anybody was awake in the building, so the chances of anybody noticing him coming or going were slim.

Maybe he'd thank her by sending a wreath to her funeral.

He got out of the car and crossed the lawn to the front door of her apartment building, the Tropic Palms, though there was nothing remotely tropical about the concrete box she lived in. He'd only walked a few steps across the grass when he stepped in a mushy pile of dog shit.

It figured, he thought. God was reminding him what a stinking mess this business with Gustavo Reynoso had been from the start. At least the work in Texas had gone smoothly and had been some fun, too.

Magar stopped at the door, put a gloved hand on the wall to steady himself, and, raising one foot at a time, used the edge of the brick planter box full of fake flowers on either side of the entrance to scrape the shit off the bottom of his running shoes. He'd need a hose to get the stuff out of the treads.

Satisfied that at least most of it was off, he went inside, crossed the courtyard to the stairs, and quietly went up to Margo's apartment door. He looked around to make sure nobody was watching from their windows, removed a lock pick from his coat pocket, and opened her door in about two seconds. It wasn't exactly a high-security building. He took one more look around, wiped his feet on her welcome mat, and slipped inside her apartment, closed the door gently behind him, and locked the dead bolt.

Magar positioned himself beside the door so he could break Margo's neck as soon as she came in, drag her body into the bathroom, strip her naked, put her corpse in the bathtub, and start the shower.

The apartment smelled of fried eggs and coffee and it made his stomach growl. He decided he'd stop at the Bagel Nosh on Wilshire for breakfast after the killing. A jalapeño cheese bagel, a couple of eggs, and a hot cup of coffee would be a nice way to finish off the morning and his career as a field agent. He was heading straight back to Moscow today and, he was certain, to a desk job some place where a jalapeño cheese bagel would be impossible to find. He was going to savor every last bite.

CHAPTER FORTY

Ian Ludlow's House. Malibu, California. November 14. 6:30 a.m. Pacific Standard Time.

Ian slipped out of bed, careful not to wake up Mei, who lay naked on her back, snoring away. He put on his bathrobe and trudged to his office, nodded good morning to the skeleton in the corner, then sat down at his desk, powered up his computer, and checked out the news on CNN.

He learned that, during the night, Vibora cartel assassins crossed the border and attacked Eli Tanner's ranch, killing over two dozen members of his militia. Now the president of the United States, outraged by the attack, was on his way to Dunn, Texas, to meet with the grief-stricken families of the victims.

Ian switched to the Fox News site and pulled up a video clip of Dwight Edney, reporting from Los Angeles, with images of the coroner's wagons and sheriff's department vehicles at the Tanner ranch as his backdrop.

"Jim-Bob Sanderson was the only survivor of last night's massacre. He joins us now from his hospital bed in Houston to tell us about the horror he witnessed and the atrocities that he endured." Edney turned to face the big screen behind him, which showed a man bandaged like a mummy, with only his eyes and mouth visible. "How many assassins were there, Mr. Sanderson?"

"It was too dark for me to count," Jim-Bob said. "But if I had to guess, I'd say fifty or sixty. Some of them was naked, like Navajo Indians, covered in the blood of the men they'd already killed."

It was too dark for him to count the men, Ian thought, yet not too dark to see they were covered with blood. How did that work? It was a contradiction in his story that he knew Edney would let slide.

"Where were you when they attacked?"

"I was on foot patrol around the perimeter of the Tanner family home and the bunkhouse area," Jim-Bob said. "When the Jeeps sped in, I thought it was our guys, coming back in to change shifts, but it was the Viboras, using the vehicles they took from the men they'd killed out on the spread. The Viboras started lobbing grenades everywhere and shooting anybody that came out of the buildings."

"What did you do?"

"I started shooting at them, of course," Jim-Bob said. "I must've killed half a dozen of them before I ran out of ammo and they wrestled me down, still swinging, gouging, scratching, biting, and clawing. Whatever I could do."

"You weren't going down without a fight," Edney said.

"I've got rattlesnake blood in my veins."

Ian had no idea what that meant.

But Edney nodded, so apparently he understood. "Then what happened?"

"They stripped me stark naked and dragged me in front of their leader, the Golden Devil."

"You're referring to the Viboras' top assassin," Edney said, "a man with gold-capped teeth, each one symbolizing a family that he's slaughtered and a mother that he's raped."

The mention of a killer with gold teeth made Ian think of Jaws, the towering killer with metal teeth in *The Spy Who Loved Me*. Perhaps the movie was closer to reality than he'd ever imagined. The thought tickled something in the back of his mind.

"Yeah, it was him, covered in the blood," Jim-Bob said. "He told me he was letting me live to deliver a message."

"What was that message?"

"He said this is what will happen to anyone who stands in our way. Your border means nothing to us. We'll take Texas the same way we took Mexico."

"Chilling," Edney said. "What happened next?"

"He ordered his men to throw me on a cactus."

"They crucified you," Edney said. "On a natural cross."

That was a stretch even for Edney, Ian thought. But he had to admire the audacity of reaching for a Christ metaphor.

"That's right," Jim-Bob said. "Then they gathered up their dead and went back into Mexico, leaving me there to bleed."

Edney grimaced, feeling Jim-Bob's pain. "You, sir, are a hero and a patriot. On behalf of a grateful country, I thank you for your bravery and your sacrifice."

"Just doing my duty," Jim-Bob said and saluted, though Ian wasn't sure why. Perhaps he was saluting the American flag that was entwined graphically in the show's logo, which took Jim-Bob's place on-screen as the set's backdrop.

Edney turned to the camera. "This was an act of war, the massacre of innocent civilians on American soil by the armed soldiers from the drug cartel that controls Mexico, a terrorist state on our open southern border. How many more American men, women, and children have to be slaughtered before we retaliate? How long can the United States of America allow these craven assaults on its citizens, its sovereignty, and basic human decency?"

Ian clicked off the video. The attack on the Tanner ranch, and Edney's colorful rhetoric, didn't surprise him. They both felt like natural escalations in the story, raising the stakes, increasing the pressure, and advancing the plot.

But what was the plot?

He glanced at the James Bond movie posters on his wall as he often did while thinking about a story. One of the posters was for *You Only Live Twice* and depicted a tuxedo-clad Sean Connery in his stocking feet using only his big toes to clutch a rafter and dangle upside down above Blofeld's secret base in a volcano as it explodes. He felt that mental tickle again, as he had earlier when he'd thought about Jaws. What was his subconscious trying to tell him?

Before he could give the tickle, or the questions about the Vibora attack, any consideration, there were multiple electronic beeps and several windows opened up simultaneously on his computer screen, displaying the video feeds from his security cameras around the property.

A landscaping crew, wearing wide-brimmed hats and covering their faces with scarves to protect them from the dust, were clearing brush with Weedwackers on his neighbor's hillside behind his house and were working their way down toward his fence.

Ian thought it was odd. November wasn't usually the time of year for brush clearance and it was also very early in the morning to be starting such noisy work. On the other hand, this was basically the countryside, homes were far apart, and noise wasn't usually an issue.

His computer dinged again and several video windows opened up with live feeds from his front-yard security cameras. A landscaping truck with a tarp over its bed pulled up across the road from his house. A black-haired white woman and two men got out of the truck. This drew his attention simply because he couldn't remember ever seeing a woman on a brush clearance crew before. He used his mouse to zoom in on her as she and the two men walked back to the truck bed and pulled something out from under the tarp.

All three of them were holding AK-47s.

CHAPTER FORTY-ONE

Oh shit!

Ian quickly pulled back the zoom, as if that would put some actual distance between him and the shooters.

He grabbed for his desk phone, brought the receiver to his ear, and dialed 911.

And that was when the dial tone went silent and electrical power went out in his house.

His computer screen flickered for an instant before the backup batteries kicked in. He'd installed the batteries to give him an extra few minutes to save his work in case of a power outage.

On-screen, he could see that the landscapers on the hill behind his house had put down their Weedwackers and were now carrying drip torches, the kind firefighters used to create backfires.

His bladder suddenly felt like it was going to burst as he realized what was happening.

They're going to burn down my house.

With me in it.

His landline was dead so he grabbed his cell phone off the desk but there were no signal bars on the screen. Either the hit team outside had a signal scrambler or he was simply the unlucky victim of the lousy cell coverage in the Santa Monica Mountains. Either way, he was screwed.

He glanced at the feed from the cameras in front of his house. The woman aimed her AK-47 at his door while the two men with her took positions around the portions of the house that didn't back up to the flaming hillside.

And in that instant, he saw the newspaper story that would be written about what was unfolding:

Landscapers clearing brush with gasoline-powered Weedwackers accidentally sparked a raging wildfire that spread rapidly through the parched Santa Monica Mountains and took the home of Ian Ludlow, who perished in the blaze along with a houseguest, reportedly Wang Mei, the actress he helped flee from China.

These people were here to kill them . . . and he knew with absolute certainty that if he and Mei tried to leave the house to escape the flames, they would be gunned down.

He really, *really* wanted to pee.

But what he did instead was dash to the bedroom and yank Mei out of bed.

"Get up!" he yelled. "Hurry!"

Half-awake, naked, and irritated, she swore at him in Chinese.

He ignored her tirade, grabbed her bathrobe off the floor, wrapped it around her, and tightly clutching her arm, practically dragged her to the courtyard outside, which was hidden from view on the hill by the smoke and several large oak trees that had survived the explosion that had burned down his house before.

Fucking assassins, Ian thought. Why do they all hate my house?

"I'm freezing. What's wrong?" she said. "Why are we outside?"

"There's an armed hit team surrounding the house and they are setting it on fire," he said. "They will shoot us if we try to leave."

He felt silly actually saying "hit team" in conversation, but that was what it was, and they didn't have much time. They were minutes away from being burned alive and he urgently had to piss. They had to get moving.

"They've come for me," she said, wide awake and frightened now. "I knew they would. How are we going to escape?"

"We aren't," he said.

Ian led her to a large boulder in the center of a flower bed and, to Mei's astonishment, lifted it up with one hand. The boulder was fake, an elaborate hatch on hydraulic hinges, and as she stepped closer, she saw that opening it had activated lights that illuminated a metal staircase that led twenty feet underground.

"What is this?" Mei asked.

"A survival bunker," Ian said. "Ronnie Mancuso has one just like it at his 'end of days' property in the Nevada desert and another at his home in Tarzana. That's how I got the idea to get one of my own."

It wasn't on any blueprints or construction permits for his house. He'd had an out-of-state crew of professional survivalists, recommended by Ronnie, build it for him and he'd kept its existence a secret.

"Will we be safe from the fire?" Mei asked, glancing at the embers that were now showering the back of the house.

"The bunker is made of high-gauge steel and is encased in concrete. It's built to withstand explosives, nuclear winter, chemical attack, and biological warfare. A wildfire is nothing."

At least he hoped so. He'd never had an opportunity to put the claims to the test. But she took him at his word and hurried down the stairs, not that she had much of a choice.

He followed after her, closing and securing the boulder hatch behind them, and then met her at the blast door, which resembled a bank vault and had a large wheel in the center.

Ian typed his code into the keypad on the wall. "This is an airtight, military-grade blast door."

The bolt retracted inside the door with a loud clank. Ian turned the wheel, pulled the heavy door open, and reached inside to flick on the lights. He waved her inside.

"Make yourself at home," he said.

CHAPTER FORTY-TWO

Wang Mei stepped past Ian into the survival shelter. The interior was tube shaped, like the inside of a submarine, but furnished like a suite at the Four Seasons. The living room had travertine floors, Persian rugs, and overstuffed leather-upholstered furniture that faced a flat-screen television mounted on the corrugated metal wall. The open-concept kitchen had oak cabinets, high-end appliances, and quartzite countertops.

"You are full of surprises," Mei said.

Ian pulled the blast door shut, locked it, and then gestured with a nod to the far end of the kitchen, where another airtight door with a hatch wheel was standing open. "Back there are two bedrooms, a full bath, a library of books and DVDs, and a storage room with enough food, water, and other supplies to last us a decade."

The mention of the bathroom, and the water, reminded him how badly he had to piss. He hurried past her to the bathroom, closing the door behind him. For a moment, as he emptied his bladder into the porcelain dry-flush toilet, he felt both relief and peace, but the experience was short-lived.

Mei let out a short, startled scream and he knew why. He cinched his bathrobe and went to the master bedroom, where he found her standing at the foot of the queen-size bed, looking at a woman in lingerie who was sitting up against the headboard with a permanently coy smile on her silicone face and a naughty sparkle in her glass eyes.

"I'm sorry for screaming," Mei said and tentatively poked the woman's silicone leg. "She took me by surprise. Is she . . . a sex doll?"

Ian felt his face flush with embarrassment. "She was a bunker-warming gift from Ronnie."

She examined the doll's face. "She's so lifelike."

What Ian didn't tell her was that she was also an exact replica of actress Denise Richards, as she was in 1997, when she starred in *Wild Things* and was the object of all of Ian's teen masturbation fantasies, a fact he'd admitted to Ronnie years ago in a moment of drunken honesty. Even now in adulthood, with killers outside, a fire consuming his house, and his flesh-and-blood lover standing beside him, looking at silicone Denise still gave Ian a twinge of desire.

"Do you think I'm a pervert?" Ian said.

Mei shrugged. "Have you tried her?"

"Of course not," Ian said. "She's a last resort, in case I'm stuck down here alone for months or years."

"Is there a doll here for me?"

"What for?" Ian said. "I'm here for you."

"I was just teasing." Mei smiled and hugged him. "Thank you for saving my life again. I'm sorry I keep putting you in danger."

He stroked her hair and thought about what Ronnie had told him about Mei being watched, and about the assassination he'd discovered yesterday in Porto.

"I owe you the apology this time," Ian said.

"Why?"

"I'm pretty sure that I'm the one they wanted to kill."

She stepped back and looked at him. "Don't be ridiculous. You're a novelist. Why would anybody want to kill you?"

"I read an article about an American couple who died taking a selfie in Portugal. I thought learning what happened to them could inspire a Straker story. That's why Margo and I went there. But we discovered the accident was actually a murder. I think the killers found out somehow that we stumbled on to them."

And then Ian had another thought that made him want to pee again, even though his bladder was empty.

Margo was a target, too. And he had no way to warn her.

CHAPTER FORTY-THREE

Margo felt nice and loose when she got back to her building after her run. She unzipped her waist pack to get out her house keys when she smelled shit. Had she stepped in something?

She lifted her right foot to examine her shoe for dog crap and saw nothing in her treads. But she saw bits of wet poop on her welcome mat.

The poop hadn't been there when she'd left her apartment. She looked back now and saw bits of crap leading from the staircase right to her door.

There was somebody in her apartment.

Was it a burglar? A rapist? A serial killer?

Whoever it was, he could be waiting by the door right now to attack her as she came in. The possibility didn't frighten her.

It excited her.

Margo knew the smart thing to do would be to just walk away, hide somewhere, and catch the assailant when he left the building.

But that was no fun.

She took out her keys, unlocked the door, and began to push it open. But before she opened it all the way, she intentionally dropped her keys, which made a loud clatter as they hit the ground.

"Shit," she muttered for the benefit of whoever was waiting inside.

She bent down, as if to pick up the keys, but instead slipped a tiny can of pepper spray from her waist pack into the palm of her hand.

Margo hit the door low and hard, crashing it open, and dove into the room, rolled across the room, and came up in a shooting position in the galley kitchen, facing the door, where a man stood, startled by her unexpected action.

He kicked the door shut and took a step toward her. She doused him in the face with the pepper spray, blinding him. He growled in rage and pain, whipped out a switchblade, and charged her.

That was when she realized she'd made a serious tactical error diving into the galley kitchen. He was temporarily blinded, but she was boxed in, with no room to maneuver. He didn't have to see her to stab her to death. All he had to do was corner her and keep plunging the knife into her. She'd be hacked to pieces.

Margo scrambled back, reaching out wildly for something, anything, to use as a weapon and, just as he was about to stab his blade into her chest, her hand closed on the iron handle of the frying pan.

She swung the pan, smacking his skull with a satisfying crack, at the same instant she felt the knife slide into her right breast like it was made of butter.

His head whipped sharply to one side, his face smacking hard into the edge of the counter as he fell. He hit the floor on his back, his wide, dead eyes staring up at her, the bloody knife still in his twitching hand.

And that was when she realized she knew the son of a bitch.

It was Waldo!

His face wasn't all that was familiar about him. He reminded her of the first person she ever saw die, an incident that also happened in a kitchen and also involved the defensive use of frying pans.

What were the odds of *that* ever happening twice to someone?

Her chest stung. She looked down at herself with a strange sense of detachment, as if her body wasn't her own, and saw blood seeping out of a jagged tear in her T-shirt.

Margo calmly set the pan back on the stove and then lifted up her shirt and her sports bra to examine her breast, wiping away the blood with a dishrag so she could get a good look at the wound.

Waldo had stabbed her above her right nipple. The cut wasn't deep, but it would probably leave a scar, especially since she'd have to stitch it up herself. Hospitals asked questions about stab wounds and reported suspicious injuries to law enforcement.

Somehow seeing her injury made it hurt a lot more. Maybe she shouldn't have looked. She pressed the dishrag against the wound to stop the bleeding and stared down at Waldo while she considered her situation.

How did he find out about her so fast?

Her cell phone rang. Only two people had the number. Ian and the Agency. She reached into her waist pack but took a moment to catch her breath, not wanting to alarm either possible caller, before answering the phone.

"Good morning," she said cheerfully.

"It's me." It was Kelton, her handler. "I hope I didn't wake you."

"No, sir." She'd never been more awake than she was at that moment.

"I've got the information that you asked for and we've identified the man in the photo you gave us. His name is Magar Orlov. He's a GRU hatchet man."

She looked down at the Russian spy. "He was."

"What do you mean?"

"He's dead on my kitchen floor."

"How did that happen?"

"He attacked me when I came into my apartment," Margo said.

Kelton sighed. She figured he was tired just thinking about the work he'd have to do to clean up after her. "Did you have to kill him?"

"I wasn't thinking about his survival at the time. I was thinking about mine."

"That was a mistake," Kelton said. "We can't interrogate a dead man."

She realized Kelton's sigh wasn't about the mess she'd made but disappointment that she'd killed their best lead to figure out why the Russians had murdered two women in San Diego and an American couple in Porto. Now she was disappointed in herself, too.

That was when she remembered that Orlov didn't always act alone. There was at least one person watching his back in San Diego . . . and whoever it was could be going after Ian right now.

"I'll call you back," she said and disconnected before Kelton could respond.

She called Ian's house. It rang a dozen times and nobody answered. She tried his cell phone. Again, no answer. She tried texting him. No response. She called back Kelton, who answered on the first ring.

"What's going on?" Kelton asked.

"That's what I need you to tell me," Margo said. "I'm worried about Ian. Can you get your eye in the sky over his house?"

"Hold on."

While Margo waited, she put her phone on speaker, crouched beside Orlov's body, and searched his pockets. All she came up with were the keys to a Toyota and a wallet containing two hundred dollars in twenties, a fake California driver's license, and credit cards under the name "Edward Aarons."

Kelton came back on the line. "I can't get a visual on his house."

"Why not?"

"Because of all the smoke," he said. "The hill is on fire."

It didn't take long for the plume of smoke to be spotted and reported to the authorities, but the remote location of Ian's home in the Santa Monica Mountains worked in Beth's favor. She and her men were able to stay on the scene until the house was fully engulfed in flame, ensuring Ludlow's demise, and fled only a few minutes before the arrival of the firefighters. Her crew left behind their leaking Weedwackers as evidence to help investigators determine the cause of the blaze, which had quickly spread to neighboring property thanks to the embers from Ian's house and winds.

She drove the stolen truck and the two gunmen down to a diner on the Pacific Coast Highway, where she had a motorcycle parked. Beth got out, gave the keys to one of the men so he could dispose of the truck, and she rode the motorcycle south along the coastline to Shutters, a beachfront hotel in Santa Monica, and reserved a suite for herself.

Killing was exhausting work and she deserved a little vacation. But first she had one errand left to do.

CHAPTER FORTY-FOUR

Dwight Edney was enjoying a big breakfast of steak, eggs, caviar, and Dom Pérignon in his suite at the landmark Beverly Hills Hotel, which for decades had been a glamorous watering hole for the Hollywood elite until it was bought by the sultan of Brunei. The kingdom's policy of stoning gays and adulterous women made many politically correct actors and talent agents uncomfortable power-lunching in the Polo Lounge or cheating on their spouses in the poolside cabanas because they might be singled out for social media shaming for being intolerant.

But Edney didn't feel any discomfort, at least not until his phone vibrated and he saw a text from his mother, summoning him to a meeting in Baldwin Hills in one hour. It was only eight miles south, a straight shot down La Cienega Boulevard, but in Los Angeles traffic he might just make it if he left right now.

He swore to himself and pushed his plate aside, swallowed his glass of champagne, and called the valet to bring his rented BMW to the front of the hotel.

Edney arrived ten minutes early. He parked his BMW beside one of the thousands of bobbing pump jacks that dotted the vast, parched oil field in Baldwin Hills. He wasn't expecting to meet his mother here. She'd simply made the arrangements as a go-between for his unidentified local handler. This would be their first meeting. Whoever it was had chosen a good spot. It was remote, despite being in the middle of Los Angeles.

Baldwin Hills was known as the "Black Beverly Hills," not for the black gold deep below Edney's feet, but because it was home to so many wealthy African Americans. He knew that Beverly Hills also sat on top of an active oil field, but that was a dirty little secret, the pumps hidden inside fake buildings throughout the city. Even what passed for the real world in Los Angeles was just another Hollywood set.

God, he hated it here.

Edney heard the motorcycle before he saw it and he tracked its progress toward him from the cloud of dust it kicked up over the low hills. He got out of his car and leaned against it.

The motorcycle roared up the dirt road and came to a stop beside him. The rider straddling the Harley-Davidson was a woman dressed in black, from her helmet down to her boots. She removed her helmet, revealing hair dyed as black as the leather. Whoever she was, she smelled of smoke, not from cigarettes but a campfire in the woods. It was an intriguing oddity.

"There are decades where nothing happens," Edney said.

"And there are weeks where decades happen," Beth said, completing the Lenin quote that was their coded introduction.

"Everybody knows who I am," Edney said. "Who are you?"

"My name isn't important." She got off the motorcycle. "Call me whatever you like."

He studied her for a moment. "Rachel Green."

"Are you a *Friends* fan or is this a test to see how American I am?"

"Both," he said, certain now that she was an American-born sleeper agent, just like him. "Why are we here?"

"The president of the United States is meeting privately today at a high school auditorium in Dunn, Texas, with the families of the militia men killed last night by the Viboras. No press are allowed inside." Beth reached into her pocket and handed him a thumb drive. "This is a partial recording of what he told one of those families."

He made a show of admiring the tiny device. "It's amazing you were able to get this recording, considering that he hasn't met with the families yet. He's still visiting the ranch and meeting with law-enforcement officials. I guess you haven't been keeping up with the news."

She gave him a cold look. "It's the president's voice. You can broadcast it with confidence, if that's what you're worried about."

Interesting choice of words, he thought. She said it was the president's *voice*, not that it was *the president*. "Have you heard it?"

"No, but I'm told what he says is incredibly newsworthy."

"I'm sure it is or the Kitchen wouldn't be telling me to broadcast it." Edney pocketed the drive.

"This scoop will make you a media sensation," she said.

"I already am," he said. "I've got the highest-rated show on the highest-rated news network. Perhaps you didn't notice."

Even as he said it, he realized he'd made a mistake. If you have to tell someone you're powerful and famous, then either you aren't or you're embarrassingly insecure. He'd given her the edge in their relationship and he'd never get it back. And he'd probably lost any shot he might have had to sleep with her. He saw her disappointment in him on her face.

"There will be a lot of pressure exerted on you by the White House, law enforcement, and the media to reveal your source for the recording," Beth said.

"I can take it," Edney said. "In fact, I welcome it. Their outrage will just keep me, my show, and the story in the spotlight for even longer."

"You should assume that after this tape airs, you will be under total surveillance at all times," she said. "You will need to take extreme precautions."

"I'll have my office and hotel room regularly swept for bugs," he said, "and I'll be sure not to buy any more crack from transvestite hookers on Hollywood Boulevard."

Beth ignored his joke, reached into another pocket, and handed him a burner phone. "If you need me, call or text the number programmed into this phone or use the dead drop in the park across from your hotel. The drop will be checked twice a day. I will be your contact for the remainder of your time on the West Coast."

"How long will that be?" he asked.

She shrugged. "We shall see."

"What is the outcome we are waiting for?"

"You'll know it when it happens," she said. "The whole world will."

"But you already do," he said. "It would help if I knew the big picture."

She climbed back onto her Harley. "How would it help?"

"The Kitchen would gain the benefit of my perspective and expertise," he said. "I could do a better job shaping the story to achieve the desired result."

"That's your mistake, Dwight. You think that your opinion, outside of what you are told to say on television, matters to anyone in Russia." She put on her helmet. "It doesn't. To the Kitchen, you are a delivery device, a talking head who can influence an easily manipulated percentage of the American TV audience into accepting what you tell them as fact. That's all Russia wants from you."

"And what about you?"

"I am also a delivery device." Beth started up her Harley and the engine answered with its trademark guttural roar, like a rudely awakened beast that was pissed off and ready to eat.

Edney raised his voice to be heard over the motor. "What do you deliver?"

"Death," she said and sped off.

CHAPTER FORTY-FIVE

The underground bunker's air vent, a radio antenna, and a camera were hidden in a fireproof imitation oak in a stand of trees on the hillside above Ian's house. The trees were barely scorched by the flames and the camera provided Ian and Mei with the perfect angle to watch the firefighters battle the fifty-acre blaze on the bunker's mounted flat screen.

Thanks to several surgically precise water drops from helicopters and hard work by scores of firefighters, the flames were quickly extinguished before they could become a raging firestorm or take any other homes. Even so, the battle made for some exciting television and play-by-play from KNX 1070 on the radio.

Ian and Mei sat on the couch, sharing a bowl of popcorn, while on TV a group of firefighters were using spades to put out hot spots on the charred hillsides and two coroners in white jumpsuits carried a body bag out from the smoking ashes of his home.

"Who died?" Mei asked.

"I did," Ian said.

"You're sitting right here," she said.

"You know that, and I know that, but maybe it's better if nobody else does for a while," Ian said. "Especially whoever wants me dead."

"That explains why we haven't left the bunker yet, but it doesn't answer my question. Who is in the body bag?"

"The skeleton in my office."

"Won't the medical examiner discover that it's not you?"

"Eventually," he said, "but it buys us some time."

"Time for what?"

"To figure out who killed the Americans in Porto and just tried to kill me," he said. "I was lucky they came for me here, where I had a place to hide, and that we had some warning."

She set the bowl of popcorn aside and snuggled closer to him.

Watching arson investigators and Los Angeles County sheriff's deputies poke around the ashes of Ian's home for clues soon became boring to watch for both of them. Ian turned off the radio and picked a James Bond movie from his end-of-the-world DVD collection to play until the firefighters and investigators were gone and it was safe to emerge from the bunker.

Ian and Mei watched *Tomorrow Never Dies*, which starred Pierce Brosnan as Bond and Michelle Yeoh as a Chinese spy. Together, the two secret agents foiled a plot by an insane global media magnate who sinks a British destroyer and shoots down a Chinese fighter jet to provoke a war that would somehow give him exclusive broadcasting rights to all of Asia. Ian didn't understand how that would work, or how anybody at the studio could think that "broadcasting rights" was exciting stakes for a spy thriller, but by the end of the movie, he'd figured out an entirely different plot, the one he'd nearly died for.

He knew the reason for the killings in San Diego, Porto, and Texas. And the irony was, he'd not only guessed what it was before he'd stepped on the plane to Portugal, but he'd seen at least three variations on the scheme a hundred times before.

The only thing he didn't know for sure was who was behind the plot. But he thought he might know someone who could tell him. The trick would be getting him to talk.

"I could play a part like that," Mei said, intruding on his thoughts.

"Like what?" He was bewildered, as if he'd just been awakened from a nap. But that wasn't unusual for him. Coming up with a story was often like being in a waking dream.

"Her." She pointed to Michelle Yeoh, who was kissing Pierce Brosnan on a piece of floating wreckage on the South China Sea. "A Chinese secret agent. You could write the script as a starring role for me."

"I'm having a hard time lately just writing my Straker novels."

"But this would be easy." She switched off the TV with the remote.

"Writing is never easy."

"All you'd have to do is take our true story and fictionalize it," she said, climbing onto his lap, straddling him. Out of habit, he looked over her shoulder to see if *Match Game* was on. "It could be about a Chinese spy who discovers that rogue elements in her government are plotting to assassinate the president of the United States. She has to stop it."

"That would make her a traitor," Ian said.

"That's what the bad guys want people to think." She put her hands on his shoulders and began to rub herself against his groin. "But the truth is, she's doing it to save her country from making a terrible mistake."

"You're saying that she's actually a patriot." He put his hands on her hips.

"Yes!" she exclaimed, but it sounded to him more like she was confirming her arousal as she moved against him rather than mutual, creative understanding. "She teams up with an idealistic, visiting American novelist to sneak out of China and foil the plot."

Her robe fell open, making him very aware of her nakedness and his erection intruding between them. He was hard, but yet strangely unexcited. Ian uncinched his robe. "Don't you think that's a little too close to the truth?"

"It's a way to use our real-life stories, and the publicity we've already gained, and turn them into assets." She mounted his hard-on, gasping as he entered her, yet he felt detached. "Don't you see the beauty of it? Not only would this be a terrific movie, it could change the narrative about me."

"What narrative?"

Mei moved faster now, speaking between her heavy breathing. "The story that . . . I'm a rich Chinese actress . . . who fled her country to avoid being jailed . . . like her parents . . . for financial crimes . . . A movie like this could . . . *could* . . . COULD make me a heroine in fiction and reality."

"Not that there's much difference anymore," Ian said.

But Mei didn't hear him. She was lost in her evolving story and her mounting excitement. She leaned forward and gave him a rough kiss, mashing her lips against his, and then leaned back again, moaning as she took him deep inside her. "This could be great for both of us."

"How is it great for me?" He reached up and squeezed her breasts, even as she exposed a different nakedness to him besides her body, one that wasn't as beautiful. She moaned and moved with more urgency against him.

"It's a way . . . to leverage your success . . . with the Straker books . . . and the national media exposure you got with me . . . into a new series character that's practically a presold commodity." She was racing feverishly toward the climax of her pitch. "You could write the script first . . . and then turn it into a book . . . we could release . . . oh God, yes . . . release the two versions simultaneously . . . *yes, yes, YES* . . . and launch a global, multimedia franchise!"

The words were barely out of her mouth before she was rocked by a sharp, intense orgasm that made her shriek and her entire body tremble.

It was the first time in their short relationship that she'd come during intercourse before him (and, if he was being honest with himself, that any woman had). Unlike Clint Straker, who could exert total control over his orgasms, Ian was usually too early or just in time. But today he was distracted by several realizations:

- The actress he was sleeping with was only using him for her own selfish reasons.
- Professional assassins were hunting him down.
- He'd uncovered a vast, deadly conspiracy that threatened the future of the United States.

Incredibly, this wasn't the first time he'd been in any of these situations. It was just the first time they'd happened all at once. It was very stressful.

On the other hand, it was also thrilling.

Somehow, he'd become a man who routinely evaded trained killers, saved America from certain doom, and bedded beautiful actresses without coming too soon.

Maybe he was an action hero after all.

Ian pulled Mei down to him, kissed her hungrily, and rolled her over without pulling out so that now he was on top of her. Still hard. *Straker* hard. She gasped and grabbed his ass.

"Enough foreplay," he said. "Let's get this party started."

CHAPTER FORTY-SIX

"Welcome to a special broadcast of *The Real Story*, live from Los Angeles," Dwight Edney said, tapping his Montblanc pen on the neat stack of papers on his desk as he stared into the camera. "This morning, the president of the United States visited Dunn, Texas, where dozens of innocent Americans protecting our border, our liberty, and the virtue of our women were massacred in cold blood by a Mexican death squad."

Video of the president walking somberly past the rows of body bags lined up in the makeshift morgue at Dunn High School played behind Edney as he spoke.

"After seeing the bodies of the fallen patriots, the president met privately with their families to express his condolences and the heartfelt sorrow of our nation. But that's not all that he said." Edney took a beat to let that sink in and to create some suspense. "We've exclusively obtained a secret recording of the president of the United States making an extraordinary vow to the weeping child of a dead patriot. Here it is, complete and unedited."

A picture of the president appeared behind Edney as the audio played, interrupted only by the occasional whimper and sniffling of a child.

"This is America. I promise you, sweetheart, that I won't let this atrocity stand. We know where this son of a bitch Giron is hiding. He thinks he's safe in Mexico, but he's not. We're going to bin Laden his ass. If Mexico has a problem with that, I'll make their pissant country our fifty-first state and name it after your daddy."

Edney nodded in agreement through the whole speech and, when it was over, hammered his fist on his desk. "God bless America!"

Top Chef Catering. Khimki, Moscow Oblast. November 15. 2:00 a.m. Moscow Standard Time.

The reaction, domestically and internationally, to the secret recording of the president of the United States was immediate, loud, and strong. Within minutes of Edney's broadcast, news anchors, political pundits, members of Congress, state governors, foreign leaders, big-name CEOs, terrorist groups, trade unions, and celebrities of all kinds (athletes, rappers, chefs, actors, house-flippers, Kardashians, comedians, super-models, and Real Housewives) passionately expressed their approval or outrage in tweets, press releases, and live television interviews.

On top of that, the Kitchen's hundreds of internet soldiers were working to amplify the president's recording, and the themes it conveyed, across every conceivable social media platform, large and small, in the United States. Seconds after Edney's broadcast, they began posting thousands of premanufactured tweets, infographics, and news stories that quoted fake statistics showing overwhelming, wide-spread, enthusiastic support for the president's remarks across every political, ethnic, religious, and racial spectrum. The stories also drew emotionally compelling parallels between Mexico's horrifying attack on Texas and—depending on the target audience—9/11, Pearl Harbor, the Holocaust, the Lockerbie bombing, Benghazi, the assassination of John F. Kennedy, the assassination of Martin Luther King, the Munich Olympics Massacre, the Charles Manson killings, the Iran hostage crisis, the crucifixion of Jesus, and the premature cancellation of the original *Star Trek*.

In his tenth-floor office, Morzeny opened a celebratory bottle of champagne and filled two crystal flutes for himself and Cannon. It had been a long but eventful day.

"Congratulations," Morzeny said, offering Cannon the glass of champagne. "The operation is a tremendous success. The fake recording was a brilliant idea and adding the sound of the weeping, heartbroken child was the masterstroke."

"Emotion is key to getting the audience invested in a scene," Cannon said.

"You're the greatest director who ever lived. You're directing history. It will only be a few days now before the invasions of Belarus and Georgia, the first big steps toward the glorious rebirth of the Soviet Union. There's already talk at the Kremlin about honoring us both with the Gold Star medal as Heroes of the Russian Federation."

It wasn't quite an Oscar, but Cannon would make do. Even so, he felt the celebration was a bit premature. The final act hadn't played out in America yet, though it was inevitable now, and there were still a few strands of the story that hadn't been tied up. He didn't like that. Ludlow and French were dead, which resolved one unexpected plot twist, but Magar Orlov had disappeared. That dangling subplot wasn't in his script.

"Any word from Orlov?" Cannon asked.

"None. He's undoubtedly gone rogue, not that I blame him," Morzeny said. "After his mistakes in Portugal, his career as a field agent is over and he knew it. The best he could have hoped for was a desk assignment and that was intolerable for him. A top field agent is like a shark. He has to keep moving or he dies."

"So now what happens?" Cannon finished his champagne. He didn't like it much. He preferred Scotch.

"We find him and kill him. He chose a better way to die. We should all be so lucky."

How typically Russian, Cannon thought. Tragic and morose at heart. But it was understandable. They lived in Russia. They didn't have much to be happy about. The sun didn't shine as bright here as it did everywhere else. Cannon could attest to that. It seemed that the Moscow skies had been cloudy and gray ever since he'd arrived.

But now, after getting his epic revenge on America, the sun would at least feel like it was shining brighter on him.

CHAPTER FORTY-SEVEN

"I didn't say it," the president said, pacing furiously in front of his desk. "Not one fucking word of it."

Healy looked around at the others sitting in the room—Chief of Staff Loretta Jones, Attorney General Ritchfield Douglas, and Secretary of State Ted Delsey—and they clearly didn't believe the president, either.

"With all due respect," Douglas said, "a preliminary audio analysis by the FBI's top forensic experts confirms it's your voice."

The president got in the attorney general's face. "Are you calling me a liar, right here, in the Oval Office?"

Douglas didn't flinch. Healy had to admire him for that.

"I'm just relaying the facts as we know them," Douglas said.

"The only fact is that the recording is a fake," the president said. "I don't know how they did it, but it's not me."

"Whether it's real or not—" Healy began.

"It's not real," the president interrupted. "How many fucking times do I have to tell you people?"

"—it's consistent with how you actually feel," Healy continued. "You already ordered the AG and me to find out where Giron was hiding so you could launch a strike."

"By law enforcement, not the military and with Mexico's cooperation," the president said.

Secretary of State Delsey spoke up. "The president of Mexico has already informed me, in very strong terms, that he would consider an air strike or a military incursion a violation of their sovereignty and an act of war."

The president laughed. "That's supposed to scare me? That limp dick can't even stand up to the cartels on his own soil. What chance would he have taking on the United States? Besides, our economy is the only thing that's keeping Mexico alive. If they can't fight us militarily, what else are they going to do? A trade embargo? Cut off their exports of heroin and crack? That'd be a win-win."

"That, sir, is exactly the attitude I'm talking about," Healy said. "The recording accurately reflects it."

"Which is why, if I *did* say what's on the fake recording, I would own it," the president said. "The fact that I'm not, and dragged you all in here for an emergency meeting, should tell you something."

It was a strong argument, Healy thought. But it could also mean that the president was simply embarrassed about being recorded saying something so politically raw and incendiary, even if it happened while he was justifiably emotional and trying to comfort a grief-stricken child.

"Why not own it anyway?" said Jones, the chief of staff. "Isn't dropping a bomb on Arturo Giron what you want to do?"

"What I want to do and what is legal, moral, and in the best interests of our country are two different things," the president said. "If I do this because some bastard put words in my mouth, then I am letting someone else use me to further their own agenda."

"But you want to do it anyway," she said. "So what difference does it make?"

"Because it undermines our foreign policy," Delsey said with authority, though his past experience in the field of international relations was limited to being CEO of the world's largest snack food company, selling cookies and potato chips to every country on earth. Healy didn't respect him, but he agreed with him.

"We can't let an unknown actor, perhaps a foreign adversary, use the president of the United States as their puppet," Healy said.

"But in this situation, he's not being used," Jones said. "He happens to agree with what he didn't say."

"Maybe that's intentional, making it easy for the president to go along with what they want this time," Healy said. "This is a test. If the president acts on the threat he didn't make, it will embolden whoever is responsible for this to do a recording next time that is more incendiary and counter to our domestic and foreign policy objectives."

The president nodded. "Who knows what words the bastards will put in my mouth. They could have me singing Pitbull's latest song."

"But the long-term negative consequences of calling the recording a fake could be far worse," Jones said. "It acknowledges that it's possible to perfectly replicate your voice. This revelation will sow doubt among the American people about the authenticity of anything they ever hear you say in the future."

"Nobody will ever trust what I'm saying again unless they actually see me saying it," the president said.

"Even video will be suspect," she said. "If your words can be faked, why not your image, too?"

"We know the world can accept a president who isn't factual or truthful but not one who isn't real." The president took a seat behind his desk and let the implications of his choices sink in. "That's dangerous territory."

Healy thought about all the possible ways he could use voice-imitation technology in covert ops. There was enormous potential for undermining foreign governments, disinformation campaigns, discrediting people, and simply destroying lives. It was a shame the technology had been used on them first. Which begged the question, who did it and why?

The president glanced at Jones. "What are you hearing on Capitol Hill?"

"Your bin Laden comparison was apt and powerful," she said. "I'd say you have bipartisan support for aggressive action, and those who won't back a military strike now will definitely line up behind you once the deed is done, assuming it's a success."

"I didn't make the bin Laden comparison because that wasn't me on the recording," the president said.

"Of course, sir," Jones said. "My mistake."

"But nobody got pissed at Obama when he sent the SEALs into Pakistan to blow bin Laden's head off," the president said.

"Pakistan was upset," Delsey said.

"They were harboring bin Laden, just like Mexico is making Giron warm and comfy," the president snapped at him. "In the end, bin Laden was dumped in the ocean, Pakistan did nothing, and the world learned that Lady Liberty will shove her torch of freedom up your ass if you fuck with us."

Now Healy wondered if the recording was a trial balloon launched by the chief of staff and if the president's claim now, made in the privacy and sanctity of the Oval Office, that it was a fake was merely political theater, a backup plan to protect himself if the public reaction to what he said was negative.

"You're still enjoying the patriotism bounce from the assassination attempt on you in Paris," Jones said. "Anyone in Congress opposing you risks coming across as anti-American. Also, while there may be some opposition, nobody wants to appear to support drug lords. It's hard to see how this could go wrong for you."

"We could take casualties, or civilians could get killed," Douglas said. "Or Giron, who reportedly has a new face, could slip away without being noticed or recognized and make a mockery of us."

"There's always risks," the president said to Douglas, then looked at Jones. "How long until you have poll numbers on public opinion?"

"End of the day tomorrow," she said.

"Make it noon," the president said, then looked at his CIA director and his attorney general. "I want to know how Edney got this recording or if he made the damn thing himself. Do it quietly for now."

"Why quietly?" Douglas said.

"Because whether I disavow the recording or not, we need to know who wants to turn me into their bitch." The president shifted his gaze back to Loretta. "Tell the Pentagon I want strike options on my desk by morning and each one ready for immediate deployment on my order."

"When will we know your decision?" Delsey asked.

"If you see missiles streaking over the Rio Grande at noon tomorrow," the president said.

CHAPTER FORTY-EIGHT

Somewhere in Nuevo León, Mexico. November 15. 6:30 p.m. Central Standard Time.

There were things Arturo Giron liked, and didn't like, about all the attention he was getting on the TV, which he'd been watching in bed almost nonstop for the last twenty-four hours.

He didn't like being framed for the massacre in Texas, or that it was supposedly retribution over an inept drug-smuggling operation that, even if it had succeeded, was an insult to the Vibora cartel. He didn't like being told that Mateo, the Golden Devil, hadn't been able to find the mysterious woman who'd created this farce. And he didn't like seeing a piece of American white trash claiming to have single-handedly gunned down a dozen of his men, even though the Viboras had nothing to do with the attack.

But he did like the terror that the massacre evoked, in Mexico and in the United States. It added to the Viboras' mythical stature, making them more respected and feared. Even the bit about his men being half-naked and drenched in blood burnished the Vibora legend. However, Arturo didn't like Mateo getting so much of the international spotlight. It might go to Mateo's head and embolden him to mount a coup while Arturo was physically weak and politically vulnerable, which was why Arturo always kept a loaded gun and a knife under his sheets at all times.

What Arturo really disliked was the possibility of the US military coming after him. That bin Laden stuff was some scary shit. The Americans went into Pakistan to shoot that camel-fucker. Compared to that, crossing the US-Mexico border to cap him would be as risky as the secretary of defense sending a secretary to Starbucks to get him a latte.

Arturo wasn't convinced that the Americans actually knew where he was, but if they did, running wasn't an option. It would put him out in the open and make him an easier target for his adversaries in Mexico. And he'd seen footage on TV of American drones killing terrorist leaders and bomb-makers driving in their cars. No, he'd stay right where he was.

"Mateo!" he yelled. "Get in here!"

The Golden Devil slipped into the room so quickly and quietly that Arturo wondered if he'd been in the room all along. "Yes?"

"Have you seen the news?"

"I caught a few minutes between murdering families and raping mothers," Mateo said.

He was joking, but Arturo knew he'd done his share of both. He just didn't memorialize the occasions with gold teeth. The killer didn't have enough teeth to make that practical.

"We need to prepare for an attack from the Americans," Arturo said.

"You want me to bring in more men and weapons to fortify the compound?"

"Absolutely not," Arturo said. "That will draw the attention of the Americans and tell them where we are, if they don't know already. Gather all the women, children, and old people from the village and bring them here. Tell them it's a feast, to thank them for welcoming us to the community, and that I won't take no for an answer."

"You're going to use them as human shields."

"Let's just say I like being around people," Arturo said, "and I'm feeling lonely up here."

Ian Ludlow's Bunker. Malibu, California. November 14. 4:47 p.m. Pacific Standard Time.

The smoke in the air combined with the fog rolling off Santa Monica Bay to block out most of the sun and make it prematurely dark outside. Ian and Mei tentatively emerged from the bunker wearing camouflage fatigues and hiking boots, their path through the blackened rubble illuminated by the headlight beams from a white Toyota Camry. Margo casually leaned against the car, watching the couple approach.

"What are you doing here?" Ian asked.

"I've been waiting two hours for you to come out," Margo said. "You really should put a doorbell or a brass knocker on that fake boulder."

"Wouldn't that defeat the purpose of hiding the entrance to my secret bunker?" Ian said, watching his step as he worked his way to her, Mei following a few feet behind him.

"It's hardly a secret," she said.

"Only to you," Ian said as he reached her, "and that's because you know Ronnie."

Margo pulled him into a hug, startling him. "I'm glad you're alive."

"I'm happy to see you, too."

She sniffed his neck and pushed him away, wrinkling her nose. "You reek of sex."

"It's my cologne. Old Spice. Very manly stuff."

"What I'm smelling isn't manly." She looked past him at Mei, who joined them. "Speak of the devil."

"How did you know we'd be here?" Mei asked.

"I knew how impressed Ian was with Ronnie's man cave," she said. "I figured he'd build one for himself as soon as he got a chance."

Ian gestured to the Toyota. "New ride?"

"It's a stolen car that was being used by Waldo, the Russian spy who tried to kill me in my apartment this morning," Margo said, clearly enjoying the shock on Ian's face. "I decided it would be best if they thought he'd succeeded."

They being the Russians.

It was the *aha* moment for Ian. He half expected to hear a dramatic music sting to underscore it. The whole bad-guy plot made sense to him now. He understood how the killings of the two women in San Diego, the murders of the American tourists in Porto, and the shootings in Dunn, Texas, fit together and what they were supposed to accomplish.

It was all part of an elaborate Russian plot.

The only piece that was missing for him was the final incident that would instigate Russia's bloody, geopolitical endgame. He hoped that was because it hadn't happened yet, which meant there might still be time to stop the United States from falling into the trap.

Margo continued with her story. "I took Waldo's car and left my Mini Cooper in its parking spot and the Agency will make sure that nobody knows, at least for a little while, that it was actually his corpse, not mine, that was carried out of the building in a body bag."

Mei looked at Margo as if seeing her for the first time.

"The Agency will have to do the same for me," Ian said. "The ME took away the skeleton in my office."

Margo studied him for a moment and broke into a big smile. "I have no clue what is going on but you've figured it all out. I can see it on your face."

"Yes, I have, at least for the most part, and it would make an incredible Straker novel," he said. "Maybe my best one yet."

She wagged a finger at him. "I told you this would happen."

"We need to go somewhere safe and contact Healy."

Mei took Ian's hand. "You can call him now and then we can all hide in the bunker until it's over, whatever it is."

"I'm not staying down there with you two," Margo said. "I'll be trapped while you fuck all day."

"You could join us," Mei said and gave Ian's hand a squeeze. "That way, we all get what we really want."

"You think I want you," Margo said.

"Desperately," Mei said, "and Ian wants you."

Ian and Margo both knew that last part was true.

"What do you want?" Margo asked Mei.

"Both of you wanting me."

"You're definitely an actress. All you care about is being the star," Margo said and looked at Ian, who was picturing all the possible couplings. She knew it and gave him a shove. "Get real. Do you have another idea where to go?"

"I do," Ian said. "But you're not going to like it."

"I love it already." Margo aimed her key fob at the car and the trunk popped open. "Anything is better than being buried alive in a three-way with you and Norma Desmond."

CHAPTER FORTY-NINE

Margo drove the Toyota, with Ian and Mei spooning in the trunk, to the gates of Ronnie Mancuso's house in a cul-de-sac in Tarzana, a San Fernando Valley neighborhood that was once part of author Edgar Rice Burroughs' estate.

Ian wasn't sure if it was really necessary that they hide in the trunk or if it was actually just Margo's way of getting back at Mei for her lurid suggestion. But he figured it was better to be safe than sorry, as his grandmother used to say.

"This is like that scene in *Out of Sight* with Jennifer Lopez and George Clooney," Mei said, pressed against Ian's back. "Except I'm a much better actress than her."

"And I'm better looking than George Clooney," Ian said.

She bit his earlobe and gave it a tug with her teeth. "Are you patronizing me?"

"Are you saying I'm no match for George?"

Ian obviously wasn't, unless Clooney had gained forty pounds, so Mei released his earlobe and wisely dropped the subject.

Margo rolled down her window, rang the buzzer, and gave the finger to Ronnie's wall-mounted security camera.

The wrought iron gates yawned open and she drove up the cob-blestone driveway that snaked up through the manicured garden to a Spanish Mediterranean mansion with a six-car garage. One of the garage doors was rolled up, revealing an empty space.

She parked the Toyota between a silver 1964 Aston Martin DB5 like James Bond's and KITT, the jet-black 1982 Pontiac Trans Am from *Knight Rider*. The other cars in the brightly lit, spotless showroom garage were a *Smokey and the Bandit* 1977 Trans Am, a *Starsky & Hutch* 1976 Ford Gran Torino, and one of the Batmobiles from the Batman movies. The once-empty space the Toyota occupied had belonged to the original *Hollywood & the Vine* bright-green 2011 Ford Crown Victoria, which was being used again on the rebooted series. The car had also helped save her and Ian's lives once, and played a very public role in exposing a dark conspiracy, which only added to the vehicle's notoriety.

Margo waited until the garage door closed to pop the trunk. Ronnie bounded into the garage wearing camouflage fatigues, combat boots, and a holstered Glock as Margo, Mei, and Ian got out of the car.

"Once more unto the breach, dear friends, once more," Ronnie declared and thrust his hand out to Margo for a shake. "Are you girded for battle?"

She stared at his hand. "Do you still masturbate three times a day?"

"That's like asking if I still breathe."

Margo ignored his hand and looked at Ian. "I thought you said he wasn't crazy anymore."

"He never was. It's the rest of us who are delusional," Ian said. "We blithely go through life pretending that we're anonymous, that nobody cares what we are doing, saying, reading, or thinking when we know that all the electronic devices we have are constantly spying on us but we tell ourselves they aren't."

Ronnie fist-bumped Ian. "Truth, brother."

"We're all living in China," Mei said, "but you American sheep just don't realize it yet."

Ronnie fist-bumped Mei. "Truth, sister."

"I hope insanity isn't contagious," Margo said, "or I'm doomed."

Ronnie turned to Ian. "I've had the news on all day. TMZ is reporting that you're dead. I was mourning you, man. But then I got Margo's call saying you're alive and on the run again. Not only am I relieved, I'm pumped. Who are we taking on this time?"

"Russian Intelligence," Ian said. "They've targeted us for death because I've stumbled into a massive covert op that could tip the balance of world power."

"You're the man." Ronnie clapped Ian on the back. "They don't know who they're dealing with."

"Did you notice that Ronnie immediately accepted your answer?" Margo said to Ian. "That's crazy. A rational person would be skeptical."

"Rationality and skepticism are about as useful as trying to suck on an alligator's tit," Ronnie said. "Nine times out of ten, it will get you killed. Besides, what he says is true, isn't it?"

"Yes," Margo said. "But you're missing the point."

"I'd say you are, honey," Ronnie said. "We're in a crisis situation. Stop trying to reconcile your attraction to me with your sapphic vows and man up for your country. Let's go inside."

Ronnie led them into the house. Ian and Margo lagged behind.

Margo whispered to Ian. "Is this the best idea you have?"

"It worked out for us before," Ian said. "By the way, do you have a copy of those sapphic vows? I'd love to read them."

"Let me remind you that I've got a license to kill and I'm not afraid to use it."

"When do I get one?"

"You aren't even ready for a learner's permit."

Ronnie took them down a short hallway to the main foyer, which was two stories high with a grand staircase in the center and a domed skylight. It was a bachelor pad with six bedrooms, six baths, two kitchens, a home theater, a wine cellar, and a bomb shelter.

"Pick any bedroom you want and help yourselves to anything in the kitchen, the bar, the wine cellar, or the gun vault," Ronnie said. *"Mi casa es su casa."*

Ian could hear the voice of the president of the United States coming from the home theater, which was right off the foyer.

"We know where this son of a bitch Giron is hiding. He thinks he's safe in Mexico, but he's not. We're going to bin Laden his ass. If Mexico has a problem with that, I'll make their pissant country our fifty-first state and name it after your daddy."

The words chilled Ian to the bone. *This* was the flame that would light the fuse on Russia's explosive global plot.

"No!" Ian dashed into the home theater, past the art deco ticket booth and the vintage popcorn machine, to the four-row auditorium, where CNN was playing on the big screen. Wolf Blitzer, Jake Tapper, and a panel of assorted reporters and pundits were sitting at a table, their backs to a window that overlooked the White House. Wolf faced the camera.

"Dwight Edney was the first to air the president's bombshell recording on his show this afternoon. Within minutes of the broadcast, the president of Mexico warned the United States that, and I quote, 'any military action against our country will be countered with appropriate force and will result in grave consequences.' Those are strong words. We will be looking at this crisis from all sides with our panel of experts. But first, let's tackle the big question." Blitzer turned to his panelists. "Are we on the brink of war with Mexico?"

"Yes, we are, and it's exactly what the Russians want," Ian shouted at the screen. "It's a James Bond movie, don't you see? It's *You Only Live Twice*, *The Spy Who Loved Me*, and *Tomorrow Never Dies* all over again."

"You know Wolf can't hear you, right?" Margo said, picking up a remote and muting CNN.

"Of course it was Edney who got the recording," Ian said. "The same way he got the scoop on Gustavo Reynoso before his corpse was even cold."

"Because he's a real journalist, a truth seeker," Ronnie said, "not a hand puppet for the New World Order like all of the other TV talking heads."

"Because he's a Russian spy," Ian said.

"No, no, not Dwight," Ronnie said, shaking his head. "I don't believe it."

Margo laughed. "Says the man who believes every crackpot idea he's ever heard."

"I believe it," Mei said.

"Only because you hate Edney for seeing right through you," Margo said. "He may be a Russian spy, but he's not stupid."

"Here's the *real story*, as Edney likes to say," Ian said. "The Russians set up the Gustavo Reynoso killings, the shootings of the drug mules, and the massacre at the Tanner ranch. Then they fed Edney all of the facts, the fake truth, that they created to support their story."

And that was exactly what it was—*a story*. Ian was sure of it. The character-based, narrative structure of the plot was rooted too much in the basics of storytelling for it to be anything else. Or for some bureaucrat to have cooked it up. This had to be the work of a writer.

Did Ian have an evil twin?

"Dwight might've been duped," Ronnie said. "But I can't believe he was actually in on it."

"Edney is the lynchpin of their plot, the hero of their story," Ian said. "They have to control him or the plot could collapse. It's his job to whip up public outrage and exert increasing political pressure on the president to attack Mexico."

"You guessed this a week ago and I blew you off," Margo said. "We could have been way ahead of this scheme if I'd listened."

"Don't blame yourself. I didn't take the idea seriously, either," Ian said. "I've got to learn to trust my creative instincts."

"So do I," Margo said.

"I don't understand," Mei said. "What does Russia get out of a war between America and Mexico?"

"Belarus and Georgia," Ian said. "It's no secret that right now the Russians are amassing troops and weapons along their borders for their annual military exercises. But the truth is they aren't games. It's real. They're just waiting for us to attack Mexico before they invade."

"Why wait?" Mei asked.

"So the Russians won't have to worry about any military, political, or economic blowback from the United States," Ian said. "How can we possibly criticize Russia for invading their neighbors when we've just bombed Mexico?"

"It's brilliant," Margo said. "Get the United States to start a war so they won't intrude in yours."

"It's certainly a better reason to provoke a war than trying to win broadcasting rights in China," Ian said, "or wiping out life on earth to create an undersea civilization."

"NATO won't stand for the Russian invasion," Ronnie said.

"They won't have a choice. NATO can't battle Russia without US support," Ian said. "Russia will take Belarus and Georgia . . . and Ukraine, too."

"If that happens, it's only the beginning," Ronnie said. "The commies won't stop until they've resurrected the Soviet Union from the dead, establishing a zombie superpower that feeds on brains."

"*That's* the Ronnie Mancuso I know," Margo said. "Batshit crazy. But I've got to ask, why are they going to eat brains?"

"It's a metaphor," Ronnie said. "It's the emergence of the New World Order. Freedom of thought will be eradicated. You'll think whatever they want you to think or, more likely, what they *program* you to think. They'll take our brains, get it? We can't let that happen."

"We?" Mei said. "You mean the four of us?"

"Hell yes," Ronnie said.

"Be reasonable, Ronnie," Mei said. "How can we possibly stop the United States from attacking Mexico and the Russians from invading three countries?"

Ronnie tipped his head at Ian. "Ask him."

Ian thought about it. There was only one way to stop the story from playing out the way it was written. He had to write a new script.

"The Russians wrote a James Bond movie," Ian said. "I'm going to write an episode of *Mission: Impossible.*"

CHAPTER FIFTY

The plot came to Ian right away because he'd seen it a couple hundred times before on *Mission: Impossible* and it always worked. It was field tested. Well, at least it was on television. Why couldn't it work in the real world, too?

"How far along is preproduction on my episode of *Hollywood & the Vine*?" Ian asked Ronnie.

"They've locked the exterior locations, reserved the Gulfstream set at Air Hollywood, and started casting the other parts."

"Perfect, give me your phone," Ian said. Ronnie handed him his iPhone and Ian began typing on it. "Here's a list of things I'm going to need you to get from the show's makeup and special effects departments. I also need you to buy six wireless webcams, four burner phones, four sets of Bluetooth earbuds, and four laptop computers, with cash. Try to avoid surveillance cameras."

"Who do you think you're talking to?" Ronnie said. "I always use cash and never go shopping without being in disguise."

"Because you're a celebrity and don't want to be recognized," Mei said.

"Because I want to be free," Ronnie said. "Nobody should use credit cards or expose their faces to any surveillance cameras unless you want the government and every corporation knowing about everything you're eating, drinking, wearing, watching, and using."

"I don't think the government cares what cookies I'm eating," Margo said, "or what brand of tampons I'm using."

"They certainly do," Mei said. "China has a database that tracks the fertility, health, employment, financial security, and marital status of every woman in the country from age fifteen on up and ranks them by their 'breed readiness.' Whether you're physically fit or menstruating is important data to them. So yes, they care about your cookies and tampons. I was one of the most breed-ready women in China, by the way."

"Of course you were," Margo said. "And proud of it."

"Here you go," Ian handed the phone back to Ronnie, who looked at the list and nodded in approval.

"This is going to be fun. Anything else you need?"

"Weapons," Ian said. "What have you got?"

"Anything you could possibly want," Ronnie said. "Except nukes."

Margo grinned. "Do you still have a rocket launcher?"

"After what we went through last time," Ronnie said, "I've got two."

"Last time?" Mei looked at Ronnie incredulously. "You've done this kind of thing before?"

"If you're asking if we've ever saved our country from going down in flames and stopped the New World Order from rising up from the ashes of liberty to stomp on our bones with their jackboots of tyranny," Ronnie said, "the answer is yes."

"Here's what I have in mind," Ian said, and quickly pitched his plot as if he were in a network meeting. It took only five minutes to lay it out. "Can you do it?"

"Putting on a show is what we do every day for a living," Ronnie said, gesturing to Ian and Mei, then looking at Margo. "But he's asking for a lot more out of you. Our lives will be in your hands. What we need is a stone-cold killer and what we're getting is a dog walker who sings in bars. Do you even know how to hold a rifle?"

"I've got hidden talents," Margo said.

"I can vouch for that," Mei said, catching both Ian and Margo by surprise. "She can kill and won't hesitate to do it."

Ronnie looked between the three of them and shook his head. "Hot damn. One of these days you're going to have to tell me what really happened in Hong Kong. But right now, the clock is ticking. Mei and I will be back in two hours with the party favors."

As soon as Ronnie and Mei were gone, Margo called Healy.

The director of the CIA listened to Ian lay out the Russian plot. Ian's conclusions seemed credible to Healy, especially given the president's claim that the recording on Edney's show was fake and his own doubts about the Viboras being part of the foiled drug-smuggling operation.

"You may be right, but it's not actionable," Healy said. "It's all conjecture."

"The dead Russian spy on my kitchen floor sure looked real to me," Margo said. "We can tie him directly to Gustavo Reynoso, the two murdered women in San Diego, and the dead American couple in Porto. They are all real, too."

Healy wasn't used to field agents arguing with him, but that was part of what made Margo special. She wasn't a typical agent and therefore achieved unique results.

"All that is true. However, there's no evidence that proves Edney is a spy or that any of what you've uncovered is tied to a Russian invasion of Belarus and Georgia," Healy said. "We'll investigate Edney and get more intelligence on Russia's military buildup. But what we have now is not enough to convince the president not to order an air strike or a ground assault on Mexican soil."

"When is the attack going to happen?" Ian asked.

The answer to that was a military secret, and sharing it with Ian Ludlow, a civilian, could qualify as an act of treason, but Healy felt it was worth the gamble.

"Noon tomorrow at the earliest," Healy said. "Can you get the evidence in time to prevent a war?"

"We're going to try," Ian said. "It's probably better if you don't know what we're doing. I'm not even sure that I do. I'm writing the script as I go along."

"That's the way it usually is in this business," Healy said. "Is there anything we can do to help?"

"I need a Russian translator who can be constantly available to us by phone between now and noon tomorrow," Ian said. "I also need all of Edney's contact numbers and a back door onto his network web page."

"No problem," Healy said. "Anything else?"

Margo spoke up. "I'd feel better if we had more firepower. Do you have a few field agents here you can spare to watch our backs?"

"Absolutely not," Healy said.

"We're trying to prevent two wars," Margo said.

"Now it's *two*?" Ian said. "I felt enough pressure when it was just one."

"I think an invasion counts as war," Margo said.

"I don't think so," Ian said.

"What would you call it then?" she said.

"An invasion," he said.

"Which is war," she said.

It was like listening to a bickering married couple, Healy thought, and about as productive.

"I can't send backup because you're off-the-books agents," Healy said before their argument could continue. "Officially, you don't exist. Besides, if whatever you're doing goes wrong, it could put the Agency in an untenable position, legally and politically. Now we have total deniability."

"If any of us get caught or killed," Ian said, "the secretary will disavow any knowledge of our actions."

"Who is the secretary?" Healy asked.

"I don't know," Ian said. "It's what the boss on the recording says to Peter Graves on every episode of *Mission: Impossible*, right before he wishes him luck and the tape explodes."

"This isn't a TV show," Healy said. "This is reality."

"You say that like there's still a difference."

Considering the situation, Ludlow was right. There was really only one thing Healy could say to that.

"Good luck," he said.

CHAPTER FIFTY-ONE

Fox Studios. West Los Angeles, California. November 14. 8:47 p.m. Pacific Standard Time.

It was easily the best day of Dwight Edney's life. He'd broken one of the biggest news stories of the century. He would be remembered as one of the greatest journalists in history because he'd broadcast the secret presidential recording that plunged America into a war with Mexico.

The war hadn't happened yet, but Edney realized that was the Kitchen's goal. It hit him while he was on camera, doing his fifteenth or sixteenth live interview with another network from his show's set. He'd remembered what Rachel had said to him in the oil field.

"You'll know it when it happens . . . The whole world will."

Edney fumbled whatever he was saying on camera, but he quickly caught himself and continued on autopilot, parroting back the same answers he gave the previous fourteen or fifteen times. But once the interview was over, he had to take a break to think things through.

Edney left the studio and went outside to get some air and to ask himself why Russia wanted America at war with Mexico.

And then he figured that out, too. He'd played a pivotal role—no, the *key* role—in Russia's first steps toward resurrecting the Soviet Union.

As a mindless puppet.

He'd had no idea what he was doing. He was essentially reading the lines he'd been given, an actor in someone else's drama who couldn't even be trusted with the full script.

And suddenly the greatest day of his life didn't feel so great anymore. He was a fraud, and so was the story that guaranteed his place in American and Russian history.

It made him sick.

That was when his cell phone rang. He answered it. "Edney."

"This is Ian Ludlow and I desperately need your help."

Edney recognized the voice, but it didn't make sense. One of his producers had told him Ian had died in a fire that morning. "I thought you were dead."

"I'm not, and as soon as the killers find out, they will hunt me down. At best, I only have a few hours to live," Ian said, his voice quivering with terror. "You're the only person who can save me."

"Why me? I humiliated you on my show."

"Because you were right. I was a fool thinking with his dick," Ian said. "Wang Mei used me. But it wasn't to escape jail in China for financial crimes or to become a star in America like you thought. All of that was a cover story so she could deliver sensitive intelligence to the CIA that her father stole from the highest levels of the Chinese government. You were duped, too. She used you, and your show, to help sell her story to the CIA."

Edney's heart raced, like someone had just jammed a syringe into his chest and given him a hot shot of adrenaline. "She *defected*?"

"That's what she wants the CIA to think," Ian said. "But it's a double cross. She's actually a Chinese spy on a secret mission and I can prove it. That's why they want me dead."

"Who?" Edney asked.

"Chinese intelligence," Ian said. "You're the only one who can help me."

Yes, he was. And it was incredible.

Five minutes ago, Edney had been a bitter fraud, a puppet who had no actual involvement in the history-making manufactured news story that he'd broken.

But now here was his chance to break another major story, one that was *true*, one in which *he* was the driving force, not an actor playing a part in the Kitchen's contrived script. And broadcasting the startling news only hours after his last blockbuster revelation would prove to America, to the Kitchen, and to himself that Dwight Edney actually was a groundbreaking journalist for the ages.

The call was a genuine Godsend.

"What's your evidence?" Edney said.

"The files that Mei had on the microSD card that was embedded in her thigh," Ian said. "I copied them all."

In her thigh?

This was great stuff.

"Come down to the studio and I'll put you on the air," Edney said. "We'll unpack this story together for the American people."

"No, no, no," Ian said. "I can't risk stepping out of hiding and anybody seeing my face. The Chinese have eyes and ears everywhere. They can take control of every security camera and cell phone in Los Angeles. You need to get me and take me somewhere safe."

"There's no place safer for you to be than in front of fifty million people," Edney said. "They wouldn't dare come for you on live television."

"Come alone," Ian said. "If you can get us back to the studio alive, I'll reveal everything."

"Where are you?"

"The Fashion Square Mall in Woodland Hills," Ian said. "It's abandoned."

"Of course it is," Edney said. "You're a writer. Don't you know that meeting in abandoned places is a cliché?"

"Because it works. It's a huge space with lots of places for me to hide and I'll be able to see you without you seeing me," Ian said. "The door to the old Barnes & Noble will be unlocked. Walk through the store into the center of the mall. I'll reveal myself when I'm satisfied it's safe. Be here in an hour or you'll never hear from me again."

Ludlow hung up. Edney went straight to his car, but a thought occurred to him as he got into the driver's seat. If Ludlow was right, and he was being pursued by Chinese assassins, then Edney was making himself a target, too.

I could get killed.

He didn't want that to happen. Fortunately, he'd recently met someone besides his mother who specialized in death.

Shutters on the Beach. Santa Monica, California. November 14. 9:27 p.m. Pacific Standard Time.

Beth Wheeler was relaxing on a chaise lounge on the deck of her ocean-front suite, watching the moonlit, crashing surf and nursing a glass of white wine, when one of her two burner phones vibrated on the table beside her. Dwight Edney was the only person who had the number of that phone. The other phone was for the Kitchen.

"Central Perk," she said.

"Very funny," Edney said. "I need your help."

Edney didn't sound scared to her. He sounded excited. That worried her. "What's going on?"

"Nothing to do with the war we just started," he said, a smug superiority creeping into his voice. "Something new has come up."

"I don't work for you, Dwight."

"Trust me, the Kitchen will be thrilled about this," he said. "I just got a call from Ian Ludlow, the novelist who helped the actress Wang

Mei get out of Hong Kong last summer. They were guests on my show. Someone tried to kill him this morning by setting his house on fire."

She sat up, alert. She had a dozen questions, starting with:

How did Ludlow survive?

Does Edney know I tried to kill Ludlow . . . and why?

Is Ludlow playing Edney?

Is Edney playing me?

But the question that she decided to ask was far less incendiary than those and was posed with weary disinterest.

"Why should I care?"

"Because Wang Mei is a Chinese double agent sent here to trick the CIA. Ludlow can prove it and that's why the Chinese want him dead," Edney said. "He's willing to tell all on my show. It will humiliate American intelligence and that's going to thrill the Kitchen."

That was encouraging news. It meant that Ludlow didn't know who actually tried to kill him or that he was handing himself over to the assassins he was running away from. It also meant that Edney was still clueless about Ludlow stumbling onto the Kitchen's operation and that she was involved in a bungled assassination attempt.

Those were very, very lucky breaks for her. And that made her very, very nervous. Luck wasn't something she believed in.

But she didn't have time to ponder her discomfort. She had to kill Ludlow right away and it would probably be impossible to make it look like an accident now. She also had to kill him before Edney could get him on television.

There was no way Edney would go along with that, at least not willingly. He was too self-centered to sacrifice a scoop that would make him even more famous for the good of their primary mission. She decided that the easiest thing to do would be to just put a bullet in Ludlow's head the moment she saw him and worry about Edney's reaction afterward.

"I still don't see what you need me for," she said.

"Ludlow is hiding because he's terrified that Chinese assassins are already hunting for him again. I'm on my way to get him at an abandoned mall in Woodland Hills. I have to show up alone or he's in the wind. I doubt the Chinese have any idea where he is, but if there are killers around, I need you to watch my back and make sure we get out alive."

"I'm not your bodyguard," she said.

"Maybe not, but I'm the Kitchen's biggest asset in this country. They need me now more than ever. If Ludlow and I get killed, how do you think they'll feel about that? Especially if it happens on your watch?" Edney said. "But if we pull this off, it's going to be a huge win for our side. And if I mention to our friends that I couldn't have done it without you, we'll *both* be heroes."

"We already are," she said.

"I'm doing this with or without you," Edney said. "Are you in or not?"

She sighed. "Where are you meeting him?"

"The Fashion Square Mall in Woodland Hills," he said.

He was already on his way and it would take her at least forty-five minutes to get there. The timing was lousy and she didn't like it.

"Don't go in until I text you that I've arrived," she said.

"I don't want to see you."

"You won't know I'm there," she said. "Unless there's some killing that needs doing."

CHAPTER FIFTY-TWO

The Fashion Square Mall. Woodland Hills, California.
November 14. 9:55 p.m. Pacific Standard Time.

Edney drove once around the mall and discovered that it wasn't entirely abandoned. The ground floor of a former department store was temporarily occupied by the local post office and an AMC movie theater was still in business on the opposite end of the mall. The rest of the mall between those two anchors was derelict and decaying.

The post office was closed, but the movie theater drew enough cars that Edney was confident that Ludlow wouldn't notice if Rachel showed up. Of course, that also meant that the Chinese hit squad could be around, too. Edney was glad he'd thought of calling Rachel to watch his back.

The Barnes & Noble was on the other side of the mall from the movie theater. He parked in front of the bookstore, its windows blackened and its sign long gone, leaving only the sun-scorched outline of the lettering on the filthy brick facade. A tattered banner advertising discounted Halloween costumes and decorations, a remnant from a pop-up store that had occupied the space for a few weeks, dangled above the doorway.

Edney checked his watch. It was 9:55 and still no text from Rachel. The minutes were ticking away. He'd lose Ian in five minutes if he waited for her and that was a risk he was unwilling to take.

He got out of his car, looked around the empty parking lot, and approached the front door of the store. The door opened with a rusty squeal and he stepped inside. The interior was lit by a few fluorescent ceiling lights that cast a piss-yellow glow over the black spray-painted partitions, scattered monster masks, plastic jack-o'-lantern pumpkins, and spilled candy corn left behind by the pop-up Halloween store.

Edney made his way through the store and out the back entrance to the center of the murky mall, sporadically lit by freestanding construction lamps set up in various spots throughout the vast space and powered by long lengths of extension cord.

There was something strangely postapocalyptic about walking through the abandoned mall, a place that had once been so full of people and commerce. Some of that energy lingered in the air like static electricity and he could still smell the grease that stuck to the walls from the deep-fried meals prepared in the food court.

Ludlow stepped out from underneath the escalator in front of Edney. The author was wearing soot-smeared camouflage army fatigues that did the opposite of what they were designed for—they made him stand out against the white walls around him.

"Are you sure you weren't followed?" Ian said.

"Relax," Edney said. "I couldn't have led them here. The Chinese have no reason to be watching me."

"You're wrong. I'm not the only one who knows that Mei didn't fool you," he said. "She knows it, too."

Edney hadn't thought of that. "She thinks you're dead and she isn't going to know you're not until she sees you on my show. Let's get out of here."

Edney and Ian started toward the Barnes & Noble when Wang Mei emerged from the darkness of a Restoration Hardware store in front of them. She was dressed in black and pointing a gun with a suppressor on it at them.

Edney let out an involuntary squeal of terror, which he knew wasn't very manly or brave, but he'd never been in a situation like this.

Mei laughed. "Oh, Dwight, I wish America could see you now, exposed as the quivering coward you truly are."

They were all out in the open, Edney thought, so why the fuck doesn't Rachel shoot this snotty bitch?

"I risked my career and my life to help you and it was all a lie," Ian said. "You were just using me to create your cover."

"Who do you think you're kidding? You only did it to sell books and get me into bed," she said. "We used each other. But at least you didn't have to fake your orgasms."

"I just had to choke back my laughter at your terrible performances. You looked like you were trying not to sneeze," Ian said. "I don't know what you're worse at, acting or spying."

She shot him four times.

Ludlow jittered backward, spurting blood from his chest, and crumpled to the floor.

Edney squealed again, shocked by the violence, and looked up from the writer's bleeding corpse into the black eye of Mei's gun.

Where the fuck is Rachel?

Obviously, she was a no-show. He'd have to talk his way out of a bullet.

You can do it!

"Listen to me, Mei. Your mission has failed. But it isn't too late to salvage something for yourself and your country out of this disaster."

"How do you figure that?" Mei asked. That was a good sign. She was listening, not shooting.

Be calm. Be confident. Don't squeal.

His phone vibrated in his pocket. It had to be the text. Rachel was here. All he had to do now was stall.

"Come on my show, reveal how you fooled the CIA and our government. It will humiliate America in the eyes of the world and erode the trust of foreign powers in our intelligence operations. You will have succeeded, at least in part, in your mission of undermining our country. But if you kill me, you will be wasting that golden opportunity for redemption."

"But it will make me feel a lot better." Mei aimed her gun at his head. "I want to see you die."

That was when she jerked twice, her eyes went wide, and her hand went limp. Mei dropped the gun and seemed to melt onto the ground like the Wicked Witch of the West doused with a bucket of water. She toppled forward and Edney saw blood oozing from two holes between her shoulder blades.

Mei had been shot.

Finally.

But he didn't want to be caught here with two dead bodies. He ran toward the Barnes & Noble, nearly colliding with Rachel as she emerged from the store wearing a dark hoodie.

She grabbed him by his lapels and slammed his back against a pillar. "You idiot. You should have waited for me to get here before you came inside. What the hell were you thinking?"

"The clock was ticking," he said. "I didn't want to lose Ludlow. But I lost him anyway, no thanks to you."

She seemed confused. "What do you mean? Where's Ludlow?"

This was why she was essentially a hired gun, Edney thought. She was too literal minded for any assignment more complex than delivering a package or shooting a target. Even the simplest form of abstract thinking was beyond her.

"I didn't mean it literally," he said. "I was talking about my news story. Ludlow is still on the floor where Mei shot him. You took your sweet time shooting her."

She pulled a gun from inside her jacket. "I didn't shoot anybody."

Every sphincter in his body closed so tight he was hermetically sealed.

If she *didn't shoot Mei, then who did?*

He pressed his back flat against the pillar and would have crawled inside of it if it was possible.

"Oh my God," Edney said. "Ludlow was right. I led the Chinese assassins here."

"Get out," she said, scanning the second floor for snipers. "I'll cover you."

Edney dashed into the Barnes & Noble and didn't look back.

He wasn't doing a very good job of looking ahead, either, because he didn't see the man in the *Scream* Halloween mask standing beside one of the black partitions.

But Edney definitely felt the blow to the back of his head and everything went dark. His last thought was:

So this is death.

CHAPTER FIFTY-THREE

Edney's story about the shooting didn't make any sense to Beth. If Wang Mei was killed by Chinese snipers, why didn't they shoot Edney and Beth, too? They were out in the open, easy targets.

It was that question, and the need to confirm for herself that Ludlow was dead, that made her go deeper into the mall and investigate. She tried to use pillars for cover as she made her way to the two bodies, but it was pointless. By nature, shopping malls were big, open spaces, even more so when they were abandoned, and Ludlow and Mei were out in the middle. There weren't many places for her to hide if she wanted to see the bodies and a sniper wanted to shoot her.

So why was she still alive?

Maybe they were already gone, Beth thought. Or maybe they'd spared Edney because they didn't care what he reported about what happened. They just couldn't let Ludlow or Mei talk.

She kept her eyes on the upper level, trying to guess where the sniper was perched based on where Mei's body fell. But the more she thought about it, the more convinced she became that she was alone with the two bodies.

Beth walked out into the open and approached Ludlow's body.

At first, everything had gone according to Ian's script. It was easier for Ian to act his part than he'd thought it would be, given that he wasn't an actor, and Mei gave a better performance than any part he'd ever seen her play before. Perhaps that was because there was more truth to the dialogue he wrote for their scene than he'd intended or realized.

Even the timing of the special effects had worked as planned. Margo had been watching them from a storefront on the second floor. When Mei fired the prop gun, Margo used a remote control to explode the packs of red-dyed corn syrup under his shirt to coincide with each shot. Margo also activated the blood packs under Mei's shirt, creating the illusion of Mei being shot with a silenced rifle.

Edney ran off and that was when Ian stole a peek and saw things had gone dangerously off script. The woman who'd tried to burn him alive had showed up. He'd thought her arrival was a possibility, of course, but now his eyes were squeezed tight again, and he was trying not to breathe, as she approached him with a loaded gun.

Ian could sense her getting closer. He could almost feel her body heat, but he knew it had to be his imagination.

If she thought he was dead, she would just walk away. But if she thought he was alive, he was a dead man.

Or she might shoot him in the head anyway just to be safe and he would die whether he took a breath or not.

No blanks and corn syrup this time.

His life was in Margo's hands.

As Beth got closer and saw all the blood, she figured that Ludlow had died from bleeding out, if nothing else. There was no reason to complicate the story that the two bodies would tell by finishing him off with a bullet from a third gun. And yet something didn't feel right about the tableau of death in front of her.

No, it wasn't a feeling. It was something more tangible than that.

It was the smell.

There were two fresh corpses in front of her but she didn't smell the copper scent of the blood, or the ammonia of urine or the sulfuric stench of shit from bladders and bowels expelling their loads in death.

It smelled like a candy store.

"Edney has no experience with killing, but I do." Beth raised her gun and pointed it at Ian's head. "Death doesn't smell sweet."

Margo pinned the crosshairs of her sniper's scope on the woman's head and was about to fire when she remembered Kelton's rebuke.

We can't interrogate a dead man.

Margo abruptly shifted the crosshairs to the woman's shoulder and squeezed the trigger.

The bullet's impact shattered the woman's shoulder, broke her hold on her gun, and knocked her to the floor.

Ian heard the woman's cry of pain, the heavy thud as she hit the ground, and the clatter of her gun skittering across the tile.

He opened his eyes and saw her facing him, her body curled on her left side, her right shoulder, chest, and arm covered with blood.

She was grimacing, not with pain but with murderous fury. Their eyes met, then her gaze shifted from Ian to the gun on the floor between them.

"Fuck you," she said and lunged for the gun.

At that same instant, Mei sat up, blocking Margo's view of the injured woman through the scope. Margo couldn't take a shot without killing Mei.

Ian went for the gun, too, getting hold of the grip with his syrup-covered hand just as the woman clutched the barrel. She tried to tug the gun away from him and he squeezed the trigger.

The bullet tore through her hand and blasted into her face, blowing off the back of her skull.

Ian screamed and scrambled away from the dead woman and Mei vomited, covering the dead woman with puke. He almost threw up, too, out of sympathetic reflex, but he managed to contain the impulse.

Instead, he averted his gaze and got to his feet, careful not to slip in the puddle of corn syrup he'd left behind.

Mei wiped her mouth with her shirtsleeve and got to her feet. "Who was she?"

The second female assassin I've killed, he thought. But he didn't say that.

"One of the killers who burned down my house."

Mei glanced at the corpse. "She was right about the smell."

And, he thought, she'd also given him a great title for his next Straker novel.

Death Isn't Sweet.

CHAPTER FIFTY-FOUR

It felt to Edney like his skull had been cleaved with an ax. Of course, if that were true, he wouldn't be alive to experience the pain, so he took it as a good sign. He wasn't dead.

But what had happened? Where was he?

He opened his eyes. At first everything was out of focus. He blinked hard, fine-tuning his world, and saw that he was sitting in a small, luxuriously appointed private jet. It was dark outside his window, water streaking across the glass, and he could hear the low rumble of the engines.

A man who looked vaguely familiar sat directly in front of him, sipping a cocktail. He had curly brown hair, a bulbous nose, and bushy eyebrows, and he wore a blue, half-zippered, pullover cable-knit sweater, a dress shirt with a button-down collar, and tan corduroy slacks. There were two white AirPods in his ears as if they were jewelry.

"*Teper' vy v bezopasnosti, tovarishch, i idete domoy,*" the man said with a friendly smile and the worst Russian accent Edney had ever heard. "*Khotite vypit?*"

"I don't speak Russian," Edney said, though if he did, his accent would probably be just as awful as this guy's.

"That's sad," the man said. "The CIA was there tonight. We had to get you out fast before you were exposed. Sorry it had to be this way. But you're safe now."

Now Edney knew who'd shot Mei. It had been the CIA.

But who was this guy? And why was he speaking Russian?

"Who are you and where are we going?"

"I am an American-born Russian spy, just like you, and we are finally going home." The man raised his glass to Edney and took a sip. *"Pozdravlyayu."*

Edney's vision had cleared but his mind was still fuzzy, clouded by pain and disorientation. The man wasn't making any sense.

"You're taking me back to New York?"

The man shook his head. "Tonight, the United States bombed the Vibora base in Mexico. War is imminent between the two countries and so is our invasion of Belarus and Georgia. Your fake news and my efforts on the ground in San Diego and Texas staging everything all paid off. Our work here is done. We're going to Moscow."

Moscow?

That single word cleared Edney's mind fast and the adrenaline spike of anger it provoked dulled much of his pain.

"I'm not going to Moscow," he said.

"You're already on the way."

"Turn the fucking plane around," Edney said. "I can't go there."

"After what happened tonight, our bosses believe the CIA will start digging and discover who you really are," he said. "So I was ordered to exfiltrate you, forcibly if necessary, before that could happen."

"The Kitchen is overreacting," Edney said. "There's no reason to believe my cover will be blown."

"You don't realize how lucky you are. You're returning to the home-land as a hero of the Russian Federation," the man said. "There's a Gold Star medal waiting for you. After your years of fighting the good fight, you've earned your freedom."

Freedom? In *Russia*? What the hell was this guy talking about?

"I'm a cable television superstar," Edney said. "I've got an apartment overlooking Central Park. I've got millions of dollars in the bank. I'm not leaving all of that behind."

"We're both free and alive. I'm going back to a one-bedroom apartment, a subsistence pension, and an arranged marriage. But you'll get a dacha on the Black Sea, a fortune in rubles, and your own show on Russia One if you want it. What do you have to whine about?"

Was he joking? What he was suggesting was outrageous. No, it was worse than that. It was unconscionable.

"I didn't claw my way to the top of American television and become stinking rich to throw it all away for obscurity, exile, and poverty. I'm at the height of my global power and influence. I'm Dwight fucking Edney!"

The man set his drink aside and leaned toward Edney. "I know who you are, but apparently you've forgotten. You're a servant of the Communist Party. You will do whatever they think is best for the cause, and if that means going home, that's what you will do."

"I belong in the United States," Edney said. "That is my home and that's where I can do the most good for Russia."

"It's not my decision. I'm just following orders. You can take it up with our bosses when we get home." The man stood up. "Make yourself a drink and relax. It's going to be a long flight."

The man walked past him to the back of the plane and went into the bathroom.

Edney couldn't believe what was happening. Going to Russia wasn't a reward for him. It was punishment.

What was he going to do there? What kind of life would he have? Pure shit, that was what.

He'd rather take his chances in America than flee to Moscow.

Besides, the Kitchen was wrong. They didn't understand how the media worked or what constituted truth in the United States. His cover wasn't blown. If anything, it was burnished. He was an intrepid journalist meeting with two sources, one of whom the CIA had murdered to keep her quiet. That was a great news story and it showcased him doing his job.

If the CIA accused him later of being a Russian spy, he could say it was fake news, laughably manufactured by a desperate intelligence agency to distract people from their assassination of a double agent who'd humiliated them. It was a story he was confident he could sell on camera and that his millions of viewers would believe.

And if he couldn't pull it off, so be it. He'd rather end up in federal prison than on Russian television.

Edney stood up, marched to the cockpit, and banged on the door. "This is Dwight Edney. You need to turn this plane around."

There was no answer. He yanked open the door.

The cockpit was empty.

Out the window, dead ahead, he could see a giant fan blowing against four sprinkler heads mounted on upright pipes. Behind the fan was something familiar to him that he saw every day, but seeing it now horrified him to the bone.

He saw the walls of a studio soundstage.

The fan shut off and so did the water. They weren't necessary anymore. The show was over.

He stepped out of the cockpit, his dizziness returning, but it wasn't from the blow to his head. It was from the blur of cascading realizations and what they meant.

Edney walked to the rear of the plane and opened the bathroom door. But there was no bathroom. He stepped out onto the soundstage.

He looked over his shoulder. The airplane fuselage was surrounded by a black backdrop that hung like a shower curtain from a track on the ceiling.

Ahead of him, he saw a director's chair and a table with four laptops open on top of it. He stepped up to the computers and looked at the screens.

They all showed angles on the now-empty interior of the plane and each computer was livestreaming its feed to a different site: YouTube, Facebook, Twitter, and his own page on the Fox site.

Just as the full impact of what that meant hit him, his phone vibrated in his pocket. He took out his phone and brought it to his ear. His hand was shaking.

"Now everyone has truly seen the *real story* with Dwight Edney," Ian Ludlow said.

Edney took a seat in the director's chair. "Where am I?"

"You're at Air Hollywood, a studio that specializes in airplane set interiors," Ian said. "It's three blocks from the Fashion Square Mall, in case you'd like to walk back to your car. Or you can just wait where you are for the FBI or your Russian comrades or CNN to show up. I'm sure someone is on the way. The feed isn't hard to track."

It didn't matter to Edney who showed up. He was finished regardless. His eyes teared up. "Why did you do this to me?"

"Because you were rude to us on your show."

"You're lying. There has to be more to it than that," Edney said. "Who are you working for?"

"I'm just a writer who likes to tell a good story," Ian said and ended the call.

CHAPTER FIFTY-FIVE

Warner Center Office Park. Woodland Hills, California.
November 14. 11:08 p.m. Pacific Standard Time.

Ian removed the SIM card from the burner phone, tossed the phone out the window of the Toyota, and turned to Margo, who was driving the four of them back to Ronnie's place.

"This is exactly how each episode of *Mission: Impossible* ended," Ian said. "All that's missing is the closing theme."

"You're obviously Jim Phelps, which makes me Rollin Hand, master of disguise," Ronnie said from the back seat, peeling off his fake nose and eyebrows. He turned to Mei, who sat beside him. "Which makes you Cinnamon Carter."

"I have no idea who she is," Mei said.

"Neither do I," Margo said to her. "But you were terrific. It was your best performance ever."

"Thank you," Mei said. "That means a lot coming from you."

Mainly because it was the first genuinely nice thing Margo had ever said to her.

Ronnie took off his curly-haired wig and tapped Margo on the shoulder. "You're Willy."

"Isn't that a man?" she said.

"He was the muscle and you're a really tough broad."

"Nobody says 'broad' anymore."

"Because it's been a long time since any woman deserved the compliment," Ronnie said. "You do."

"It's not a compliment," she said.

"I still can't believe Dwight was a traitor." Ronnie settled back into his seat and looked at Ian. "I was hoping right up until the end you were wrong about him. Is there nobody left we can trust?"

"Not on TV," Ian said, tossing the SIM card out the window. "The world has changed. Truth is fiction and fiction is fact."

"If you're right, then you're at the leading edge of our new reality," Ronnie said. "You've proven that you're a master at combining the two. That's a superpower, buddy. What are you going to do with it?"

"Write another Straker book," Ian said.

"That's a waste," Ronnie said.

"It's what I do," Ian said.

"It's what you *did*. You're Straker now," Ronnie said. "You're an actor who has become the part that he plays. Just like me."

Margo looked at Ronnie in the rearview mirror. "You're half-plant?"

"I attract bees and I weep uncontrollably whenever I see firewood," he said. "What does that tell you?"

"That you're off your meds," Margo said.

"What happens now?" Mei asked Ian.

"You go back home with Ronnie tonight and shoot your episode of *Hollywood & the Vine* next week," Ian said. "What you do after that is up to you. It's about time that you wrote your own story."

"What about us?" Margo asked him.

It was the question Ian expected Mei to ask, and he was relieved that she didn't because he didn't have an answer for her. But the question had an entirely different meaning coming from Margo and he knew exactly what to tell her.

"We're going to pretend that we've just returned to Los Angeles after being away for weeks on a research trip to Madagascar," Ian said, knowing that the CIA could easily, and quickly, create a data trail with airlines and hotels that would support his story and hold up to any scrutiny.

"Why are we doing that?" Margo asked.

Ian smiled. "So we can make the shocking discovery that we're dead."

Top Chef Catering. Khimki, Moscow Oblast. November 15. 9:05 a.m. Moscow Standard Time.

There was a long, crushing silence in the tenth-floor conference room after Kirk Cannon, Leonid Morzeny, and the six generals, all sitting around the table, watched Dwight Edney walk out of the airplane set and the livestream broadcast ended.

It felt to Cannon like they'd just watched an episode of *Mission: Impossible*. All that was missing was the shot of the IMF team driving away, leaving behind the African dictator they'd toppled, or the Eastern Bloc spy network they'd destroyed, or the Asian king they'd deposed with their clever con.

Which was why Cannon was certain a writer like him was behind the scheme. It *had* to be Ludlow, even though the author was dead. The novelist must have cooked up the plot before he was killed.

"I've never seen anything go viral so fast." Viktor scrolled through some numbers on his laptop screen. "The number of times the captured video is being reposted globally on social networks is increasing exponentially every sixty seconds. It's going to be the most-watched, most-shared video ever made."

"How did this go so wrong?" asked Evgeny, picking at the scabs on his chewed fingers.

Cannon turned to Morzeny. "Because you were right about Ian Ludlow. What we just saw was scripted. Ludlow must have been working with the CIA all along."

"That's ridiculous," Morzeny said. "What's more likely is that the CIA was already suspicious of Edney and, thanks to your damn script, we exposed him to the enemy. We gave him too many damaging scoops, and that intensified the CIA's scrutiny. But giving that fake recording of the president to Edney, rather than to an objective journalist we didn't control, was your big mistake. It confirmed their suspicions about Edney. They didn't have time to actually prove their case, so they mounted this con as a desperate, last resort to prevent the president from starting a war."

That made sense to Cannon, who believed they were both right, not that it made any difference at this point.

"What happens now?" asked Petrov, raising one of his gargantuan arms, as if he were waiting to be called on in class.

"A catastrophe for Russia," Cannon said. It was easy for him to see how the story would play out.

"The United States, the United Nations, and the entire international community will condemn us in the strongest possible terms. Russian diplomats and citizens will be expelled by the thousands from countries all over the globe," he continued. "NATO will immediately accept all the remaining former Russian republics into their alliance and vastly increase the number of missiles aimed at us. Russian assets in the West will be frozen or seized, brutal economic sanctions will be levied against us worldwide, and our economy will be crippled, creating poverty and social unrest throughout our society that could provoke another revolution."

"I think you're right." Morzeny sighed and stood up. "And all of it will be a result of our epic failure. How do we live with that?"

He looked at each man in the room, his sad gaze lingering on Cannon for a long moment, and then he walked out.

Viktor turned to his mentor and idol. "What do you think will happen to us?"

Cannon thought the answer was obvious. "We're done."

"Yes, but what does that actually mean?" Evgeny asked, taking a break from chewing off the tip of his left pinkie, drops of fresh blood on his chin. "Will we be fired? Exiled? Killed?"

Those were good questions.

Cannon looked out the window to ponder the answer and saw Leonid Morzeny's graceful swan dive off the roof, the laces of his untied Air Jordans fluttering like streamers in his wake.

POSTSCRIPT

In the days immediately following the livestreamed outing of Dwight Edney as a Russian spy, the following occurred:

Dwight Edney was arrested by the FBI and charged with treason. He agreed to cooperate with authorities to avoid a death sentence.

Cloris Edney was arrested while attempting to board a flight to Qatar, which has no extradition treaty with the United States. She refused to cooperate with authorities.

The president of the United States declared that the "secret recording" that Edney had aired was a fraud and that the deaths of two American tourists in Porto and the killings in San Diego and Dunn, Texas, were the work of Russian spies trying to provoke a war with Mexico. He congratulated the Justice Department's "innovative use of social media" to expose Edney's treason.

Top Chef Catering's covert activities came to an immediate end so they could focus their full attention on making cheap, inedible meals for Russian schoolchildren, hospital patients, and the military. Morzeny's former "generals" were retained as full-time dishwashers.

Kirk Cannon took a new position as creative director of the Chernobyl community theater.

The entirety of Dwight Edney's testimony was classified for national security, so nobody was aware that Ian Ludlow, Margo French, and Wang Mei were involved in his downfall. The secrecy also allowed CIA director Healy to give Vice President Penny fake intel to feed to his Chinese masters that falsely exposed several hard-line party members as Russian spies, leading to their summary executions.

Vibora leader Arturo Giron and Mateo, the Golden Devil, were murdered by the villagers they'd brought into their compound as human shields against a US attack that never came. The villagers pillaged the house and pulled out Mateo's teeth for the gold caps.

Jim-Bob Sanderson got his own nightly talk show on Fox in the time slot formerly occupied by *The Real Story*.

"The Bad Seed" aired and became the highest-rated episode in the history of *Hollywood & the Vine*. Wang Mei was promptly signed as a recurring character and began a torrid affair with Ronnie Mancuso. Their affair became public when an explicit sex tape of the two of them was "stolen" and a portion was "mysteriously released" on the internet, making Wang Mei a household name in America.

Margo French returned to Camp Peary in Williamsburg, Virginia, for additional training in weapons, self-defense, and spy craft.

Ian Ludlow moved into the Oakwood apartments in Universal City while his house, which had been burned down by assassins for a second time, was being rebuilt again. He started writing a new Straker novel and began a desperate search for affordable homeowners insurance.

ACKNOWLEDGMENTS

I would like to thank Gracie Doyle, Megha Parekh, Kevin Smith, Dennelle Catlett, Kyla Pigoni, Sarah Shaw, Gabrielle Guarnero, and Megan Beatie for their enthusiasm, creativity, and hard work. Their efforts are a big reason why Ian Ludlow's adventures didn't begin and end with *True Fiction*.

The blurring line between fiction and reality was a very real problem for me while I was writing *Fake Truth*. It seemed like every day I was forced to decide whether to re-plot my story so my fiction would still be fiction or just keep going, reality be damned. I decided to keep writing and ignore the news, or I'd never finish the book.

I don't know how much of this book has become reality in the time between when I finished writing it and when it ended up in your hands. My fear is that a lot of it has . . . and you're thinking that either I am too unimaginative to come up with original ideas or my novel was intentionally "ripped from the headlines" like a *Law & Order* episode. Neither is the case. I really made this stuff up.

However, the community of Dunn, Texas, is fictional and named after my friend author Robert E. Dunn, who created the fictional Texas town of Lansdale, named after author Joe R. Lansdale, in his book

Dead Man's Badge. I tried to use fictional Lansdale as my setting, too, but couldn't make it work geographically. So I created Dunn instead.

Fake Truth was written in many places, from Billings, Montana, to Porto, Portugal; from Bois-le-Roi, France, to Green Bay, Wisconsin; from Calabasas, California, to Birmingham, Alabama . . . and in the skies in between. Ian and Margo were my constant travel companions for six hectic months in my life. I hope you've enjoyed their company as much as I have.

ABOUT THE AUTHOR

Photo © 2013 Ron Scarpa

Lee Goldberg is a two-time Edgar Award and two-time Shamus Award nominee and the #1 *New York Times* bestselling author of more than fifty novels, including the Ian Ludlow series (*Killer Thriller* and *True Fiction*), the Eve Ronin series (*Lost Hills*), fifteen Adrian Monk mysteries, and the first five books in the internationally bestselling Fox & O'Hare series (*The Heist, The Chase, The Job, The Scam,* and *The Pursuit*) cowritten with Janet Evanovich. He has also written and/or produced dozens of TV shows, including *Diagnosis Murder, SeaQuest, The Glades,* and *Monk,* and cocreated the hit Hallmark movie series *Mystery 101.*

As an international television consultant, he has advised networks and studios in Canada, France, Germany, Spain, China, Sweden, and the Netherlands on the creation, writing, and production of episodic television series. You can find more information about Lee and his work at www.leegoldberg.com.